A STORM LIKE IRON

KINGDOM OF BETRAYAL
BOOK THREE

EVERLY FROST

JULIAN MADDEN

DISCOVER THE EVER REALMS

Seven series. One world.

Suggested Reading Order:

Bright Wicked
Storm Princess
Assassin's Magic
Soul Bitten Shifter
Supernatural Legacy
Dark Magic Shifters
Kingdom of Betrayal

In the silence before darkness breaks, destiny is forged.

PART ONE
THE GIRL IN THE SNOW
TEN YEARS AGO

CHAPTER I
TEN YEARS AGO

The forest is quiet, but the air is heavy with danger.

Snowflakes drift from the thick canopy of twisted branches overhead as I creep through the brittle undergrowth.

My hunting knives are drawn and ready, one in each hand. My footfalls are silent. Years of hunting in these mountains have taught me how to move between fallen branches and navigate around debris without making a sound.

Twenty paces to my left, my father and brother stay close together, moving silently as a team. Like me, they're wearing thick, fur coats that conceal the handmade leather armor underneath.

Even with the warmth of the fur, falling snow chills my cheeks and nose. I've learned to live with the cold and survive despite it.

Across the distance, Father signals to the tightly gathered trees that rise up about thirty paces directly ahead of us, where the morning sunlight doesn't reach and the shadows are deepest.

Small signs indicate the presence of the creatures we're

tracking. Smudges of black ooze across the ice in front of the trees, the density of the unusually lush leaves, the way the branches lie low, and the soft rustle within them.

Father holds up his hand for me to halt and I immediately draw to a stop.

A moment later, Thoren—my brother—steps quietly to the left, taking up position behind the trunk of a tree situated thirty paces from our target. Crouching in the crisp snow built up around its base, he retrieves an arrow and nocks it to his bow.

He gives our father a nod to indicate that he's ready.

Thoren is thirteen. Four years younger than I am. But he's nearly as tall and broad-shouldered as I am, and this isn't his first hunt. Father and I have been training him since he could pick up a bow and he's proven to be a fast learner. These days, he can shoot an arrow even more accurately than I can.

Which is just as well because Father wants him as far from the fight as possible.

Two hours ago, before we left the safety of our home deep within the heart of the mountain range, Father reminded him: Stay back, shoot from a distance, let Erik do the cutting.

I have no issue with that, except that the deadly creatures infesting this part of the mountain have become more unpredictable over the last few months. If Thoren can't defend himself up close—if he isn't used to getting blood on his hands and on his face—he'll be in trouble if the creatures get past me.

Thoren seems to sense my anxiety, glancing across the distance, his gray eyes bright with concentration.

He cocks his head, as if to say: *Stop worrying, Erik.*

I'll never stop worrying.

It's fear that brings me out here every day, hunting the beasts that lurk in this forest.

Fear of running out of food. Fear that the creatures will start nesting closer to our home and kill us in our sleep. Fear that they'll destroy the last of the untainted wildlife that still survives in this part of the mountain range.

Or worse, fear that the dark magicians who live within the walled city at the base of the mountains will discover our existence.

Blacksmiths.

Their infectious magic has poisoned the environment across the mountains, rending and tearing at all natural life. They've turned ordinary, peaceful animals into malformed distortions of their original forms. Predators have become irrationally violent beasts that kill for sport instead of food.

Now, Father gives the signal for me to continue forward.

It's an approach he and I have followed time and time again, and it's as natural to me as breathing.

I go in first.

Father covers my back.

Thoren stays under the cover of trees and picks the creatures off from a distance.

Of course, there was a time when Father took the first strike.

But he soon learned that telling me to hang back was pointless.

He drops to a crouch twenty paces back from the lush trees, both of his hunting daggers drawn and ready. He and Thoren have similar coloring, both blond-haired and gray-eyed. I, too, inherited Father's eye color, but I have my mother's dark hair.

As I continue onward, the boughs up ahead appear densely packed, but it's a dangerous illusion. The wall of greenery is as unnatural as the destruction the Blacksmiths have wreaked on this land.

Know your prey.

Father's training informs every step I take out here on the mountain. His father trained him—not in fighting strange creatures like we do now, but in fighting other men. But he brought all of those skills with him and passed them on to me.

He doesn't talk much about his past, except to make sure we understand that he escaped that life for good reason. Thoren was only a baby at the time, and I was too young to remember much at all. Sometimes, in the dark of night, I recall the runes etched into the side of the longhouse where I slept as a small child and I smell the scent of blood on my father's hands when he carried us away from his clan.

I shake off the memories, clearing my mind.

Carefully, I study the leaves on the trees ahead, noting the darker-black smudges on the snow in front of the leafiest one.

The creatures we're hunting are nocturnal and far weaker in the morning just after they've fallen asleep. Their hearing is also poor, but they can sense vibrations. The time of day makes it possible to creep up on them, but only as long as we're as quiet as a breeze.

If it were night, they'd be swarming us already.

As for how many there are, it's impossible to tell when they're so aptly camouflaged within the tree's foliage.

The only way to find out is to strike.

Focusing my mind, I exhale into the crisp air, grip my knife, and remind myself I can reach for my bow and the arrows on my back if I need them.

I crouch into position, raise my hand, and steady my heartbeat.

Then I give the signal.

Now.

Thoren's arrow flies through the space directly above my head and hits the foliage dead center.

Shrieks fill the air, high-pitched and piercing, making my hearing buzz.

In that same instant, all of the emerald-green leaves burst outward in a storm of wings and claws.

I have barely a second to make out the features of the critters now screaming toward us. Each one has leaf-shaped wings, bright green, but beneath the wings, their skin is dark gray, like a corpse's. Their faces sport multiple eyes: black, soulless, and packed together like a spider's.

They fly low, no higher than the top of the tree from which they're swarming, since their body weight doesn't allow them to gain any greater height.

We call them 'butterflies', but they're a far cry from the few real butterflies I've ever seen.

Thoren's arrows fly quick and fast, taking down two of the creatures within the seconds that it takes me to drop even lower and avoid the creatures' claws as they soar through the air above me.

The butterflies aren't my target.

They're a distraction I trust Father and Thoren to take care of.

My focus is on the monster that was hiding behind them.

CHAPTER 2

I move fast, ducking beneath the butterflies, aiming for the central tree's trunk.

My focus is on the part of the trunk that drips with black liquid, oozing thickly but freely now that the butterflies have lifted off the wood.

I've barely made it five steps when a chunk at the base of the tree separates from the rest of the wood, appearing as if the tree trunk is unraveling, twisting and turning at an impossible speed.

The transition ends with four of the low-lying branches descending and rotating toward me, now resting on the snow in a pouncing stance.

Together with the legs, the monster's head and body separate from the tree, parts of what appeared to be branches sticking up and fanning out from its shoulders like spines.

This beast may seem to have formed from the tree, but it isn't made out of wood. It was simply devouring the tree's bark and cocooning itself within it.

It's flesh and blood, a monstrous version of a snow leopard.

Only Blacksmiths could take such a beautiful animal and turn it into a dark creature such as this.

Its eyes are milky white, the color its fur ought to be, as it takes one look at its surroundings and immediately focuses on me.

It leaps right at me, its black teeth bared, sharp enough to tear me apart. It doesn't make a sound. It's a silent predator that doesn't waste its breath on snarling or posturing, only survival.

Hell, there's a part of me that relates to that.

I dart to the right, throwing myself beneath the creature as it sails in my direction. My left hand flies upward and I aim my blade for the soft flesh where the leopard's front leg joins its body.

Usually, I can pierce a limb this way, ram my blade into the animal, and hobble it, bringing it to its knees. Then I can kill it swiftly.

I have no desire to cause it unnecessary pain.

But this leopard's hide is thicker than most.

Despite my accurate aim, my knife glances across its skin without cutting it or even drawing blood.

Damn!

Worse than not bringing it down is the fact that it's now facing my family and I'm several paces behind it.

I run and leap at the leopard's back even as it regains its balance after my hit knocked it off course.

Up ahead, my father has brought several of the butterflies down with his hunting knife. The blade drips with gore. He ducks and rolls beneath the low-flying claws of one butterfly to leap up into the air at another, then rams his dagger through its pale body, bringing it down.

Thoren's arrows fly quick and fast, but if my dagger couldn't pierce the leopard's hide, then his arrows won't, either.

I can't let the beast reach either of them.

The time it took the leopard to regain its balance is all I need to land on its back and knock it down, my dagger slashing toward its backbone, right behind the sharp spines jutting from its shoulders.

I didn't expect to do much damage, although I hoped I might. My intention is only to keep its focus on me and away from my family.

The leopard stumbles for a split second before it gets its feet under itself again. Its focus whips back toward me, its teeth gnashing as it spins and tries to reach me.

I know I need to throw myself off its back, but I take a chance to deflect its bite with one blade, using the opportunity to strike at its eye with the other.

It's moving too fast and my dagger misses its eye socket, but to my surprise, the blade pierces the beast's temple.

A weak spot!

The dagger slices across the leopard's face, cutting in line with its movement before I listen to my survival instincts. My muscles bunch, preparing to carry me backward in a leap, but that's when I realize I let the beast get too close.

The cut across its temple is deep enough to cause it significant pain but too shallow to lead to its death.

Its jaws snap at my forearm, its teeth closing around my limb and slicing through my leather armor.

A shot of fear strikes through me.

I can't let it tear off my arm!

My other dagger flies toward its temple in a desperate bid to kill the beast.

But I can't get the angle right.

The blade glances across the creature's face as its teeth pierce my skin.

Pain shoots through my arm.

At that moment, a blur of gray appears at the corner of my eye. A predator of teeth and claws and unparalleled speed leaps at the leopard's back.

Thud!

The wolf we call 'Skirra' rams into the leopard, whose jaws open a heartbeat before it tumbles across the snow, leaving a trail of black liquid behind it.

I crash back into the icy ground, my heart pounding as I roll to regain my footing.

Skirra is fast and strong, gnashing at the leopard's face as he fights it with a fury that only a predator can achieve.

Snarls and claws and slashing teeth. Blurs of movement.

I watch with my heart in my throat, prepared to jump into the fight as soon as I see an opening.

Skirra is family, too. His pack followed my father from the far north to these mountains, where Skirra was born. We named him for his frightful speed and the terror that strikes our hearts to see him fight.

Thank the stars he's on our side.

I take the briefest moment to check my arm, my heart sinking to see the gashes through my fur coat and armor, and the blood seeping between them.

The leopard has the scent of my blood now. If it escapes, it will follow us home and bring others of its kind with it.

I didn't intend to let it live, but now the consequences of not killing it are far worse.

Only once before did we make the mistake of leaving a leopard alive after it had tasted our blood—Father's blood, in that case—and we will never do that again.

I grip my daggers tightly, crouching and waiting for my chance to re-enter the fight. I can't risk slashing Skirra by accident, but my fear is growing.

The leopard is twice Skirra's size, and I can't stand by and let it get the upper hand.

I'm preparing to jump back into the fight when the two animals crash across the clearing and knock into a nearby tree.

The leopard hits the wood first and Skirra's claws slash across its belly, spilling blood.

Another weak spot!

But it will be far harder for me to strike its stomach without exposing myself to its claws.

With a loud snarl—the first it's made—the big cat darts to the side before Skirra can latch on to it again and races away through the trees.

At the corner of my vision, Father is covered in black ooze, but Thoren is still safely located behind the far tree. There are only a few butterflies left and I trust Father will finish them off soon enough.

He must have seen the blood on my arm because his sharp command reaches me a split second later. "Go, Erik! Go, now!"

I'm racing across the snow before his shouts fade.

I have no choice.

If I don't kill the beast now, my family will be in terrible danger.

The leopard is fast, but the cut across its face must be messing with its ability to orient itself because its path is more erratic than I expected. I didn't think I blinded it when I stabbed at its eye, but I could be wrong.

Skirra rushes after it, giving chase far faster than I can on my human legs. But I have a few tricks up my sleeve, especially with Skirra's help.

Up ahead, the wolf leaps at the leopard's back, bringing it down, both animals tumbling through the debris once more. When the leopard jumps free, it heads toward the thicker undergrowth, where Skirra has steered it. It's a harder path for the monster to travel.

I cut across the clear ground, veering right of the thicker trees, my arms and legs pumping as I sprint down the incline.

I'm horribly aware of the mark notched into the bark of a

tree to my left. It's a mark that indicates the boundary of our safe zone.

Father notched out the boundaries years ago and drilled into us the importance of never going past them. Traveling beyond this line of trees takes me closer to the walled city and risks detection by the Blacksmiths.

But once again, I don't have a choice.

Speeding along the track, I take advantage of the sharper downward slope to increase my speed, hurtling forward. Much farther ahead of me, I can make out some sort of snowy clearing, but it's difficult to see what lies beyond it.

For now, my focus is entirely on the sounds of the predators crashing through the foliage to my left and the fact that I'm now ahead of them, where I need to be.

Veering sharply in their direction, I swiftly deposit one of my daggers into its sheath, freeing my left hand.

The leopard shoots from the undergrowth right into my path.

I leap for its back, my left arm stretching for the spines across its shoulders, my fingers closing around one of them.

My intention is to gain enough of a hold that I can reach forward and ram my hunting knife into its right temple and end this monster once and for all.

The leopard is strong enough to rip me off my feet and carry me with it for all of three seconds before I realize my mistake.

Suddenly, the terrain that I couldn't see before is rushing toward me.

A yawning chasm. The edge of a ravine.

I catch sight of snow drifts below me before the leopard leaps out into thin air, taking me with him.

CHAPTER 3

I have no time to think, only to respond by instinct.

My left arm bunches, muscles flexing as I shove myself as hard as I can away from the leopard. At the same time, I let go of my hunting knife. Wherever it lands, so be it.

I'm moving at breakneck speed as I plummet downward, my hands whipping back to snatch my bow and an arrow, which I nock in one swift movement.

The force of my shove has pushed the leopard slightly sideways.

I twist toward the leopard and let the arrow fly, praying that it will strike true.

My arrow arcs across the air and that's all I see before I hit the ground.

There's no such thing as soft snow when falling from a height.

My body crunches against the icy drifts. But I don't have time to register the pain or shock of the impact.

All I know is that I didn't break any bones—or if I did, I'm still functioning despite that fact.

The leopard smacks into the ground only a few paces away from me, the arrow jutting from its stomach right where I aimed it—into one of the cuts Skirra's claws had already made.

Snatching up my remaining dagger, I swing myself toward the leopard, lunging as fast as I can while the beast snarls and struggles to get up.

My knife meets its temple and I ram the blade down.

Then I throw myself in the other direction, tumbling clear of its thrashing claws.

I come up into a crouch, my blood rushing in my ears and my breathing rapid as I wait for the leopard's next move.

I'm aware of Skirra landing nimbly a few paces away. He must have paused at the top of the ravine but only for a second. His ability to leap and land so easily is just another testament to his wolfish nature.

He rushes to my side, growling and snapping his teeth at the leopard, slowly calming as the beast stays down.

Its chest stops rising and falling and its eyes... finally become vacant.

I sigh into the silence.

This leopard may once have been a beautiful creature, not a mindless predator.

I quickly assess my surroundings, taking stock of the sharp cliff faces twenty paces away on either side of me, the way the ravine curves both ahead and behind me so I can't see much beyond the immediate clearing, and the way the breeze whistles softly as it flows through the chilled air.

Now that I've ascertained there are no immediate threats in the vicinity, I rise to my feet and approach the leopard carefully, watching to make sure all life signs are gone before I take a knee beside it.

I press my hand to its shoulder behind its spines and close my eyes for a moment.

My father didn't bring all of his peoples' beliefs and

customs with him, but acknowledging the strength of a fierce creature, before its spirit departs, was one of them.

"You have a strong spirit and you fought well," I murmur to the leopard. "May you fill your belly in the Hall of Warriors and sleep by the warmth of the eternal light."

Opening my eyes, I retrieve the arrow from its body. Then I lean back and finally check my arm.

Damn. The puncture wounds are worse than I thought.

Skirra, too, is bleeding from a slash across his shoulder, presumably from the leopard's claws or teeth.

A bite from any of these malformed animals can sicken the flesh and cause it to rot, but a bite from a leopard can bring on the sickness faster.

I check my left hand, but the abrasions where I gripped the creature's rough spine are superficial.

I'll have bruises from my fall but nothing in that regard that won't heal within a week.

I have a choice to make now, about whether or not I should access the light in my heart to speed the healing process or take the chance that my body will heal itself.

It's a power that my father's people revere and spend their whole lives building and cultivating. A spark of light that all humans have, but few are aware of. Even fewer know how to use it.

My father's people do. They are Einherjar, the ones who fight with light. His father taught him how to cultivate and harness his deep light, and he taught Thoren and me.

But our light is limited and as such, it shouldn't be used unnecessarily. Judging by the shallow depth of the punctures in my arm, I have a little time to decide. I'll seek my father's wisdom first.

In the meantime, I need to check Skirra's wound more carefully and then get back to my family.

Bending to Skirra, I check the gash, relieved to find it isn't deep and the blood within it is a healthy red color—no sign of the black sludge from the creature's body.

I'm about to rise to my feet when Skirra gives a soft whine, an uncharacteristically fearful sound.

His eyes are forward, his head lowered toward the ground, his focus on the curve in the ravine fifty paces away.

I study the terrain near the curve more carefully, making out lumps in the snowy ground ahead, but it's difficult to see what they are from this distance.

The breeze continues to waft through the ravine and I'm suddenly aware of how eerie it is. There's a heavy pall that carries a dark scent I can't place.

Skirra whines again, his body stiff before he lurches forward.

"No, Skirra," I whisper, but I may as well tell the breeze to stop blowing.

I'm at his side within seconds, retrieving my fallen knife along the way.

As we draw nearer to the curve, I struggle to make sense of what I'm seeing on the ground.

Strips of white material. Odd protrusions rising up through the surface of the snow.

We turn the corner and my lips draw back.

Pure horror freezes me to the spot.

Ahead of me, the ravine is deeper and its sides are more sharply inclined.

Human bodies lie beneath a thin layer of ice, each one wrapped in white cloth that doesn't appear to have kept their arms or legs tight enough to their sides. Hands, knees, even heads protrude up through the powdery snow.

It's a dumping ground.

A fucking pit into which bodies have been thrown.

My stomach is empty of food and thank the gods for that.

"Fuck," I whisper, trying to process the cruelty I'm seeing.

The bodies look thin. Many have scars. They appear to be all ages, from children to the elderly.

This can only be the work of Blacksmiths. *Fucking Blacksmiths.*

From what we know of them, they keep humans as servants and frequently work them to death.

A deep rage sparks within me, a blind heat that threatens to darken the light in my heart, but I clamp down on it.

I need to get the fuck out of here.

This pit is far enough from the city that the snow falls here, freezing the bodies and alleviating the stench of decay. But it's close enough that it must be only half a day's travel by wagon.

Far too close to their city.

It's also a place that the Blacksmiths must frequent and that makes the risk of discovery even more dangerously high.

I'm backing away when Skirra suddenly falls silent, his soft snarls coming to an abrupt halt.

His ears prick up and he edges closer to the bodies.

"What is it, Skirra?" I whisper, wishing I had his sense of smell and hearing.

With a soft yip, he prowls ahead, skirting around the parts of the bodies that protrude upward and navigating toward a lone tree that grows out of the right-hand side of the ravine.

The tree's trunk is situated at the point where the slope meets the ground, the wood thickly curved at the bottom as if it began by growing outward before it turned upward toward the sun.

I trust Skirra's instincts, so I follow him, although I can't deny that my own instincts are telling me to leave as quickly as possible.

Keeping my eyes on our surroundings and staying alert for the sounds of anyone approaching, I pull my fur sleeve over my mouth and step carefully around the bodies. The snow seems to be smothering some of the odor, but not all of it.

Closer to the tree, I make out what looks like silver threads caught in the bark partway up its trunk.

My forehead creases. *What are they?*

Up ahead, Skirra takes the final distance to the tree at a run and starts digging at the frozen earth beside it.

I continue to check our surroundings as I move, listening carefully above the sound of his scrabbling, wary of the silence now that the breeze has stopped.

As I draw closer, the bright threads I spotted against the tree's bark become clearer.

They look like spun silver. The finest metal.

But not heavy, like metal would be; some of the threads lift in the breeze.

I'm close enough to reach out and catch several in my hand to keep them from floating away.

That's when I finally see what rests on the other side of the tree.

First, a pale shoulder and an arm, both bare and exposed to the elements. Then the side of a slender torso clothed in a beaded dress that catches the light, a garish sparkle in this place of death.

And strands of silver hair falling across a face that snatches the breath from my chest.

Her eyes are closed, her head is tilted toward her left shoulder, and her cheeks are pale.

I've never seen anything as beautiful as this woman.

Or as terrible as the thick streak of dried blood that extends from her forehead down the left side of her face.

Her chest rises and falls as she quietly breathes into the frosty air.

She's still alive.

CHAPTER 4

I have to get her out of the snow.

Dropping to my knees beside Skirra, I dig frantically into the ice that's piled up around the woman's body and is currently burying her to her hips.

If I don't free her, she'll continue freezing to death.

I can't yet tell where her legs might be. They could be stretched out in front of her or folded beneath her. Either way, the freshness of the snow built up around her waist tells me she was dumped here recently, probably in the night.

Whoever brought her here left her to die.

They would have known she was still breathing, but they fucking left her to perish. She can't be any older than I am.

The burning fury that I've been pushing away since I first saw the bodies in this pit rises again. The heat of anger comes, once again, from my heart and the well of light that exists within it.

But always, I hear Father's warning in my mind: Your deep light is finite. Once burned, it's gone.

So again, I push it down.

The outline of the top of the woman's legs becomes visible and it's finally apparent that they're folded beneath her.

But I also now realize that, while her right hand rests across her stomach, her left hand is fully submerged in snow.

Fingers and toes are the most vulnerable to the cold and the first to succumb to flesh death.

Her left hand could be black with it already.

If it is, the only way to stop the rot from entering her blood would be to cut off the affected limb.

Her feet are in danger too, but possibly less so because there's a chance some of her body heat has filtered down to them.

The impulse to take hold of her torso and wrench her out of the snow is strong, but if I don't free her hand first, the upward pressure could snap her frozen fingers right off.

I pull at the ice as fast as I can, taking glances at her face, hoping she'll open her eyes.

The fact that she isn't shivering and doesn't respond at all to our presence or our actions tells me she's far gone, caught in a death-like sleep that will certainly take her to the gods if we don't get her warmed up—and carefully. Sudden heat can be as bad as no heat at all.

Skirra continues to dig beside her legs, making soft, whining noises. He doesn't scratch her despite his frantic movements as he burrows into the impacted ice around her body.

Despite my bond of friendship with him, he's a wild creature. I don't command him. He does as he pleases. But he seems as determined as I am to help her.

Finally, I free her hand, taking care to lift it gently, slowly bending her arm at the elbow.

Her fingers are blue and icy cold, but I'm relieved to see that the black rot hasn't set in yet.

Even as relief fills me, so does a new wave of anger.

There's a ring of red around her wrist and, when I glance at her other hand, I see abrasions around that wrist, too.

She must have been bound at some point. In a similar sign of cruelty, some of her hair must have been torn out, since the loose strands are now caught in the tree's bark.

Swallowing my anger, I focus on freeing her from the ice.

Carefully, I slide my hands around the sides of her hips and legs, working my way around her folded knees and back to her ankles, seeking her toes, checking that the ice isn't clinging to them.

Her skin is brutally cold, leaching the warmth from my hands as I work, but I don't resent the transference of body heat.

In fact, I need to give her more of it.

My leather chest plate will stop my body heat from reaching her, so as quickly as I can, I draw back; remove my scabbard, my coat, and the chest plate; and pull only the scabbard and coat back on again.

I check that my hunting knives are safely sheathed and I roll up the leather chest plate and squish it into the quiver with my arrows before I replace that on my back.

Finally ready, I gently leverage each of her limbs upward, scratching at the ice where I need to free her further. Now certain that the ice won't tear her skin or her body, I slide my arms behind the woman's back, pull her up against my chest and onto my lap, and close my coat around her.

She's heavy in my arms in the way that the dying carry a weight that seems to pin them to the ground.

I grimace as my body heat races away from me and my heart pumps harder to counter the cold she brings with her.

Blowing out an exhale, I steady my mind and focus on breathing. On the strong beat of my heart. The knowledge and certainty that I am warm.

I *will* warm her.

Carefully, I draw her left hand up to my chin, trying to be careful not to bend her fingers yet. I press her fingertips to the warmth beneath my jaw until my skin cools and her hand is a little less cold.

Then I bring her fingertips to my lips, exhaling softly across them, a continuous, gentle warmth.

I know I can't stay here for long.

Only a few minutes more.

Maybe not even that.

Skirra has settled beside me, but now he rises and snarls in the direction of the city, making a low hum of sound in his throat as his lips pull back from his teeth.

I recognize that snarl as a warning.

I can't hear what he can hear, but there's urgency in his growl.

We need to move.

Determined to keep her against me and within the folds of my coat, I draw to my feet and consider all the exits from this ravine.

The path I came from has steep inclines on both sides, but it curves toward the north, which would be better, direction-wise, even if it's impossible to ascend. The other way curves toward the south—toward the city—but the incline is gentler.

With the woman in my arms, I don't have much choice.

Skirra seems to know it too.

He darts along the southern route. Ignoring the sharp pain of the wound in my arm, I follow Skirra at an awkward jog, leaving the horror of the dumping ground behind.

To my relief, the ravine curves again, this time northward.

Soon enough, the terrain on my right evens out a little and I can take the ascent as a run, relying on my leg muscles to power me up the slope.

As fast as I can, I reach the peak and race north through the trees.

I've never been so happy to leave a place behind. Not only because of the sheer horror of the location, but because even a half mile from the Blacksmith's city is too close to the danger it poses.

Keeping the woman close, her head supported against my chest, I run back toward the location of the initial fight, where my father and brother will be waiting.

Skirra races ahead of me, stopping at intervals so I can catch up.

Finally, we burst back into the clearing, but I pull up short, skidding to a halt at the carnage ahead of me.

CHAPTER 5

The snowy clearing is covered in black ooze.

Butterfly bodies are strewn everywhere, far more of them than we were fighting earlier. Far more than there should be.

A pack of wolves growls and snarls, picking their way through the fresh meat, but I relax a little when I recognize each of them.

Skirra's pack is as ferocious as he is.

I let out my breath with a full rush of relief when I see my father—apparently unharmed—bending to examine something on the ground ahead while Thoren runs toward me.

"Erik!" My brother knows not to shout, so his exclamation comes at a loud whisper.

"Thoren, what happened?" My question is urgent as I quickly do a visual check of him for wounds. With my hands full, that's all I can do.

"More butterflies." His face is smeared with oily goop while the visible parts of his cheeks are pale. When I left, he wasn't close enough to the flying beasts to end up with any of the substance on him, but now it's all over his skin and clothing.

His focus darts over the woman in my arms—what he must be able to see of her around my coat, that is. Maybe part of her arm, her torso, some of her hair, the top of her head, her general shape.

His eyes widen. "Erik, who is that?"

My own question cuts across his. "How were there more butterflies? They don't build nests near each other."

There's only ever one nest within a certain radius and we already ascertained there were no other nests near the first one.

Thoren points to the southeast but doesn't take his eyes off the woman. "They swarmed from that direction. Something must have disturbed them. The wolf pack came running, too. Together, we took all of the butterflies down."

The fact that the butterflies swarmed from the southeast is concerning. They won't willingly take flight during the day unless they're trying to escape a threat. It's how we can target single nests, picking them off one at a time.

"Father thinks it could be Blacksmiths." Thoren's voice is breathless as he continues speaking in a whisper. "We were just making sure Kori was okay and then we were coming to find you."

Kori is one of the male wolves.

The pack across the way parts at that moment, giving me a clear line of sight to my father.

I can now see that he's crouched beside Kori—a wolf with pure-white fur. Most of the wolves are dark gray like Skirra, but a few of them have the whitest of pelts. It gives those wolves an advantage in the snowy terrain, but it also makes it easy for me to see the blood matting Kori's right shoulder.

The Blacksmiths' destruction of life has decimated the wolf population, making Skirra's pack extremely rare. They might even be the last of their kind, but I want to believe there are other wolves in the north or far to the south.

Across the way, Father rises to his feet and I'm relieved when Kori jumps up too, appearing to be okay.

Skirra doesn't leave my side, but several of the other wolves mill around Kori in the distance.

"Kori will be fine," Father says as he hurries toward me.

There's always a moment when I come back from a fight that I see fear in his eyes.

Fear that I've returned hurt.

Fear that he won't be able to help me.

It's normally only the briefest moment before it gives way to relief.

Today, his tension grows.

"Thoren said there could be Blacksmiths in the forest," I say when Father nears me.

To my knowledge, at least for the duration of my life, Blacksmiths haven't ventured into these snow-laden mountains in the northwest. But then, I didn't know they had a dumping ground on this side of the city, either.

Father doesn't respond to my statement.

"Erik." His voice is tense and low and I don't miss the way he seems focused on the strands of the woman's silver hair that have escaped my coat. "What have you got there, Son?"

He stops several paces away from me—farther away than Thoren, who's now right beside me.

My father and I stand eye to eye, but he dwarfs me in size, his shoulders and chest broader than mine.

"I found her freezing to death," I say. "She was in a pit surrounded by human bodies. A fucking dumping ground. I fell into it chasing the leopard. But I got her out of there and I think she has a chance of staying alive."

Still, his voice is low and tense and he remains focused on her hair. "You're okay?"

"The leopard got me. I'll need you to take a look at the puncture wounds. But I'm fine for now."

"Good," he says. "Because you're taking her back."

I blink at him. Shake my head.

I can't have heard him correctly.

"*What?*"

Father's expression hardens and his jaw clenches. "You're taking her back to where you found her and you're going to leave her there. Then you're going to forget you ever saw her. Do you understand me, Erik?"

"No," I say, bluntly and immediately. "How could I ever understand such a barbaric order?"

It's that kind of brutality that caused my father to leave his people in the first place and now he's telling me to put this woman back into that pit and let her die?

"Erik." Father's expression remains hard, but the fear behind his eyes grows stronger. "This woman is our enemy. She can only bring us death."

I glance down at the pale face tucked against my chest. The way she's nestled against me, it hides the dried blood from the wound across her forehead.

My disbelief is intense. "How?"

How could she bring anything but peace?

My father's response is full of fear. "Because she's a Blacksmith."

CHAPTER 6

A Blacksmith?

I've never seen one of them up close to know if she has any of the physical traits that might be particular to them. Although... the color of her hair is unusual... but it's not unknown for humans to have hair so silvery white...

More than anything else, it doesn't make sense to me that her own people would hit her, bind her, and leave her to die in a pit of decaying bodies.

My immediate response is filled with denial. "Why would they kill one of their own?"

"It happens." Father is unwavering. "If they left her in that pit, then it means they want her dead."

My brow furrows because the way Father's talking... "You knew the pit was there?"

His jaw clenches, but he continues to hold my gaze. "The safe zone exists for a reason, Son. It's not something I ever wanted you to see."

I know that everything he does—every decision he makes—is to keep us alive. We're caught between two worlds: the one we left behind and the one of which we skirt the edges.

"Regardless, they'll check up on her body," Father continues. "They'll discover she's gone and come looking for her. That puts us all in danger."

My brother's interjection is quiet. "What if they already did? Came looking for her, I mean." He gestures around at the butterflies. "*Somebody* disturbed these butterflies."

Father gives this some thought but says, "It's too soon. Erik only just brought her here and the butterflies were disturbed earlier than that." He scratches his chin. "Unless there's a chance she fell into the pit? Maybe she ran off into the snow and lost her way? If her people are out searching for her, then, yes, it could have been they who disturbed the butterflies."

I shake my head. "There's blood on her face where she was struck—"

"But by what? A fist or a falling tree branch?"

"—and rope burns around her wrists."

At that, Father falls silent. Then, "Rope burns, huh?"

"Yes, sir."

He exhales heavily. "Then they want her dead and there's nothing we can do about that. I'm sorry, Son—"

"*I'm not taking her back.*" My voice snaps across the air, more loudly than I should have spoken when danger lies in every part of this forest.

My arms close tightly around the woman, and the anger I've been pushing away is rising far too fast.

Thoren takes a step away from me.

My father's eyes widen and his lips part with a sharply indrawn breath.

Both of their faces have drained of color.

Father's left hand rises in a wary gesture while his right hand moves to the hilt of the hunting knife resting at his waist.

"Erik." His voice is tense, heavy with a fear he's never shown when he looks at me. "Your deep light is burning, Son."

I stiffen, only now aware of the sapphire tinge at the corner of my vision. The light I'm trying to keep caged must be glowing beneath my coat and across the edges of my jaw.

Well, at least this small spark of light will banish any sickness that might have otherwise taken hold from the leopard's bite. I can sense the warmth in my arm as it cleans my blood. No need to seek my father's opinion about that any longer.

But using more than a spark is too much.

Deep light builds more slowly than it burns. I can't afford to waste any of it.

With great determination, I push it down; a difficult task when every instinct in my body is raging at the idea of putting this woman back into that pit.

Across from me, my father's expression is slowly changing.

The crease in his forehead smooths out, and he considers me with a solemnity that replaces my rage with a cold dread.

I wait for him to repeat his command, to insist that I return her to the hellish snow where I found her.

My deep light fades when the silence between us draws out.

Even the wolves have fallen quiet. Skirra's face is turned up to mine. They're all watching me.

Finally, my father speaks again and now his soft statement carries a weight I haven't heard in his voice before.

"Your deep light must be drawn to her," he says, exhaling heavily into the crisp air. "I cannot ignore this. *We* cannot ignore this. I may have left my people behind, but not my beliefs. The gods give us each a destiny, but few of us have the courage to follow it."

He inclines his head at the woman. "It's your destiny to keep this woman alive."

Then he casts a meaningful glance at Thoren and the wolves. "Just as it's our destiny now to follow your path wherever it leads. Be it life or death."

With that, he turns and scoops up a sack in which he will have loaded as many butterflies as can fit.

I'm frozen to the spot, trying to process the finality in my father's words, the heaviness in his tone, and the resolve in his eyes before he turned away.

I want to speak, but I don't know how to articulate the sudden turmoil I feel.

Father swings the sack over his shoulder. "We'll take the rocky path home so we don't leave tracks," he says. "The wolves can finish off the rest of the game here. Thoren, I want you to watch our backs and brush off any tracks we leave. Erik will carry the woman. We'll get her to the cabin and out of the cold. Then we'll figure out what to do."

Without another word, he sets off ahead of us, surveilling our surroundings as he goes. Thoren hurries to pick up a fallen branch, which he'll use to sweep across our footprints when we need to walk in the deeper snow.

I keep my brother in my sights while he follows close behind me.

My father's declaration has brought a weight to my heart.

For him to speak of destiny... and in a way that implies my path will now determine my family's future...

It feels as if a great fist has closed around me.

A fist of my own making.

It will take us half an hour to reach the rocky path where our tracks will be concealed, then another hour and a half to head deep into the mountains to finally reach our cabin.

Skirra stays at my side while several of the wolves, including Kori, follow closely, their footfalls light and quick. The rest of the pack stays behind, but they'll come to the cabin when they're ready.

Along the way, Thoren walks mostly backward, swishing the branch across our path, working hardest where our feet sink deepest, ensuring that, as the snow falls, it will quickly fill the finer crevices left by the branch.

All the while, I worry that the woman's breathing is too shallow, that her feet and hands are too cold, and that the rot could still set into her fingers and progress to her arm.

Every step takes too long.

Ahead of us, my father's back remains tense. His surveillance of our surroundings constant. He glances back at us at regular intervals, checking on us too.

He took us away from his clan to keep us safe. He has done everything since then to ensure we survive.

Now, I've put us all in danger.

But even as doubts creep to the edges of my mind, all it takes is a glance at the woman's face for my misgivings to vanish again.

She needs to live.

Every spark of my deep light tells me that.

I have to keep her alive.

CHAPTER 7

Finally, we reach the mountain pass where our cabin and several storage buildings are hidden. Father built them along the side of the mountain closest to our right. Although there's a clearing around them, they sit behind a thick camouflage of bordering trees. In fact, if I didn't know the buildings were there, I would easily overshoot them.

The cabin itself is a rectangular building, not large, but it resembles the longhouses of Father's clan with modifications to camouflage its shape against the mountain.

Its door is on the far side, where the mountain curves a little. It means we have to walk along its long side to reach the entrance. Father designed it that way to make it harder for an attacker to gain immediate access to the inside while allowing for turrets along the roof from which we can defend ourselves.

On that side, there's also a smokehouse for curing meat and a small forge for working metals. We keep all of our extra weapons and belongings within the cabin itself.

Each of the buildings is vented so that any smoke from the fires within them flows across the face of the mountain and disperses well before it becomes visible in the sky. The last thing we want is a white plume funneling upward like a beacon leading to our home.

As we approach the windowless and doorless side of the cabin, Father hoists the sack of game into a wooden structure filled with snow that sits at this end. It will keep the meat fresh until we can cure it. Once the butterflies are cleaned, they make a good stew. They're our main source of meat during winter and keep us from starving.

He quickly gestures us inside the cabin. "Thoren, get up to the eastern turret in the roof and watch for intruders. Erik, bring the woman to the hearth."

While Skirra follows me inside, Kori and the other wolves remain outside, all of them seemingly on edge as they stay on their feet, sniffing the air and gathering around the long side of the cabin.

As soon as we enter the building, Thoren reaches for a fresh quiver of arrows from the stash of weapons hanging on the wall inside the door. He also snatches up a cloth, wiping at the goop on his face while he hurries across the interior, past the hearth in the middle of the floor, and up the steps on the opposite side to the loft that runs around all four sides.

There are two more smaller set of stairs—barely more than ladders—positioned at equal distances along the right-hand loft. Those ladders lead up into the shallow turrets built within the roof cavity. Each turret has a long but narrow opening that will allow him to scan the forest from side to side and fire arrows in any direction.

It's still warm inside the building. The hearth is built up around the sides as high as my knees, so the fire within it stays safely contained and we can leave it glowing while we're absent.

Father is a few steps ahead of me, his daggers remaining sheathed at his waist as he drops to his knees on the fur beside the hearth and begins stoking the fire.

We were moving fast to get here and my breathing remains labored as I hurry after him and lower myself to my knees on the same large fur he's resting on.

Because we sleep around the hearth, there are already multiple furs rolled up nearby. There's also a metal bucket filled with cooled boiled water, and a basket containing clean cloths. We prepare the water and cloths in advance in case we come back injured.

"Let me see her." Father turns from the fire and reaches for the edge of my coat where it covers the woman's face.

The tension in his jaw increases. "She can't be older than you, Erik. Barely more than a girl." His brow furrows more deeply. "It concerns me that someone this young would have angered her leader so much that he'd cast her out. Whatever she did, it must have been grievous in his eyes."

The Blacksmith who rules the city is named Malak Ironmeld. Stories about him reached Father's clan all the way in the north, none of them good.

Apparently, there was a time when Blacksmiths would travel beyond their city, forging alliances with other peoples. They were peaceful then. So peaceful that they considered the Einherjar way of life to be brutal and abhorrent.

Malak changed all that. Now, according to my father, the Blacksmiths have surpassed even his people's proclivity for brutality.

If Malak hates this woman, then Father could very well be right—he'll check on her body.

Strange, though. If he really wanted her dead, why didn't he place guards around the pit to ensure she perished?

My more immediate concern is the fact that she still hasn't stirred. "She should have woken up by now, shouldn't she?"

Father's brow creases. "The blow to her head may have caused more damage than we can see. Or the object that struck her could have been magical. It may have had an unnatural effect on her. I don't know enough about the more complex impacts of Blacksmith power—other than the obvious consequence of striking metal against flesh and bone."

I already know the answer to my next question, but I ask it all the same. "Could I use my deep light to help her?"

Father's expression softens. "Son, you know you can't. Our light can't be transferred to another being, no matter how much we may want to give it to them. We can only use it within our own bodies."

He clears his throat before he continues. "Other than the head wound and the marks around her wrists, is she hurt anywhere else?"

"Those were the only wounds I saw."

He presses his lips together. "What you saw might not be all."

Damn. "I'm certain there are no deep cuts that could be life-threatening," I say, reflecting on the fact that there were no visible pools of blood on her clothing or on mine where I held her close.

Father pauses but then nods. "Okay, then. I'll clean the head wound now. Keep her close to your body for warmth."

My father leans back on his heels and reaches for the bucket and the basket of cloths. He dips the tip of a cloth into the water before he lightly wipes her forehead, studying the wound as he works.

"Her skin is split, but the cut is shallow," he finally announces, dropping the bloodied cloth into a second, empty bucket. "As for other wounds, you need to check to be sure, and then you need to get her completely warm."

He's matter-of-fact as he continues. "Thoren will stay up in the turret. I'll go outside and keep watch. If she has any other injuries that need cleaning, call me. If there are no other wounds, then your body heat is most important to her survival.

Undress her, get your shirt and heavy pants off, and wrap yourself up in furs with her."

Undress her? My forehead creases. "I don't have her permission. What if she wakes up? She'll be frightened."

I don't want her to regain consciousness, only to find herself bound in furs with me and to think I might have hurt her.

Thoren's voice suddenly calls down from the turret at the near end of the loft, proving that he could hear our conversation. "To see *your* ugly face up close?"

He pops his head through the opening at the top of the ladder, grinning at me from within the shadows. "If I were a woman who woke up next to you, I'd stab first and ask questions later. Just make sure there are no blades handy and you'll be fine."

I grimace. "Yes, thank you, little brother."

"Happy to help," Thoren calls before his head disappears again.

Father speaks quietly. "If she wakes up, give her space. Tell her what happened and how she got here."

He rises to his feet. "She won't live to see the end of the day unless she's warm. Your body is a heat source that will keep her alive. She doesn't have time for you to wrestle with your honor, Son."

The cold grips her. The deathly sleep will kill her. She can't fight it on her own.

I have to fight it for her.

CHAPTER 8

I give my father a nod.

He heads to the door as he speaks. "At all times, control your thoughts. The decisions you make will determine whether or not she lives."

Reaching for his sword and its scabbard, he pulls both onto his back. "Call me when you're ready. I'll come back and boil cloths for her feet and hands for extra warmth."

As soon as the door closes behind him, I extricate the woman from my coat and lay her carefully down on the large fur.

Even though I wrap part of it around her, I'm aware of the way her body cools now that she's apart from me. It's like she can't retain any heat at all—like she's frozen all the way to her heart and mind.

I only know what my father told me about Blacksmith magic. They don't have the deep light that our people have learned to harness. Their magic is the oldest of the old— creation magic that they access through their hammers and bands of metal they wear on their bodies. When they have contact with their power, it makes them far stronger and faster than humans.

But there isn't any visible metal on her.

No hammer and no bands around her arms. No jewelry of any kind.

Quickly, I remove my bow and quiver from my back and set my hunting knives safely down at the end of the hearth.

Then I start checking her over, examining her head and neck first, relieved that I didn't miss any injuries there.

Keeping the fur partway over her, I roll her onto her side and reach for the clasps at the back of her dress, acting fast to peel it off her back and arms, touching her only when and where I need to.

I freeze as her back becomes fully visible.

Her skin is as pale as snow and as smooth as the sharpest blade, but it's covered in welts.

Ten brutal cuts crisscross her skin, stretching from her shoulders to her hips. As I slide the material down, I discover more welts across the backs of her legs.

They look like the kind that would have been made by a switch.

My jaw clenches and I try to swallow the instant rage that pushes at my deep light.

These wounds look old. They're already scabbed over and the skin around them is yellow. They would have been inflicted days ago—well before whatever altercation put her in that pit.

Was she beaten for days before they threw her in there?

Another careful look tells me there's healing skin near the new cuts. Older switch marks that indicate beatings over time.

Nearby, Skirra gives a soft whine, padding up to the woman's back and sniffing at her broken skin. He gives a soft growl, angry in a way I wish I could mimic.

When I check the rest of her torso, there are no welts across her front, although there's a fist-sized bruise across her midriff. That bruise, like the cut on her forehead, is fresh.

I picture the punch that would have forced the air out of her chest, followed by the blow to her head that would have knocked her out.

My hands are shaking with fury by the time I place her dress at the side of the hearth and wrap her up fully in the fur.

The fire is now at her back, its warmth constant, but her skin remains cold.

I snatch up a few clean cloths to wipe my face before I peel off my shirt, swap my heavier pants for a loincloth, and slip inside the fur with her. Then I pull her close, both of us on our sides, her torso against mine, my upper arm wrapped around her side and back.

Skirra rests down at my back, as if he's pushing me toward her, his head resting against my side.

The woman's body is so cold that I shiver.

Even though she's naked in my arms, I have no thoughts other than a rage that has nowhere to go.

Hers is the not the body of someone who is loved.

Her face is not the face of someone who smiles. There are no laugh lines. Only dark rings under her eyes.

If I could change that...

I shake myself.

She might not survive this. She might not wake up. And even if I can keep her alive, the path ahead will be dangerous.

Without delay, I lift my voice to call quietly to my father, and he appears in the doorway a few moments later.

He lowers a satchel to the floor inside the door before he hurries to the fire. "Any other wounds?"

My voice is tight. "Somebody beat her with a stick. The welts are healing over, but there are older marks that indicate it wasn't the first time."

Father pauses at that, his lips pursing before he sinks to the fur. Silently, he sets about boiling water, the flames making his features bright.

I inherited many of his features: his eyes, his jawline, and his physique, but he told me that I have my mother's heart.

"You have a choice to make now, Son," he says, speaking quietly as he focuses on the water, using tongs to dip a cloth into it. "The wolves are unsettled. The Blacksmiths have never ventured this far northwest, but the chances of them passing us by without an altercation are slim. We have a few hours at most until they track us here."

My focus flickers to the satchel my father left at the door. A rolled-up fur rests on top of it and a fresh quiver of arrows sits beside it.

I've remained conscious of Thoren where he's concealed in the turret—and the fact that he hasn't sounded any sort of alarm —but it's only a matter of time.

"Life is a series of choices," my father continues. "Some barely nudge the course of our destiny. Others push us far away from what we want."

I exhale slowly, trying to stave off the inevitable decision that lies ahead of me.

The only decision that will keep my family safe: to leave them.

As much as I try to push at it, I know I already made my choice when I pulled this silver-haired woman out of the snow.

I take a deep, shaky breath, determined to calm the fears rising up within me, only for my chest to fill with the scent of her hair.

It's a soft, sweet and calming fragrance. The fine strands tickle my chin and my cheek. Her head fits perfectly in the crook of my neck while her arms are folded between us.

Her hand rests on my heart, binding me to her with every thudding beat.

CHAPTER 9

I don't have to speak my answer.

My father gives me a single nod, his expression never changing, but within his eyes...

Damn. I can't decipher what he's thinking or know what he's feeling.

His expression is that of a warrior who has seen too much death and felt too much loss and is prepared for more of both.

He speaks quietly, as if he already knew my answer before he asked. "I've readied the sled so you can carry her on it. You won't have Thoren to cover your tracks, so you'll need to choose the rockiest paths, where the sled won't leave deep marks that can be followed. Those paths will be harder to travel but safer for you both."

My voice is hoarse. "Father, I—"

"Whatever direction you choose, don't travel too far east. The fae rule those lands and you can never trust a fae. *Never.*" He gives me a stern look. "Do you understand?"

I take a quick breath. "Yes, Father."

"The same goes for the north. If you travel too far north, you'll encounter our old clan. If you're lucky, they'll kill you quickly, but they'll take their time with her. You know this already."

I suppress the cold chill slipping down my spine. "Yes, Father."

"Stay west," he says. "Find humans and hide among them. Keep her hair covered until you can figure out a way to mask its color."

"I will," I whisper.

He reaches out to squeeze my shoulder through the rug, his eyes appearing faded now. "Remember always that your deep light is finite. If you choose to call on all of it at once, it will give you the strength and speed of ten men and deliver you glory in death."

His grip tightens. "If you choose to die in this way, the Valkyries will come for your soul and deliver you to the Hall of Warriors."

A little light flares once more in his eyes before it fades again. "But make no mistake: Your deep light is like a flame consuming wood. Once burned, there's no escaping the death that follows. Whatever you do, don't burn out your light unless you're certain that death is inevitable."

Releasing my shoulder, he jabs at the wood in the hearth. The blue runes inked across his hands are stark and clear in the firelight. They're the marks of the Einherjar. Marks that neither Thoren nor I wear because we weren't old enough to get them before we left our clan and since then, he made the decision that we wouldn't be inked.

The wood crackles and I picture the gleaming portions crumbling into ash as inevitably as death will come to me if I choose to burn out my light.

"I understand," I say.

At that, Father turns to the cloths in the pot. He uses the tongs to drain each cloth, one at a time, allowing them to cool and testing them against his own face before he gestures for me to extricate the woman's hands so he can wrap them.

Silence stretches between us as he works, and I'm conscious of the quiet from within the turret. Thoren will have heard our conversation and be processing all of this too.

Father breaks the silence as he presses the cloths to the woman's left hand.

"There's one more thing I need to tell you." He pauses. "It's about Thoren's mother and how she died."

Thoren's mother was our father's second wife after my mother died. It was the circumstances of Thoren's mother's death that caused our father to leave his clan, but he would never speak about the details.

My focus flickers back to the turret. If there's something Father hasn't told us about Thoren's mother, then Thoren should be the one to hear it.

As if he reads my mind, Father quickly says, "Thoren already knows. It was his right to hear it first."

My forehead creases. "Okay?"

Father continues working on the cloths as he speaks, his focus down, his movements careful. "She wasn't a member of our clan or of the clans with which we were allied. She lived in a village that we conquered."

I can't hide my surprise. "She was a captive?"

He nods his blond head and looks me in the eye. "The moment I saw her, my light was drawn to her. Her family was slaughtered, but I swept her up before she could be killed or worse."

Apprehension fills me at the fact that he's telling me this story now—a story that started with his deep light, just as my light was drawn to the woman in my arms. I don't remember Thoren's mother. I was too young at the time.

"I treated her well. Protected her." Father's forehead creases, but he looks more bemused than angry. "I tried to teach her my people's ways, but she hated our customs. She was outspoken. She never failed to speak up when she witnessed injustice or cruelty."

He finishes wrapping the woman's hands and starts on her feet. "I was their leader, so I started making changes. Small changes. Little things. Until the day she smiled for the first time. I never forced her into my bed or even asked her to come to it. She came to me. That was when I believed that she had chosen me and was content."

His hands become still. "Soon after Thoren was born, a rival from another clan challenged my leadership."

I know enough about my father's people to understand that a challenge for leadership involves a fight to the death.

"I wasn't worried," Father says. "I'd watched him fight and knew I could beat him. We made a square, but in the middle of the fight, he knocked me to the side, where one of his supporters stabbed me in the back."

Again, I know enough about his clan's culture to know that a square is sacred. Nobody else is allowed to interfere.

"I stumbled," Father continues. "My rival saw his chance. He went for the killing blow to my heart."

Father covers the woman's feet in the fur again and leans back on his heels, his fists clenched on his knees. "Thoren's mother darted from the crowd and stepped between us. She took the blade that was intended for me."

My heart sinks at what he told me.

Father meets my eyes. "You know what that means in my people's culture."

I nod. "She shamed you."

His gaze is piercing. "A warrior must face each blade. By sacrificing herself, she took away my honor. Without honor, I was forced to forfeit my clan. Even though I was left alive, my rival won."

He gestures to the wall of weapons inside the door and the

spot above them all where his war hammer rests. The wooden handle is broken and splintered, and now I understand that it wasn't broken in battle, but as a deliberate act by his opponent when he lost his honor.

His jaw clenches. "She knew our customs. She knew the consequences. But what I will never know... is if she did it because she loved me and didn't want me to die. Or if she did it because she finally saw her chance to take revenge for her slain family."

His focus falls now to the woman in my arms. "Be careful of your enemies, Erik. Particularly the ones you keep close."

My heart is cold.

This woman is my enemy simply because of who she is. What she was born to be. Not by choice.

But when she wakes up, what will she choose?

And how will I know if what she *appears* to choose reflects her heart?

Father rises to his feet. "I'll check on Thoren. Then we'll fetch her some warm clothing." He exhales heavily. "Then it will be time for you to go. You can make good ground before night falls."

I put voice to a question that's now squeezing my chest. "When will it be safe for me to come back?"

"That will be up to her," Father says. "And whether or not she wants to get you killed."

CHAPTER 10

Without another word, Father heads up to the turret, speaking quietly with Thoren before I hear them decide to switch places.

Thoren hurries down the stairs and drops to his knees beside me, nudging up against Skirra.

My brother's expression is pale and drawn, every glimmer of happiness gone. "You'd better come back, Erik."

With that, he jumps to his feet and hurries to the far end of the cabin, where we keep our spare clothing. Moments later, he reappears, his arms full of garments.

He deposits two sets of fur-lined clothes beside me and taps one of the piles. "These should fit her."

I recognize the items as clothing he recently outgrew. He's shot up over the last few months and could end up taller than me.

I beat back the realization that I might not have the chance to see that happen.

He doesn't say anything more and I know better than to push a conversation with him. On the rare occasions that he chooses silence, breaking it doesn't do anyone any good.

He pours himself a cup of steaming water from the pot before he retrieves his bow and arrow and disappears outside. I catch sight of Kori, the white wolf, padding up to him before the door closes.

The woman's arm twitches against my chest, drawing my attention back to her.

I study her face carefully in case she's about to open her eyes.

I prepare the words I need to speak: *I found you in the snow. You were dying. If you want to leave, you can.*

She doesn't move again.

It seems she isn't waking, after all. The tremor in her arm must have been reflex. Perhaps her muscles were remembering how to move.

I'm suddenly conscious that my lower shoulder feels damp, and when I adjust my position a little, I'm surprised to find tears leaking from her eyes.

I check her face again, but she hasn't woken up.

Maybe the leaking of tears is a good sign.

Maybe it isn't.

She's warmer than she was before and a slight color has returned to her cheeks.

I'm torn between the need to keep her warm and the threat that will come to my family's door if I linger here with her.

Closing my eyes for a moment, I inhale again the scent of her hair and listen to her breathing, deeper than before.

Deep enough.

Keeping the woman as covered and warm as possible, I shimmy away from her, nudging Skirra out of my way.

Reaching for my warmer clothing, I pull it on as fast as I can.

Then I take the garments Thoren brought, keeping the woman as wrapped in the fur as possible while I dress her in the cloth tunic and cloth pants first, followed by the fur-lined coat and pants.

I pull the boots over her feet and mittens over her hands but leave the cloths wrapped around her hands and feet to keep as much warmth in as possible.

Finally, I cocoon her in the fur she was already lying on.

All the while, Skirra remains nearby, watching me and giving a soft whine every now and then. He was insistent about digging her out of the snow and now it seems he's as unrelenting about staying at her side.

"It's up to you if you come with me," I say to him, even though I know he won't understand me. He'll probably think we're going on a hunting trip like we often do, at the end of which we'll return home.

While he watches me, I hurry over to the satchel my father prepared, checking its contents before I arrange my weapons in their sheaths—my hunting knives at my waist plus my bow and arrows at my back.

Returning to the woman, I lift her into my arms, fur and all, sensing a little more life in her body, as if her soul is no longer trying to flee its physical cage.

I call quietly to my father, who appears from within the turret and descends the stairs.

"Quickly now, Erik," he says, an urgency in his voice that sends cold apprehension through me.

"The wolves?" I ask, following Father to the door.

"Most of them darted away a minute ago," he says, still holding his bow, its quiver now resting in the scabbard at his back alongside his sword. "They must have sensed something close. You need to move."

Outside the cabin, Thoren waits on the frozen ground a few paces from the door, an arrow nocked to his bow, his attention focused on the trees to our left. If the Blacksmiths are coming from the south, that's the direction from which they would first appear.

Kori has stayed at his side, the wolf's blue eyes bright as he snarls softly.

"The other wolves went that way," Thoren says, inclining his head in the direction his bow is pointed. "I'll keep watch."

I head for the sled that waits on the ground directly in front of me.

At the same moment, a howl sounds in the distance.

It's an eerie cry from a single wolf that's picked up by the other wolves until the forest is echoing with their calls.

Their combined howls send shivers down my spine, and I try to calm my movements while Father and I strap the woman onto the sled. It has raised edges, so she won't easily slide off either side, and the leather straps will ensure she doesn't get knocked off if we traverse rocky terrain.

Of course, she'll feel like a prisoner when she wakes, but that's the least of my concerns right now.

Keeping her and my family alive is what I care about.

Within my mind, I'm berating myself. I never should have brought her back here. I should have split off from my family and found another way to get her warm.

I should have—

My father's hand on my shoulder halts my thoughts. "Erik."

I glance up at him.

"Destiny," he says with a stern look that speaks volumes.

"Father, I'll remember everything you taught me." My throat tightens too much to continue speaking.

He draws me upright and pulls me into a warrior's embrace. "May the stars watch over you, Son."

Then he turns away, taking Thoren's place on watch so that my brother can come to me.

I don't miss the tears in his young eyes.

I fight the burn of my own tears as I pull my brother into a hug. "You *will* see me again."

He gives me a nod, even though he must know it's a promise I might not be able to keep.

I crouch and reach for the straps attached to the sled.

I'm about to pull them onto my shoulders when Skirra edges away from the woman for the first time, growling savagely in the direction of the trees directly opposite the cabin —farther to the right than the direction Thoren was focused on.

Father tenses, his eyes narrowed at the trees. If it's indeed the Blacksmiths who have alarmed the wolves, and not one of the monstrous predators that lives in this forest, then it seems they're coming from that direction. Which means they probably circled around, scouting the cabin's surroundings, ascertaining the terrain.

It means they're smart. I can't underestimate them.

Suddenly, the chorus of howls stops.

We're left in an abrupt, sharp silence that feels heavier with every passing second.

A breeze kicks up, tugging at the snow on the trees, swirling at the ice on the ground.

Then there's a soft, scrabbling sound in the distance.

It stops. And once again, an unsettling quiet falls over the forest.

I want to believe that there's some kind of beast out there, not Blacksmiths, because then I would be confident we could take it down. Maybe it's another leopard, but I know that's wishful thinking. If it were a creature of the forest, the wolves would have returned to us already. We may not control them, but they know how to alert us to the dangers within these mountains.

If it's Blacksmiths, then they're moving as quietly as we do on our hunts.

I reach for one of my knives, listening carefully, unable to shake the feeling that this time, we're the prey.

That's when a shriek crashes across the air, the desperate yelp of a wolf in pain.

With it comes the *clang* of metal, a melodic ringing sound that echoes as eerily as the wolves' howls.

My father's jaw clenches and his exhale is sharp.

"I know that sound," he says. "It's Blacksmiths."

CHAPTER II

I jolt into action.

"I'll lead them away." I'm already dragging at the sled's straps and preparing to run.

My father is impossibly calm despite the disturbing howls and ringing of metal now filling the forest. "You won't be able to move fast enough."

"I have to give you and Thoren the chance to run—"

Father grabs my arm, his brow suddenly furrowed and his grip hard.

"Run?" His gaze is furious. "We will not die running. We will die in battle."

His voice is a snarl and for the briefest moment, I see the man he must have been long ago. The savagery and bloodlust that must have been bred into him.

It's a brutality I've glimpsed on every hunting trip, but it has never been aimed at me.

"That is our way, Son," he says, his glare piercing.

Without another pause, he turns to my brother, who is wide-eyed beside us.

"The wolves!" Thoren whispers, his voice sounding strangled, as if his throat is too tight to speak. "We have to help them."

"There's nothing we can do for them." The corners of my father's mouth are turned down as he demands Thoren's attention. "Pull the woman inside the cabin, then get back to the turret. You will defend our home from the roof. Do not let loose an arrow unless you know you have a killing shot. Do you hear me, Thoren? The moment you shoot, they'll know you're there and they'll come for you."

Thoren has now frozen opposite me. He's never killed a person before. Neither have I. Only beasts.

Father takes hold of Thoren's shoulders. "Erik and I will fight them here on the ground. You will stay back and shoot from a distance. Erik and I will do the cutting."

It's what he says to Thoren before every hunt.

"It's just another hunt, Son. Go. *Now*."

Thoren nods hurriedly. Without another moment's hesitation, he darts past me, reaches for the sled's straps, and takes the woman back inside, his teeth gritted and muscles bunching.

He disappears within seconds.

Father's fierce eyes meet mine. "Whatever regrets you have, Erik, cast them out. If the Blacksmiths were this close all along, they would have caught you no matter what. And then they would have made their way back to slaughter Thoren and me. We'll have a better chance of survival if we fight them together."

His expression allows no argument, but it doesn't stop my rising fear.

I tell myself that facing Blacksmiths will be like fighting the leopard. They will be smart, dangerous, and vicious.

So will I.

I reach for my weapons.

My hunting knives already hang from my belt and my bow and quiver are strapped to my back. Quickly retrieving the bow, I nock an arrow and take a knee to the ground.

Father, too, draws his bow and nocks an arrow, but he remains in a standing position so that he and I can cover different trajectories with our arrows.

It's a hunting formation we've used many times before.

"Judging by the sound of their metal, there's at least three of them," Father says, his voice low. "You can tell by the different melody each piece of metal sings. Remember that they can transform their weapons into any shape they want. A short dagger can become a spear within a blink. Don't get too close to them without a way to quickly retreat."

The way Father described Blacksmith power to me in the past, their only clear limitation is that they can't use their power on just any metal. They can only transform the metal they've tempered with their magic, which is why they carry it on their bodies. Even a piece of what appears to be metal jewelry could become a deadly object.

Skirra stays by my side, edging forward, his teeth bared as he continues growling softly.

"Stay back, Skirra," I whisper to him, but I'm not surprised when he ignores me. I have as much hope of controlling Skirra as I have of wishing the Blacksmiths would simply leave us alone.

Even so, I'll do everything I can to protect both Skirra and Kori. Their pack is the last of its kind in these mountains. Untainted by Blacksmith magic, which makes them rare and precious.

Kori remains on my father's left side, farthest from me, appearing more cautious when he stays a step behind my father.

A shadow of movement from within the turret on the roof

tells me that Thoren has taken up position there. Given what Father said about revealing his presence, I'm certain Thoren will stay concealed until he has a clear shot.

We've trained him well.

Stay back. Let us do the cutting.

My father's voice is even quieter. "No matter what they say or do, they will intend to kill us," he says. "We've lived under their noses for over a decade. They won't simply walk away from us now that they know we're here."

His eyes pierce mine. "Fight to kill, Erik. They will have no mercy for us. We must have no mercy for them."

My jaw clenches. I give him a nod before he returns his attention to the forest and so do I.

The howls and clanging have faded, and now a soft dragging sound reaches us across the distance, slowly coming closer.

And closer...

Five figures materialize between the trees, all of them wearing white cloaks that blend seamlessly with our snowy surroundings and, disconcertingly, make it impossible to see what weapons they might be carrying around their bodies.

I narrow my eyes at the forest behind them, conscious that there could be more of them holding back in the shadows.

The ones I can see are moving quietly, their footsteps as light as predators who know how to defy the undergrowth and avoid the worst of the leafy debris.

They're stealthy. Although as they come closer, I can see black smears on their cloaks, confirming that it was very likely they who disturbed the second butterfly nest earlier today.

We won't know for certain if they were out searching for the woman until we speak with them—assuming they speak first and attack second.

The central figure surges ahead of the others, a lean man whose features become clearer as he emerges from the shadows. He's only a little shorter than Father with slightly narrower shoulders.

His hair is long, straight, and a metallic copper color that catches the dappled light as he approaches the edge of the clearing. In contrast, his eyes are pale-green like leaves that don't get enough sunlight. His jaw is angular, giving his face a sharp appearance, which is compounded by the sneer on his lips.

He holds his head high, his gaze seeming to take us in within seconds; his speed slows as he nears the edge of the trees twenty paces away.

That's when it becomes clear that his right arm is stretched out behind him, a posture that's concealed somewhat by his cloak.

My forehead creases and I narrow my eyes, trying to see why.

Soon enough, he wrenches his arm forward and one of the wolves comes into view, its body sliding through the snow.

The way it's struggling tells me it's still alive, but its snout is bound shut by a copper-colored chain that extends in a seemingly continuous strand, binding the wolf's front and back legs. The chain is wrapped around the wolf's body all the way from its hindquarters up to its neck, where the metal forms a solid collar.

Attached to the collar is another, thicker chain, the end of which is curled around the man's right hand.

In the same fluid movement with which he heaved the wolf forward, he flicks the end of the chain toward the nearest tree.

Like a blade, it streaks across the air so fast that the copper chain is a blur before the sharp end hits the tree with a *crack*, embedding deep into the wood and tethering the wolf to the tree's trunk.

The wolf scrabbles furiously at the ground, trying to free

itself, while the man continues toward us without missing a step.

I fight my instinct to jump to my feet and defend the wolf, forcing myself to stay with my father, keeping my arrow pointed squarely at the copper-haired man's neck as he continues walking toward us.

It's as if he has no fear of us or our arrows at all.

"Blacksmith!" my father calls, his voice calm while his bow remains visibly taut. "Stop where you are."

The copper-haired man slows his pace but takes two more steps before he draws to a halt, his cloak swirling around his legs.

"Humans," he says, casting a dismissive glance at me before he shakes his head at my father. "Put away those pitiful weapons. They will offer you no advantage."

"Don't be so sure of that," my father replies. "Blacksmiths bleed and die as easily as humans. I know it for a fact."

As he speaks, Father turns his bow slightly, ensuring that the runes on the back of his right hand are fully visible to the copper-haired man.

The Blacksmith stiffens, appearing to quickly reassess my father, refocusing on his blond hair and then the ink on his hands. "Blond hair. Blue runes..." The corners of his mouth turn down as he mutters, "Fucking Einherjar." He spits. "Nothing more than barbarians."

Despite his contemptuous reply, his eyes betray a new wariness.

My father's declaration implies that he fought and killed a Blacksmith in the past.

I can't risk taking my eyes off the copper-haired man, but from the corner of my eye, I briefly assess my father's expression.

I'm surprised to realize... he may not be lying.

Not judging by the clench of his jaw and the steadiness of his gaze.

Killing a Blacksmith would certainly earn him a reputation worthy of a leader under Einherjar law.

But now I wonder how many secrets my father has kept from me all this time.

To the copper-haired Blacksmith, my father says, "Come any closer and I will spill *your* blood just as easily."

CHAPTER 12

The copper-haired Blacksmith rallies quickly.

"Do not challenge me, human," he sneers. "I am Kalith Silverspun. I stand at the right hand of Malak Ironmeld. And *you* are clearly outnumbered here."

As he speaks, the other four figures draw to a stop at the edge of the clearing, all of them men.

Two are positioned to Kalith's right, while the other two are on his left. They're spread out, located far enough apart that it will take seconds to adjust our aim between them all.

The one on my far right has short, bronze hair and fierce eyebrows, while the man next to him wears a beard with sharply defined edges. The bearded man's hair is a similar copper color to Kalith's hair, but his brown eyes are nothing like Kalith's pale-green irises.

Both of those men drag wolves beside them, each of the animals bound in chains. They tether the wolves to the trees with thudding cracks of metal into wood, just like Kalith did.

My father doesn't wait for the sound of the thudding cracks to fade. "I challenge whomever I wish, Blacksmith," he says, remaining scarily calm, which only makes his threat sound deadlier. "If you want to live to see tomorrow, turn around. Release the wolves. And leave."

"Not until I have answers," Kalith snaps.

My father narrows his eyes. "What answers do you seek that I could possibly give you?"

"I'm searching for my daughter," Kalith replies. "She disappeared from within our city walls last night."

His daughter?

His statement confirms Father's theory that these Blacksmiths were out searching for the woman, but this man looks nothing like her. His hair is a completely different color than her silvery tresses, although I haven't seen her eyes to know if they could be green like his.

Even if she *is* his daughter, it doesn't mean he cares for her.

I remind myself of the marks of a beating she bears across her back and legs. Somebody did that to her, and surely, a father would know about it—yet there were no signs of salve or balm or any other treatment to indicate she had been cared for.

Kalith continues speaking, his lips pinched. "She is feeble. Unable to defend herself. We fear some harm may have come to her."

Father's expression remains calm, although his question is cutting. "How does a father fail to protect his child?"

Kalith stiffens again, but this time, he glances back across his shoulder.

Unnervingly, so do the other four men, even though taking their eyes off us is a reckless move on their part.

I'm suddenly aware of another male figure, standing much farther back within the forest, right where the shadows gather.

It's another Blacksmith. It has to be. Concealed in the background like I feared they could be.

He's too far away to discern the details of his features, but I make out broad shoulders and a square jaw.

Unlike the first five, he's swathed in an inky-black cloak,

which would normally make him easily visible in these snowy surroundings, but he's staying close to the trees and somehow... *impossibly*... blending into them.

Skirra is suddenly fixated on that man. The wolf edges farther forward despite the danger of the Blacksmiths closer to us, the low pitch of his snarls telling me he's even more on edge now.

Just like earlier today, I wish I had his wolfish eyes, this time to discern the details of the sixth man's features across the distance, to see what weapons he's currently carrying, and to understand what kind of threat he poses.

Even without Skirra's senses, the hairs on the back of my neck are standing on end, a prickling sensation invading my skin.

I don't miss the way my father shifts a little, adjusting his stance, his arrow now aimed slightly between Kalith and the man in the shadows. The other Blacksmiths won't be able to read father's stoic expression, but I know his reactions well.

He's worried now.

Really worried.

Kalith and the other four men return their attention to us.

This time, Kalith surges forward, defying my father's threats and taking three steps toward us. He's now only fifteen paces away.

His tone is sharp. "I'll ask you plainly, Einherjar, and I suggest you answer truthfully: Have you seen my daughter?"

As he speaks, the others look at me as if they will enjoy spilling our blood, whether or not they have reason to.

"I've seen many Blacksmiths," Father replies. "But as for your daughter, I can't say for certain. Does she have silver hair?"

I wasn't expecting my father to mention her specifically, but I remind myself to trust him. He won't do anything that jeopardizes our lives.

At my father's question about the color of the woman's hair, the man in the background jolts away from the tree he was leaning against and begins pacing across the shadows, his cloak billowing around his form.

"She does," Kalith replies sharply, his shoulders stiffening and his gaze flickering back to the man in the shadows before he returns his attention to my father. "So you *have* seen her?"

"Yes, we saw her," Father says. "Hours ago. She was waist-deep in snow at the edge of the pit where you throw your dead."

Kalith's eyes narrow and the tension around his mouth increases. "In the pit? You saw her there?"

Father's voice remains matter-of-fact. "We were not so foolhardy as to touch her. If you wish to save her, you may want to hurry. Her hands were already black with rot."

In the background, the shadowed figure pulls up sharply. He whirls in the direction from which they came—back toward the pit, which is now a full two-hour hike down the mountain.

Kalith seems acutely aware of that man's reactions, his jaw clenching.

He lets his breath out with a snap. "You lie, Einherjar! I personally checked the pit this morning. She wasn't there."

He's lying about checking the pit. I'm not sure how I'm so certain about that.

Maybe it's the slightly desperate tone of his voice or the tightness of his jaw. Or the timing. The second nest of butterflies was disturbed while I was pulling the woman out of the pit. If it was these Blacksmiths who disturbed them, then they had already passed the pit and were well within the forest by that time.

He can't have checked the pit, because if he checked it, he would have seen his daughter in it and—

My breath stills.

I reassess the tension in his face and recall the sickening

contempt with which he spoke about her when he called her 'feeble'.

He saw her there.

He fucking saw her and left her to die. He might have even been the one who put here there.

Kalith's eyes flicker once more to the man in the background. "She wasn't there! She's *here*. She has to be."

The way he shouts, it's as if he wants the other man to believe him. I'm not sure exactly what's going on between them or what their hierarchy is, but it's clear that the other Blacksmiths are wary of the man in the shadows.

Kalith spins back to my father, declaring to the other Blacksmiths, "I will find Asha and bring her out."

Asha.

That must be the woman's name.

A deadly smile splits Kalith's lips as he continues. "But first I'll tear these Einherjar apart."

CHAPTER 13

With a *whoosh* of material, Kalith casts the coat off his shoulders.

Beneath it, he's wearing a white shirt and pants, neither appearing lined with fur, but he doesn't seem to notice the cold.

Two copper armbands rest on his left forearm while three more copper bands are wrapped around his left bicep. A copper-colored hammer is attached to a white belt at his waist.

Curiously, a fine, copper ring rests on the thumb of his right hand and an unbroken line of metal runs up the inside of his right arm all the way to the edge of his sleeveless tunic. I can't see what might be sitting beneath his clothing that could be connected to that metal line.

He moves fast.

Before I can blink, he snatches one of the bands from his forearm into his right hand. Its flat shape instantly elongates into a chain, growing in length as he spins it in the air, a blur of circular movement that makes an unearthly metallic hum.

All I manage to make out is the deadly shape forming at the

end of the chain: a cleaving knife like the one hanging in our smokehouse.

It's small enough to whip through the air while attached to the chain.

And large enough to slice right through my father's throat.

Kalith has already taken a step forward, letting the blade fly with a force that makes it shriek in the cold air. A killing scream.

His aim is perfect.

The knife streaks toward my father, the chain curving slightly as if Kalith can control its trajectory by will alone.

Father's turning and his legs are bending. I know he'll try to leap clear, but the weapon is moving too fast.

I react on pure instinct.

My arm muscles are already firing. I release my arrow, not at the flying blade, but at the uppermost chain link to which it's attached.

Clang!

The sound of the arrow hitting the loop creates an eerie echo like a plucked note. The arrow's metal tip catches the chain, wrenches the knife off course, and yanks Kalith's right arm away from his body.

With a *thud*, the arrow hits the tree behind him, right beside one of the far Blacksmiths, who takes a quick step back. The arrow takes the chain with it, pinning the chain and blade to the tree's trunk with a force that makes the arrow's wooden shaft *twang*.

I was sure the accuracy of my shot and the tightness of Kalith's grip would have wrenched the chain right out of his hand, possibly even hurt his shoulder, but neither of those things have happened.

For the briefest moment, I replay the widening of his eyes when my arrow hit the chain, the tensing of his right bicep, and then the sudden extension of the chain as if were made of liquid, not metal, giving it the length and slack needed so its sharp arc didn't pull his arm too far backward.

Damn.

Not only is it clear he can transform the shape of his metal at will, but the metal itself seems able to act like a fluid substance, practically flowing like water.

Worse, he has four more bands on his left arm and I don't doubt he can use each of them with the same deadly efficiency as he used the first one.

All of this passes through my mind within a split second as I nock another arrow to my bow, aiming it at the exposed side of Kalith's neck and letting it loose.

My father has dropped into a crouch and his arrow flies at Kalith's extended right arm, heading for his underarm where a savage cut can cause enough blood loss to lead to death.

Kalith lets go of the chain, ducking and darting at whirlwind speed.

Both arrows sail harmlessly through the air.

I don't have time to watch them land, aware only of the dull thuds that tell me they hit nothing more than the snowy ground.

I'm nocking a third arrow to my bow while, at the edge of my vision, my father drops his bow and arrow and reaches for his hunting knives.

Then Kalith rages toward me.

Another copper band is suddenly missing from his forearm. There's a glint of metal in his right hand that tells me he's holding it already.

His snarl is a whoosh of sound. "You think you can test me, Boy?"

A copper sword forms within his grip, the blade and its ornate hilt catching the light in blinding flashes as he crosses the five paces between us at an unbelievable speed.

The sword cuts through the air as he spins it so that it rests down by his side, its tip pointed forward, both of his hands on the hilt.

He reaches me faster than I can take a breath, slashing the sword forward and, because I'm still in a crouched position, aiming it straight for my neck.

With all my strength, I throw myself backward, calling on every muscle in my legs to give me enough speed to evade the killing blow.

At the same time, I pull the arrow back, hoping to shoot him at close range, where he'll have reduced time to respond.

I've moved just in time that the tip of the sword only grazes my shoulder, but its swinging arc slices across my coat and takes the blade right through my bow and arrow before I can fire.

Wooden shards explode around me, pieces of my bow and the splintered arrow flying up across my face and body. One of them nicks my left cheek. Another barely misses my right eye. My thick coat protects my chest, although several splinters end up embedded in it.

Splinters fly toward Kalith too.

But with both hands around the hilt of the sword and with its arc heading to his left, his arms are already in an upraised position to protect his face.

I hit the ground on my back, aware of a sudden blur of gray fur as Skirra leaps from the snow beside me, his teeth bared.

He knows how to take down predators—if not by the neck, then by savaging their bellies or underarms where blood will flow quickly. And, once again, Kalith's right underarm is exposed.

Before Skirra's teeth can sink into Kalith's body, Kalith's boot flies up, smashing into Skirra's jaw and knocking him back across the snow.

The wolf yelps and tumbles through the powder, kicking up snowflakes, but his efforts were not completely in vain.

The distraction left Kalith's back exposed for a few seconds —an opportunity my father doesn't squander.

He throws himself at Kalith's side, his knife stabbing at Kalith's lower back where vital organs lie.

Father's blade connects, but instead of impaling Kalith's body, there's a *clang*.

The blade slides right off Kalith's back with a ferocious shriek that sounds like metal scraping against metal.

What the...?

Kalith whirls back to my father, again moving so fast, I can hardly follow it.

The torn section of his tunic flaps apart at the back where Father cut through it, revealing copper plating resting against Kalith's skin beneath his shirt.

More metal.

But this time, it seems to be sitting against his skin like armor, hidden beneath his clothing. There's a glimmer as it appears to become liquid, moving across his back.

If he can move his metal fast enough, he'll be able to protect whatever part of his body is vulnerable at any given time.

Father is already slashing with his other knife, moving as fast as I've ever seen him move, stabbing at Kalith's face, but with the upward strike, Father's right side is exposed.

My heart leaps into my throat as Kalith's sword swings into that space.

Just in time, Father adjusts his aim, bringing his blade arm down instead of going through with the original strike.

The edge of his knife connects with the top of the sword and he pushes Kalith's weapon away. The muscles in his neck bunch, indicating how much strength it takes to ram Kalith's sword off course.

But my father isn't done.

The moment Kalith's sword arm flies wide, Father headbutts him.

Smack!

Kalith stumbles back for the first time since the fight started, lurching across the clearing and toward the other Blacksmiths.

They're all leaning toward the fight, tension simmering in the air around them. They've thrown off their cloaks, revealing that each of them is similarly dressed to Kalith in white tunics, pants, and boots.

They don't appear to wear as many metal bands on their left arms as he does. The men who chained the wolves to the trees only have two bands each on their left biceps. The men on the other side each have three metal bands, also on their left biceps.

I'm starting to see a pattern between them, the way they store their metal on their left arms and use it with their right hands.

There isn't time to study them further.

Blood streams from Kalith's nostrils, splattering his white tunic.

The bone at the top of his nose is visibly broken.

He quickly regains his balance, and a savage cruelty enters his voice.

"Fuck this," he says, his voice taking on a nasal tone now that his nose is broken.

He gestures to the two Blacksmiths on his right. "You two are with me."

Then he turns to the Blacksmiths on his left—the two who chained wolves to trees. He addresses the man with the copper beard first and the one with the bronze hair second. "Deron. Abdiel. Search the cabin. Find Asha."

With that, Kalith focuses back on me and Father.

"No matter what else we do," he snarls. "We're killing these fucking Einherjar."

CHAPTER 14

Father's chest rises and falls with a deeply indrawn breath as he sheathes his knives and reaches for the sword at his back.

As he draws it, a calm seems to settle over him once more.

He casts a quick look at me and then beyond me to the cabin.

I read his wishes loud and clear: Keep the Blacksmiths from getting inside, where Thoren and the woman—Asha—are hidden.

Father leaps back into the fight with Kalith, the sound of ringing metal filling the air while Abdiel and Deron storm in my direction.

From the way Kalith addressed them before, it seems that Abdiel is the one with bronze hair while Deron is the one with the copper beard.

They reach for a metal band from each of their biceps, at which swords spring forth within their hands.

My bow and arrow rest in splinters across the snow and my fight with Kalith forced me a few paces closer to the cabin, but

I'm still well within the center of the clearing with plenty of space to move.

I draw my hunting knives, gripping one in each hand, taking quick seconds to study the oncoming men while Skirra stays close to my right side. If either of them gets past me, Skirra will be able to give chase more quickly than I can.

They come at me fast, weapons swinging, alternating glimmers of copper and bronze.

I dart back and to the side and back again, deftly evading each killing blow they aim at me as they work in unison, fighting as if they've been coordinating their attacks for years.

It's clear from their increasingly furrowed brows and downturned mouths that, despite the way I defended myself against Kalith, they didn't expect me to be able to evade them.

But I've had plenty of practice avoiding the claws and teeth of creatures in this forest. Their blades are no different.

And with the two of them coming at me at once, they have to be mindful of each others' weapons. It seems to be slowing them down. Or at least, they aren't as fast as Kalith—and I plan to make the most of it.

I just need an opening to use my knives.

Abdiel exposes his side and I throw myself forward through the snow, sliding past him, my knife cutting across his ribs, tearing through his tunic and the flesh beneath it.

Blood splashes across the snow and he whirls on me with a roar.

Unlike Kalith, it seems this Blacksmith doesn't have liquid metal to protect him. I may not have struck the knife deep between his ribs, but I hurt him.

He slashes at me wildly, his movements erratic and furious as he splits off from Deron to rage at me.

My surroundings become a blur as I focus on his blade and the way it's transforming, becoming sharp and jagged on both sides.

The copper metal swings in a deadly arc toward me, but this time, I step inward, a dangerous move.

My left dagger flies at the side of his throat. My right dagger flies at his stomach.

Both connect, each one slicing into him.

His eyes widen and suddenly, he's trying to leap backward, where Skirra is waiting.

The wolf sails through the air, teeth bared, latching on to the back of Abdiel's neck and pulling him down to the ground.

I keep hold of my daggers as his downward momentum wrenches the blades out of him.

He screams and thrashes, trying to dislodge Skirra while his sword transforms into a dagger.

A bolt of fear shoots through me as he rams the blade at Skirra's face.

At the same time, Deron is now ploughing toward me.

I dart forward, ready to drop onto Abdiel's chest, to evade Deron and slash open Abdiel's throat before he can hurt my wolf.

That's when a volley of arrows flies through the air.

One strikes Abdiel's throat, driving all the way through his neck and knocking his head back into the snow. The second shoots through his wrist and pins his dagger hand to his own chest. And the third strikes through his eye.

Two killing shots and one to save Skirra.

Metal glints at the corner of my eye and Deron's roar meets my ears as he lurches toward me, a spear in his hands.

But another volley of arrows is already raining down on him.

I can only imagine how fast Thoren's firing them, as skillful as an archer can be.

Three arrows fly toward Deron's neck and face. As fast as he's moving, they're perfect shots.

A heartbeat before they would hit him, Deron skids to a halt, and his sword transforms into a copper shield.

The metal spreads outward in all directions.

Each arrow crashes against the shield, cracking and splintering.

I roll clear of Abdiel's body while Skirra leaps backward.

The life may have gone from Abdiel's eyes, but his death screams didn't go unnoticed, particularly not by Kalith. Across the way, he appears to freeze for a moment, a delay that costs him a cut to his arm when my father lunges at him.

But worse, Deron has spun away from me and is now focused on the roof, where the turret is concealed.

To make the shots, Thoren had to lean forward and his face was visible for a few seconds.

Instead of coming at me, Deron runs toward the cabin with a furious shout. "You're fucking dead, Boy!"

I give chase, knowing that Deron will soon be out of Thoren's range. I can't let him get inside the cabin.

I shout to Skirra, whose snout is covered in blood, but the wolf's body is already a blur as he streaks ahead of me, leaping at Deron's back just as the Blacksmith reaches the corner of the building.

The wolf's reflection across the back of Deron's shield gives him away.

Deron moves in a flash. He whirls back to Skirra, flips his shield into his left hand, smacks his now-free right hand onto his bicep to collect his final band, and drops into a crouch.

A shot of confusion streaks through me when he doesn't appear to transform that band into a weapon, simply keeping it in his hand.

In that same heartbeat, Skirra continues to fly forward, his trajectory now taking him toward Deron's head.

The Blacksmith's fist snaps out, his right hand wraps around Skirra's throat, and he shoves the wolf backward.

For the split second that Deron's right hand remains in contact with Skirra's throat—too short a time for Skirra to bite—metal bars spring out from Deron's hand.

A copper cage forms around Skirra as he sails back through the air, the force of Deron's punch sending the cage tumbling and sliding through the snow. The cage is just big enough for Skirra to stand up in with only inches on either side for him to move.

A thin metal thread stretches out from the cage, maintaining the contact between it and Deron's hand until the thread snaps, its loose end floating in the breeze.

The cage is now fully formed and Skirra is trapped inside it, thrashing and gnashing at the bars, trying to get out.

I'm caught for a moment between the need to free him and the danger to my brother, but there's no way I can bend those metal bars, not without burning out my deep light.

I have no choice but to leave Skirra there for now, but I make a silent vow that I'll come back to him.

Deron disappears around the cabin's corner and although I'm only five paces behind him, I fear he'll reach the cabin door before I can stop him.

He's completely out of Thoren's range. My brother will now have to choose whether to stay inside the turret or to move into a less confined space where he can more easily fight off an attack.

When I catch sight of three more arrows shooting from the turret toward the Blacksmiths fighting our father, it tells me Thoren has chosen to stay put. But not without more danger.

One of the Blacksmiths breaks off from that fight, his weapon transforming into a spear as he takes a step back, his focus on the turret.

Before he can let the spear fly, Kori launches himself at the Blacksmith, his jaws closing around the man's arm and dragging him down to the ground.

Then I'm around the corner and I can't see them anymore.

I'm afraid for my father.

Fearful for Thoren.

Worried about the wolves.

Also about Asha, who, for all I know, could have woken up by now.

I grit my teeth, forcing my feet to fly faster and my arms to pump harder while my hunting knives remain gripped in my hands.

As I race after Deron into the cabin, I tell myself these Blacksmiths are nothing more than monsters in this forest.

They can bleed and they can die.

We *will* take them down.

CHAPTER 15

I race inside the cabin, the warmer air filling my chest—a comfort that does nothing to reduce my fear.

Deron is still five paces ahead of me.

Sprinting forward, I rip off my coat and drop it to the floor, needing the better agility I possess without it.

Now that we're inside, the turret within which Thoren is concealed is on the near right-hand side. But to access it, Deron will have to run all the way to the back of the space, up the main stairs, and back along the right-hand loft to reach the turret's ladder.

Up ahead, now near the hearth, Deron has skidded to a halt. He's half-turned in the direction of the turrets, but the angle of his head tells me he's focused on the shadowed space beneath the stairs at the back of the room.

I can only just make out the outline of the sled and Asha's still form lying on it. Thoren must have pulled her all the way back there in an attempt to hide her under the stairs.

She's all wrapped up and, to my view, it would be hard to distinguish her from an innocuous pile of blankets, but Deron's fixation on her for a long second tells me he must have seen her.

I expect him to run in that direction. To either retrieve her or to race up the stairs to reach Thoren.

I'll barely have time to stop him, pushing myself to move faster, trying to make the most of his hesitation.

He gives a snarl and then, to my surprise, he flicks his shield down onto the floor, a connecting metal thread running between the shield and his hand.

He steps onto the shield and the metal transforms in a rush, rising upward from the floor like a tree branch. It supports his weight but becomes thinner and thinner as he reaches the top, where he will no doubt launch himself off it, over the railing, and onto the loft.

The base of the branch is also thinning, as if he intends to pull it back up to him with a snap.

I throw myself across the remaining distance, snatching hold of the branch halfway up, but with daggers in both my hands and no time to sheathe them, my grip is useless, my hands slipping.

Above me, Deron has reached the railing and is preparing to hoist himself over it, the visible bunching of his arm muscles telling me he's going to pull the metal back to himself at any second.

I do the only thing I can.

Wrapping my legs around the diminishing branch, I harness the muscles in my stomach, lean back as far as I dare, and pitch the hunting knife in my right hand as hard as I can.

As it flies toward him, I pray he doesn't have hidden armor where I've aimed it.

Thud.

The knife hits Deron's back beneath his right shoulder blade, sinking so deep into his flesh that there's hardly any visible blade beyond the hilt.

He cries out in surprise and roars in pain as his focus flies down to me. I guess he never expected me to hit him so accurately, let alone so hard. Years of throwing knives into trees has given me that ability.

While he shouts, the impact of the knife knocks him against the railing, causing him to fumble and nearly lose his grip before he throws himself over it and onto the loft.

In the meantime, I take advantage of the delay. Now that my right hand is free, I propel myself up the branch as best I can before he can retract it.

He's pulling on the metal, which only helps me ascend. Up and over the railing and onto the loft, where he's twisting and trying to grab hold of the knife to pull it out.

I deliberately lodged it where it's hard to reach and nearly impossible to remove without help. What's more, he's having trouble moving his right arm—the arm and hand he uses to control his metal.

The impediment shows in the way his copper moves more slowly, the branch sluggishly reforming into a much smaller dagger.

I've landed in a crouch on the loft, but I don't waste time.

Fear drives me to act.

I don't know what Thoren's doing right now. Certainly, I haven't heard a crash that would tell me the Blacksmiths outside have succeeded in throwing any spears or other projectiles through the turret, but then, a perfectly aimed arrow shot by one of them wouldn't make much sound.

I don't know if my father's still alive. Again, I haven't heard any shouts of triumph that might signal his death, but that doesn't mean the Blacksmiths haven't killed him.

I don't know what's happened to Skirra and Kori.

Fear for all of them fills my mind, and all I can think about is my father's warning that these men will have no mercy for us.

Launching myself upward and lunging at Deron side-on, I reach for the handle of the knife embedded in his shoulder.

He's turning toward me, the metal in his right hand

changing once more, this time becoming like liquid. It streams from his palm up his arm, across his shoulder, and down his exposed side, all while connected to his right hand by a thin thread.

It's molten and hot, the heat from it beating up at me as spikes begin to form within it. I'm close enough to them that they'll impale me across my chest like multiple spears at once.

I catch his smirk. His arrogance. His certainty. Because he must think he will now cut me to pieces at close range.

But my father trained me to kill creatures as savagely as if I were a beast myself.

Fast and brutal.

I don't give my own safety a second thought.

Wrenching the knife out of his back with my right hand, I ram the dagger in my left hand through the side of his neck, tearing through flesh and sinew, twisting and spilling his blood as I yank it back out.

Only to thrust the dagger in my right hand upward under his arm, right at the edge of the forming metal armor, ripping his veins, before I drop my weight and strike his lower back, three more times in quick succession, each strike aimed at the organs that will bleed the most.

He goes limp, his legs buckling and his head tipping to the side.

I step back and let him drop to the ground.

The metal spikes across his side remain half-formed, now silent and still like he is.

My chest heaves, my breath rasping in and out of my mouth as I stand over him, gripping my bloody weapons, ready in case he's still alive, preparing to cut him again if I need to.

Because there's nothing I wouldn't do to protect my family.

Nothing.

"Erik?"

I look up to find Thoren, frozen and wide-eyed, hovering at the top of the ladder only a few paces away.

His face is pale as he fixates on the body at my feet.

Blood pools across the loft floor and I'm certain it's splattered across my face, but somehow…

I can't feel it.

All I have is rage where compassion would normally be.

Thoren's question is strained. "Did you use your light to do that?"

I hesitate. *Did I?*

I don't want to replay the moments or second-guess how fast I moved, but I'm certain I didn't, so I shake my head. *No.*

Thoren takes a sharp breath and now I can see that his hands are shaking where he crouches at the top of the ladder and his cheeks are streaked with tears.

Fresh fear rises within me.

My question is urgent. "Thoren?"

He gasps. "We need to get out there. Father's in trouble."

CHAPTER 16

I race along the loft and down the stairs, gripping my bloodied hunting knives.

Thoren is close on my heels, his feet flying as fast as mine are. He's holding his bow, but he only has two arrows left.

I don't have time to check on Asha beneath the stairs—even though I'm worried about her. I know I wrapped her safely and I also know that none of the Blacksmiths came near her. I stopped Deron before he could go back outside and tell any of the others that she's here.

A brief glance tells me she isn't awake; she isn't struggling to free herself from the straps.

But what if she's lying there because she's stopped breathing?

I nearly turn, nearly run back to check that she's still alive, but Thoren grabs my arm, pulling me onward.

"No time!" he shouts.

The door is ajar, but because of the way it faces, I can't see what's happening within the clearing. The fight certainly hasn't moved near it.

We burst through the door, kicking up snow as we sharply turn the corner.

Finally, I can see the fight ahead.

"Father!" My shout rings out as fear rushes through me.

My father lies on the ground at Kalith's feet all the way at the other end of the clearing. It will take us long seconds to reach him.

Father is curled over his knees, a copper-colored lattice of metal pinning him down from his neck to his feet, which are tucked beneath him.

Both of his arms extend outside the lattice, but they're also tied down, metal chains pinning his wrists to the ground.

Much closer to us, Kori, the white wolf, is caged just like Skirra, their enclosures only paces apart. Both wolves throw themselves against the bars, snarling and trying to bite through the metal. Both of them are facing Father, as if they're trying to get to him.

Along with Abdiel—the Blacksmith that Thoren killed— another of the Blacksmiths lies dead in the snow near Kori's cage. That's the Blacksmith who tried to throw a spear at Thoren in the turret.

The fourth man stands near the trees, holding his left arm where blood runs down it. Father's sword is dug into the snow, tip first, beside him.

But Kalith is once more the Blacksmith whose choices I fear.

He towers over my father, a sword held in his hands and pointed down at Father's neck. Kalith's tunic is torn and his face is bloodied. He has cuts all over his body, but the sneer on his face defies his wounds.

As I run toward them, I search for the final man, the one who was standing in the shadows. I don't see him and my fear only increases because he could be a significant danger to us.

At my shout, Kalith's focus snaps to us, distracted from my father for a few valuable seconds.

He spits blood as he shouts across the distance. "Witness your father's death, Einherjar!"

We aren't close enough to stop him. Not yet.

Beside me, Thoren raises his bow, nocking an arrow even as he runs.

I'm too far away from Kalith and the other Blacksmith to hit them with my daggers, but the bow and arrows that Father dropped earlier are resting on the snow only five paces away from me.

I will my legs to move faster as I veer toward them. Will my arms to scoop them up in time, to nock the arrow and fire it at one of the unprotected parts of Kalith's chest now visible through the tears in his tunic. I tell myself I can cut him down while he's focused on my father's neck.

At the same moment that Thoren lets his arrow fly, my hand closes around the bow on the ground and I prepare to slide across the snow to snatch the quiver of arrows into my other hand and shoot as fast as I can.

I'm aware of the rush of air around Thoren's arrow, the bite of the cold snow on my arms, the tension in my muscles, and then—

There's a *clang*, a soft hum of metal, and it's coming from behind us.

Out of nowhere, a heavy object hits my back, striking my right shoulder and knocking me off course.

Pain explodes through my chest.

I can't see my back to understand what happened, but as I tumble through the snow, a single, fine line of black metal bursts through my torso, right where my shoulder meets my body.

The line is as thin as a thread, but it rapidly thickens into prongs like claws, forming multiple hooks across my chest that wrench me to a stop.

I land on my side, still facing my father, trying to get my arms under me to push myself back to my feet, but cold metal grips me across my ribs and shoulders and it's spreading with every desperate breath I take.

Multiple spikes plow into the ground beside me, pulling me down onto my stomach, pushing the air out of my chest, and pinning me to the spot.

There's a *thud* beside me and I catch sight of Thoren landing hard in the snow, black metal wrapped all around his body. It's a spider web of chains. The same kind that must be wound around me. Because of the way he's landed, I can't see his head, only his body.

A thin, metal strand drifts at the back of the web imprisoning Thoren, its loose end now floating in the breeze.

I struggle to free myself, roaring against the pain gripping my chest as I try to push at the chains that now bind me, trying to use my back to heave myself upward.

It's impossible. The prongs have dug deep into the earth as if they're rooted way down through the snow and into the soil.

I can't see who took us down, but it has to be the Blacksmith who was hanging back in the shadows.

This metal.

The way it sung in the air and now bites into my body...

It makes my head spin, a cold darkness crawling through me, stealing my hope.

Up ahead, Kalith steps back into place. I didn't see where Thoren's arrow ended up, but it looks as if Kalith moved out of its way to avoid it.

He laughs. A cruel, harsh sound as he grips the hilt of his sword and positions it over my father's neck once more.

"Accept defeat!" he shouts to me. "You will not prevail."

We made it closer to our father, and since he's facing in our direction, I can see his eyes.

He's looking right at me, as if he wants me to pay attention.

Despite the blade hanging over his neck, a look of serenity flows over him. The furrow in his brow eases and a small smile touches his lips.

I can nearly hear him reminding me: *Be careful of your enemies.*

In that moment, I know what he's going to do.

No.

I don't want him to make this choice.

I want to believe that there's another way for us to survive.

He doesn't have to do this.

But my hope is dying with every strangled breath I take and with every whimper Thoren makes, vanishing as the gap between Kalith's blade and my father's neck closes.

Death is inevitable.

There is no other way.

My father closes his eyes.

CHAPTER 17

Sapphire energy bursts around my father's body, his deep light rising in a flash so strong and bright that it fills the clearing.

It casts Kalith's shocked face into sharp relief, making his blade look dull and his hair appear dark brown, like dried blood.

With a ferocious roar, my father breaks free from the metal that was pinning him down and rolls to the side, avoiding the plunging sword.

Kalith shouts and steadies his weapon, taking a step back, his eyes wide. The Blacksmith standing behind him drops to a crouch, as if he intends to make a leap for it, although it isn't clear if he will fight or run.

Father drags air into his chest as he rises up to his full height, his eyes glowing sapphire and his muscles gleaming. Blue light flows around him in streams and that same small smile rests on his lips.

Complete calm.

The serenity of knowing he will die in battle and ascend to the Hall of Warriors to join his ancestors.

His eyes meet mine across the distance, his focus flowing across me and Thoren where we're pinned to the ground, and despite the peace on my father's face...

My heart tears apart.

He raised us, protected us, taught us how to survive, gave us his wisdom, and shared his skills.

But now his light is burning and soon he will be consumed by it. The look in his eyes tells me he's determined to free us before he perishes.

Opposite him, Kalith rips off his torn tunic, revealing the full extent of the copper armor beneath it, flowing metal that's connected to the copper ring on his right hand by a thin thread.

Father doesn't give Kalith another moment to prepare himself.

He leaps forward, a pure predator, matching Kalith's speed and strength now.

Within seconds, he's deflected Kalith's sword attacks and whirled through the snow to snatch his own sword out of the ground. The other Blacksmith, who was crouching beside Father's weapon, doesn't jump out of reach fast enough before Father's hand wraps around his throat.

There's an efficient *crack* before Father drops that man to the snow and plows back to Kalith.

Kalith backs away into the clearing, stepping closer to Thoren and me, as if he'll use the threat to our lives against our father.

Father leaps into the fight again, and I can hardly follow the strikes and parries and deflections as he beats Kalith around the clearing, sapphire light clashing with copper metal.

Kalith's metal gleams and flows, moving so fast and transforming from shape to shape so quickly that the heat from the copper radiates out from him and the snow at his feet begins to melt. The ground turns to sludge, water splashing up around them.

As they fight, I try to sense where the final Blacksmith might be—the one who used his black metal on me and Thoren. He knocked us to the ground, but he seems to have chosen to stay out of the fight *and* out of sight.

I can't tell if Father is conscious of him, too. Every time he glances in our direction, his focus is on me and Thoren, but every now and then, his gaze rests higher than us, as if the threat is behind us, quietly waiting.

I hold my breath when Kalith's weapon transforms from a dagger into a whip with a blade's edge and, when it whirls at my father, it slices through the tree trunk behind him without even slowing down.

The whooshing sound it makes turns my blood cold. The tree groans and splits a little but doesn't topple.

But Father uses Kalith's outstretched arm against him, cutting down toward it, forcing Kalith to retract his metal to protect his arm before Father slices it off.

The moment costs Kalith.

Father beats him back across the clearing, closer and closer to us, ramming his sword against Kalith's metal armor, dinting it over and over across his chest and neck and arms, and the only thing Kalith seems able to do is to protect his head.

When Father aims a blow at Kalith's face, Kalith's metal swarms up across his cheek, stopping the blade that would have sliced his head in half.

The *clang* as Father's blade meets Kalith's metal is immense and the force knocks Kalith down.

The Blacksmith hits the ground, his eyes closed, appearing unconscious.

Just as Father would ram his blade down through Kalith's now-vulnerable neck, a black spear flies out of nowhere toward Father's back.

He spins to the threat, plucks the spear from the air right

before it would hit his spine, and rams it down into the sludgy snow.

The sapphire light around him is unwavering, still burning bright while footfalls sound from behind me and the man from the shadows finally strides into view.

His black cloak swishes as he moves, and I catch sight of a black hammer resting at his waist, the same color as the metal that's wrapped around us.

Black hair falls below his shoulders and obscures his face, except for a flash of pale skin and inky-blue eyes that send a chill through me.

A single, black band of metal is wrapped around his right hand. Several black rings circle the fingers on his left hand, along with a metal covering over his forefinger that's sharp at the end and shaped like a talon.

Father doesn't miss a step as he strides to meet the dark-haired man, his sword ready. "Malak Ironmeld."

But of course. It's the leader himself. It would explain why the other Blacksmiths seemed so conscious of this man earlier.

Malak doesn't reply and, confusingly, doesn't form a weapon with his metal, silently prowling forward to meet my father, whose sword is raised.

It happens so fast that I nearly don't follow it.

Father's sword strikes down.

Malak's left hand flies up.

With two fingers, he stops my father's blade from descending and at the same time, his right palm connects with my father's chest.

"To stone." His voice is a whisper of sound, as melodic as the hum of his metal.

Malak shoves my father backward and for the first time since Father's deep light burst around him, Father stumbles.

His eyes are wide as he glances at his chest, the briefest

pause before he throws himself forward again, driving his sword toward Malak's neck.

The breath stops in my chest as a dark-gray substance washes across my father's chest, radiating out from his heart where the Blacksmith shoved him.

Dark gray...

Stone.

It's spreading quickly, rushing up Father's neck and down his legs, clothing and all, even as he struggles to drive his sword forward, his movements becoming stilted and shuddering as the stone consumes his light.

I try to shout, but my voice is strangled in my throat, my eyes wide with horror.

I don't understand how this is happening.

Blacksmiths control metal, not flesh and bone!

Malak doesn't move another step, doesn't waver, waiting for my father's sword to slowly reach his jugular before the blade shudders to a stop—its tip a hairsbreadth from cutting him.

At the last moment, my father's eyes meet mine.

Then his light fades, his face sets, a final breath leaves his lips and...

He's gone.

His body has become a statue, his left leg forward, his weapon poised to strike, every part of him turned to stone except for his sword.

He's there, standing only a few paces away from me, but his life, his soul, and his heart are no more.

I'm aware that Thoren is shouting, screaming, roaring where he lies helpless on the ground. The wolves are howling. But not a single sound passes my lips, not even a groan of horror as a chunk of my heart slides away.

The moment my father burned his light, I was forced to accept that I was about to lose him.

But not like this.
Not like this.

CHAPTER 18

I'm numb as I lie on the icy earth.

So much of the snow melted during Father's fight with Kalith that the icy liquid reaches my fingertips where my left arm is pinned to my side.

I took off my fur coat inside the building and now the cold is biting me. Probably. I can't feel much of anything.

Across the way, Kalith stumbles to his feet and Malak strides over to him without a glance at us. With his back to us, I still can't fully see Malak's face.

Kalith winces and squints, a disgruntled expression flooding his features as he squares his shoulders. "I had the situation in hand."

Malak's voice is low, a metallic hum that's somehow expressionless, yet hints at danger. "You did not."

In a swirl of black material, he turns toward the cabin. "Wait here with the captives. Keep them alive until I come back."

Kalith quickly steps into Malak's path. "I'll get her."

Malak pauses, his head turned toward Kalith, his silence glaring before he replies. "You will not."

Malak is behaving as if he knows for certain that Asha is inside the cabin. Maybe he does. After he knocked Thoren and me to the ground and while our father was fighting Kalith, he could have gone to the door of the cabin or even stepped inside and I wouldn't have been able to see him do it.

All I know is that he's as quiet as the breeze, his footsteps barely making an impact on the ground.

He walks straight past the fallen Blacksmith Abdiel, whose body remains riddled with arrows. I wonder if Malak will be as dismissive of Deron once he sees the dead Blacksmith lying on the loft.

But the fallen Blacksmiths are not my concern now.

Skirra is visible to me across the way, his head hung low, his soft whines floating across the air. Kori, too, has sunk to his belly, his teeth still gnawing uselessly at the bars that cage him. The other three wolves have remained chained to separate trees. Their affinity with my family was less, but still strong. They have all fallen silent, seeming to understand that my father is gone.

I try to see my brother, but as much as I try to twist, I can't lay eyes on his face.

I need to know that he's okay.

He's my responsibility now. No matter what happens to me, I have to protect him.

"Thoren." My voice sounds far away to my ears. "Tell me you're okay."

His only answer is his now-stifled crying.

"Thoren. Brother." My tone is more urgent. I need him to respond. "Are you hurt?"

His voice is tight. "No."

I close my eyes with relief but open them quickly.

Kalith seems to have waited until Malak turned the cabin's corner and is now crossing the distance to me.

He drops into a crouch beside me, and his right hand darts

out to grab the back of my head. "If she's here, it means someone pulled her out of the pit," he says, a low, angry snarl. "Was it you?"

His question confirms that he saw her there but must have pretended he didn't. He may have led the other Blacksmiths, including Malak, away, believing that they wouldn't find a thing except monsters in this forest and in the meantime, the snow and ice would mostly cover her up. Maybe he thought he would go back later and bury her to be sure.

I have only theories, and no concrete facts, but his contempt for her is clear. The fact that he saw her in the pit and didn't tell his leader is also clear.

I can't believe she's evil or deserves to die. Not when my light is drawn to her the way it is.

My voice is raw as I fight the resurgence of pain in my chest and the anguish I feel for my father, both pushing at the edges of my numbness. "Are you the one who beats her? Or do you stand by while someone else does it?"

Kalith draws back with a sharp inhale, but his fingers remain wrapped around my head and his movement pulls painfully at my scalp.

He darts back toward me, his whisper vicious. "What did she tell you?"

I fight the widening of my eyes.

He thinks she's conscious?

But if he believes she's conscious, he also hasn't said anything about the fact that she hasn't come out of the cabin of her own free will.

Does he think she's hiding in there?

As I consider my reply, I'm aware that his copper metal extends across his right palm and all he has to do is form a sharp blade with it to kill me.

"You'll never know what she told me," I whisper, a veiled lie, although the marks on her body spoke volumes.

Kalith snarls, his grip tightens, but that's when a soft dragging sound reaches us and Malak appears at the cabin's corner, pulling the sled on which Asha rests.

She appears to have remained unconscious, but the rise and fall of her chest is deeper now. Stronger. I'm more certain than I was before that she will wake up. The only question is when.

At her appearance, Skirra raises himself back to his feet, growling softly.

Malak pays him no attention, lowering the sled to the ground and quickly setting about releasing the straps that tie Asha onto it.

I suppose he already ascertained that she's breathing because the first thing he does is pull the mittens off her hands. The cloth wrapping becomes visible, pulled aside a little but securely fastened.

Kalith hovers nearby, but his concern sounds forced. "She's alive?"

Malak ignores him, holding each of her hands, turning them slowly back and forth. His fingers brush the wrapping before he checks her fingertips and then his hands brush over her palms and up to the rope burns around her wrists.

His back is still to me, but the time he takes with her hands tells me he's studying them.

He slowly pulls the mittens back on and rises to his feet, pausing there, his head tilted before he swings to me.

Finally, I can see his face.

I imprint his features on my mind: dark-blue eyes, a square jaw, pale skin, high cheekbones, expressionless lips. It's impossible to know what he's thinking, as his face is like a mask.

The face of the man who ended my father.

He approaches me at a slow pace, then kneels beside me and rests his hands in his lap, palms up, as if to keep the threat of his metal in full view.

"I'm going to ask you questions, Boy, and you would be

wise to answer them truthfully." His focus shifts to Thoren where he lies behind me. "Fail to tell me the truth and *that* boy will die, do you understand?"

I fight my fear.

My numbness is wearing off and with it comes a heightened awareness of the warmth beneath my chest where my blood must be pooling. The thread Malak shot through me could have done catastrophic damage already.

If so, I will choose to use my deep light like my father did.

With it, I will kill Malak.

I grit my teeth and nod. "Ask your questions."

CHAPTER 19

Malak studies me for a moment, the fingers of his left hand twitching, the black rings on them catching the light.

"The cloth around Asha's hands is what we call 'linen'," he says. "It's an Einherjar weave, far looser than the weave our machines produce, which means the cloth belongs to you."

He hasn't asked me a question yet, so I wait, my caution rising.

"Why did you wrap her hands?"

I choose my response carefully and keep my explanations short. "She was freezing. Her fingers were blue. The cloths were warm. We didn't want the black rot to set in."

"We?"

"My family."

His focus flickers to my father and then to Thoren. "But surely, she was freezing because you snatched her from our city and dragged her out into the snow. Why try to undo what you had already done?"

I can't keep the rage from my voice. "She was *freezing*

because she was waist-deep in snow when I found her in that pit—"

"*You* found her."

"I did."

"What was she wearing?"

I pause. *Why would it matter?* "A silver dress."

When I took it off her, I placed it to the side of the hearth, so I guess he didn't see it inside the cabin.

Even so, it seems to mean something to him because the muscles in his jaw tense.

"Straight from the feast," he mutters, but his attention returns quickly to me. "Why didn't you leave her there?"

I don't have an easy answer. He seems to have some knowledge of the Einherjar because of the way he spoke about our cloth, but telling him about my light feels dangerous.

Instead, I say, "Because she didn't deserve to freeze to death."

"Deserve?" Malak arches his eyebrows at me. "You couldn't possibly know anything about her or what she deserves. Perhaps she has committed atrocities too cruel and depraved to speak of. Even for us." He leans toward me. "Does her beauty convince you she is innocent of any wrongdoing?"

"No," I say. "Beauty can be deceptive."

"Then why save her?"

He's right that I know nothing about her or what she could have done or why she was in the snow or even why her own father wanted to leave her there, but I know my own heart.

"Destiny," I say.

Malak purses his lips. "Ah. Destiny. The Einherjar live and die according to the fates given to them by the gods, do they not?"

"They do."

"What fate was given to you, Boy?" he asks, peering into my eyes.

I answer as truthfully as I can. "How can I possibly know?"

"Hmph." He rests back on his heels, tapping the fingers of his left hand against his thigh for a long moment.

Finally, he says, "You saved her hands. For that, I will give you a life: yours or your brother's."

It seems he intends to let one of us live, but no doubt he will play a cruel game of choice with me.

"Two hands," I say, trying to keep the strain from my voice. "I saved them both. That deserves two lives. Mine *and* my brother's."

He considers me coldly. "But only one hand matters," he says. "Therefore, only one life can be saved."

I watched the way the Blacksmiths used their right hands to wield their metal, even swapping their weapons to their left hands so they could free up their right hands to transform more of their metal.

I exhale heavily. I can't see Thoren's face, but his quiet denial reaches me loud and clear.

"No," he says. "Not me."

He must believe that of the two of us, I have the greater chance of survival.

But I have the stronger light. If I'm facing death anyway, I will use my deep light to kill these Blacksmiths before my end. My brother will remain free.

"My brother," I say.

"No," Thoren's whisper is harsh. "No!"

Malak ignores Thoren and tilts his head at me. "Are you sure, Boy?"

"I chose to save her hand," I say, fighting the way my blood pounds in my ears. "I choose for you to spare my brother's life."

Malak's expression doesn't change. "Self-sacrifice for family." His jaw tightens again. "So very pointless."

He turns to Kalith, rising to his feet as he speaks. "Kill the younger one. Leave the older one alive. We will take him back with us."

Wait... what?!

"No!" My shout echoes across the clearing as all my numbness disappears. Rage, pure and hot, flows through me.

Kalith wears a cruel smile as he approaches, his copper metal streaming down his arm toward the ring he wears around his thumb, pooling in his palm before it shapes into a dagger.

He won't even have to remove the black metal caging my brother's body.

He'll only have to stab Thoren between the chains.

"*Stop!*" I roar, shouting at Malak's back. "What do you think I'll do if you keep me alive? Do you think you can control me?"

I thrash at the chains holding me down, not caring that the thread through my body pulls and tears.

I'm ready to call on my deep light. I'm ready to die.

"Do you think I won't slit your throat while you sleep?" I snap.

Malak whirls back to me, his voice harsh. "You wouldn't get close enough."

My own shout drowns out his. "How will you control me without my brother?"

Kalith has paused, his location now at the edge of my vision, making it difficult for me to see him, but there's no blood on the blade he's holding. Thoren hasn't cried out. My brother is horribly quiet.

"You'd better kill me, Malak," I snarl, hardly recognizing my own voice or the rage within me. "You'd better end me while you can because if you hurt my brother and leave me alive, I will hunt you." My voice lowers. "And I will end you."

Malak holds up his hand to Kalith. "Wait."

He returns to me, stooping and reaching out toward the chain across my shoulder. It's only then that I realize it's looser across my body and the side of it is covered in dirt, as if I succeeded in dislodging it.

Malak brushes a few crumbs of dirt away from the chain, his eyes narrowed and his lips pursed, but he doesn't immediately speak.

I lower my voice. "Keep my brother alive and I won't kill you. As long as he's safe, so will you be."

He considers me for another moment. Then, "Very well. We have an agreement. Your brother will live." He knocks the dirt from this hand. "You will do whatever I ask if you wish him to stay alive."

My heart is darkening and my soul is sinking at the deal I just made.

But there isn't anything I won't do to save my brother now.

"What is your name, Boy?" Malak asks.

It's a small rebellion, but I take it. "You will never know it."

He studies me again as if he's picking apart the pieces of my mind. "You fight like a wolf. You even snarl like one. And it's clear that the beasts of this forest walk beside you."

He gestures to Kori and Skirra before one corner of his mouth tugs up, the hint of a smile. "You are *of the wolves*, Boy."

Then he mutters to himself for a moment. "Vanda... *Of the...*"

His lips stretch into a full smile as he rises to his feet and towers over me. "I will call you 'Vandawolf'."

CHAPTER 20

"Do not make any sudden movements," Malak warns as he bends to me again.

With a brush of his right hand, he transforms the metal that's caging me. The prongs rip up out of the earth and snow on either side of me, dragging dirt with them, confirming how deeply they were embedded—as deep as tree roots.

I take his warning seriously, not least because the metal may be retracting from the soil, but the claws sitting directly across my chest remain and so does the thread that speared through my shoulder.

It looks like a spider sitting on my chest.

He speaks coldly. "Make a wrong move and the thread I've wound through you will cut across your body like a knife. You may sit, but do not move from that spot."

He must be confident that I'll obey him because he immediately turns his back on me to move toward Thoren.

I rise as quickly as I can into a half-kneeling, half-crouching position, ready in case I need to move fast.

In that position, I can finally swivel my head to see my brother.

His face is tear-streaked, but it's the emptiness in his eyes when he looks back at me that worries me the most.

Our father's monolith is only five paces away from us and Thoren's focus shifts to it. And then to Asha where she sleeps on the sled.

A muscle clenches in his jaw before he returns his focus to our father, remaining on him while Malak removes the prongs but leaves Thoren with the same claws across his chest.

They're tangled in Thoren's coat, the edges of which are pushed aside enough for me to see the same pool of blood across his shoulder, which means a thread must run through his chest too.

It will kill him in an instant if Malak wills it.

Malak's voice is calm as he speaks with Thoren. "I assume you will also refuse to tell me your name."

Beyond the flicker of his gray eyes to Malak, Thoren barely reacts.

"You are silent, Boy. But no less dangerous than your brother. Like the steel at the end of a quiet arrow." Malak cocks his head to the side. "You are 'Vandasteel'."

It's a strong name, but it feels like a mockery to me. Malak has given us both names that ridicule us in our powerlessness.

Once Thoren is sitting up, Malak turns back to Kalith and they quickly set about gathering up their metal, along with the metal of the slain Blacksmiths.

I watch carefully how Kalith seems able to handle and control Abdiel's and Deron's metal, using it to fashion a narrow cart that will fit between the trees. But he avoids touching Malak's dropped spear.

That could simply be because Malak is present, but the way Kalith actively gives Malak's metal a wide berth where it rests on the ground indicates he's reluctant to be anywhere near it.

The more I see the Blacksmiths use their metal, the clearer their power becomes. Every time one of them transforms it, he keeps his right hand in contact with the metal somehow—from using a continuous chain to a metal thread.

It seems their power streams from their right hands. Once they let go of their metal, like leaving the wolves chained to the trees or creating the cage around Skirra, the metal remains in that form.

It doesn't change unless they're touching it again.

As far as the cart goes, there are no horses or mules to pull it, so I'm not sure how it's going to travel down the mountain. Even on a downward slope, the snow could bog it down.

Meanwhile, Malak transforms his black spear back into a band that he wraps around his left forearm.

Then he bends to me again. "You will retrieve the bodies and put them on the cart," he says. "Likewise for the wolves in the cages. Your brother will stay where he is while you do this. This will be your first test."

Deron's body is inside the cabin, which will force me to leave Thoren outside on his own.

I grit my teeth, rising slowly to my feet before I back away from Malak and then I move fast toward the cabin, finding that I'm able to run since my legs are free of metal now and the claws across my chest don't hinder my arms.

Carrying a full-grown, adult male won't be an easy task, but I've built up enough muscle dragging large beasts to manage pulling Deron along the loft, down the stairs, across the room, and out into the snow.

At the door, I take a glance at the weapons on the wall inside it. But separating me from my brother was smart—it's what I would have done. To try to hide a weapon on my person would only put him in harm's way.

Even if I use my deep light, the chance of Malak making contact with the claws on Thoren's chest and killing him in an instant is too high.

I have to reserve my light for the moment when I have my best chance of keeping Thoren alive.

Dragging Deron as fast as I can, I hurry back to the cart to find that Thoren hasn't moved. He doesn't raise his head, but Skirra whines to me. I squash my anger, hating to see the wolves caged like this.

Malak and Kalith are deep in quiet conversation where they stand beside Asha's sled.

"I understand the shame that her powerlessness brings upon your family." Malak looks Kalith in the eye as he gives a quiet nod. "It is a heavy burden for you and Ayla to bear."

"My wife struggles more than I," Kalith says, his voice gruff. The way his lips press together and the words drag out of him tell me he didn't want to speak that truth, but I'm certain that lying to Malak would be a very bad idea. Especially considering that Kalith did it once already today.

Malak's expression remains unchanged, and yet there's a hint of steel in his eyes. "Indeed. But Asha is your daughter, and I have commanded you to keep her alive as a test of your loyalty to me."

He emphasizes the word 'loyalty' as he reaches out across the gap between them to grip Kalith's shoulder with his right hand—the hand around which the black band of his metal is wrapped.

Kalith freezes at the contact, his own arms remaining at his sides while his fingers twitch.

Malak's grip on Kalith visibly tightens. "You overlooked Asha in the pit," he says, his voice dangerously low. "Your failure cost Blacksmiths their lives. Your penance will be to return the bodies of the fallen to their families and explain how they died."

He doesn't release Kalith from his steely gaze. "But I will not compound the shame of Asha's disappearance. Our search for her began as a secret and it will continue as such."

Kalith appears to exhale with relief. "None of these men knew why we were really traveling outside the city until I met them outside the wall this morning," he says. "They didn't have any opportunity to speak of Asha's disappearance to anyone. They thought we were hunting for untainted wildlife like we have before."

"And indeed we found some," Malak says, indicating the wolves.

Kalith swallows. "The only other person who knows why we're really out here is my wife, but if I need to speak to the families..."

There's a question in his voice and I guess it's because Malak ordered Kalith to tell the fallen men's families how they died, which could include telling them the reason why.

"Nobody else has to know," Malak says. "For that reason, you will tell the families of these men that they died valiantly fighting leopards that set upon us without warning. We killed the beasts, but these men's wounds were fatal."

He waits a moment for Kalith to nod before he continues. "Your cousin will not be happy to lose his favorite brother. You should be prepared for his ire."

At that, Kalith's attention shifts to Deron, where I've pulled him to the ground near the open end of the cart.

Kalith and Deron have the same copper-colored hair. I suspected they might be related, but it sounds like Deron is— *was*—one of Kalith's cousins, which will make his death personal. At least to his extended family. Kalith himself doesn't appear to be shedding any tears.

Malak demands Kalith's attention while his voice once again becomes dangerously quiet. "You lied about the pit,

Kalith. Do not mislead me again or you will know the consequences."

Kalith's expression wipes clean and this time, he doesn't seem to breathe again until Malak releases him.

Kalith clears his throat. "What do you want to do about the other wolves?"

My ears prick up since it's true that Malak only ordered me to load Skirra and Kori onto the cart.

Malak considers the three wolves chained to trees for a moment. "Release them. I know they're here now. I will come for them if I wish."

Kalith hovers for a moment and I suppose it's because the wolves will likely attack him once they're released. Or they might simply take their freedom while they can.

Kalith harnesses his metal to cover his arms and chest, but it turns out the wolves just want their freedom, each of them leaping to their feet and rushing away, the first stopping only long enough for the others to catch up.

The rest of their pack is still out there, and I take comfort knowing they will join them.

My hands are now bloody from my task and Deron's body has left a thick, crimson trail behind me in the snow. Pulling the bodies up into the cart will be harder than dragging them across the ground, so I put off that task, setting about pulling all four of them to the base of the cart first.

Given what Malak said about blaming leopards for the deaths, I pull the arrows from Abdiel's chest.

The puncture wounds don't look anything like claw marks, and I'm not sure how they could be passed off as such.

Rising back to my feet, my chest heaving from the effort of hauling the fourth man to the cart, I find Malak gliding up to me.

He's holding out one of my hunting knives.

I eye the weapon warily until he says, "Slash." His lips stretch into an uncharacteristic smile. "Like the wolf you are."

CHAPTER 21

By the time I've pulled the bodies into the cart, I'm covered in blood, but once again, I'm numb.

And shivering despite the exertion.

The bare warmth of the midday sun has passed and now we're headed toward the cold afternoon. Temperatures may be milder farther down the mountain, but up here at its near-peak is the coldest.

My glances at Asha tell me she's warm, her cheeks now full of color. But my brother has slumped where he sits, rising unsteadily to his feet when Malak finally gives him permission.

The metal through his chest, like mine, seems to have plugged the wound and stopped most of the blood loss, but the crimson stain across his torso where his coat is pulled apart concerns me.

I heave the wolf cages onto the cart, managing to fit them side by side because they're so narrow.

Then Malak tells me to pull the sled with Asha while Thoren walks beside me and Kalith controls the cart's descent.

I watch him carefully when he links a chain of metal to the side of the cart, maintaining contact with it once more.

The cart begins to move and it isn't clear to me how it's happening until I look down at the wheels. Prongs form at the back, pushing against the snow as they grow and propel the cart forward.

In the next moment, prongs form at the front, also extending into the earth, the action of extending and retracting in sequence appearing to create the force needed to move the cart along.

It looks like simple mechanics and it would be fascinating to me if it wasn't a skill being wielded by my enemy.

I look back as we leave the clearing, an awkward action as I try not to upset the sled behind me, but I can't leave my home without one more look.

Father's monolith remains in a mighty warrior's pose, but it hasn't escaped me that his deep light was consumed within it.

I wait a beat, hoping to sense the energy within the air, the spark of my own deep light that will tell me that the Valkyrie are coming for him.

Their presence can't be detected. They have no aura and can conceal themselves so fully that even the strongest magic wielder wouldn't know they were there.

But Father always told us that if a Valkyrie were near, our deep light would spark, even if for the briefest moment.

He said it's a feeling of true peace unlike any other.

I hold my breath, but all I feel is rage.

A deep, clawing darkness that builds in strength while I try to keep it down and cage it.

I tell myself I will let it grow and conserve it, as effectively as I have built and conserved my deep light. With every battle I've fought today, every brutal conflict spent defending my family, I've also increased my deep light.

I will use it when the time is right.

I'm acutely aware of Thoren where he trudges beside me, his own focus passing backward, as if he, too, is searching for the Valkyrie's presence in the same way he might search for hope.

I turn back to find Malak watching us, his expression inscrutable.

"Your father fought well," he says, and I wonder if he's deliberately trying to provoke us.

Thoren tenses but presses his lips firmly closed, visibly holding his anger.

When neither of us responds, Malak turns back to the snowy path ahead, his black robe swishing across the ground while his hands trail from one tree to the next, turning the bark black wherever he touches it.

It takes over two hours to descend down the mountain and by then, I'm dehydrated and my muscles are cramping up. I push myself onward, determined not to stumble, even though Asha's sled seems to grow heavier and heavier. It's only because my muscles are growing wearier.

I'm certain it's what Malak wants. To push us to our limits and ensure we're as physically drained as possible before we reach the city.

When its enormous stone wall comes into view between the trees in the far distance, Kalith draws the cart to a halt and Malak tells me to set down Asha's sled.

I lower it slowly while my back, thigh, and arm muscles scream.

To Kalith, Malak says, "This is where we'll separate. I don't want anyone connecting the Einherjar with our fallen men. You will enter through the western gate on this side of the city. I will continue with our captive under the cover of trees to the northern gate and make it look like we've come from the north.

"Cover Asha completely in the fur that's wrapped around her so it appears as if you're carrying nothing more than furs on that sled. You've brought animal skins back before. Nobody will ask questions."

"And the cart?" Kalith asks.

Malak gives Kalith a hard stare. "Leave it here for now. Tell the guards at the gate to bring it in. After that, it's your responsibility."

"The wolves," I rasp, interrupting their conversation. "What about them?"

Both Skirra and Kori have settled down on the bottom of their small cages, growing silent over the last two hours. Their haunted eyes are weighing heavily on me.

These proud, wild beasts should never be caged.

Malak steps toward them. "They will come with me." He gestures to Kalith. "Kalith, you will retract the cages and I will muzzle the beasts so I can control them."

I can't stop my protest as I glare at Malak through the sweat dripping down my brow. "They're wild creatures. They can't be controlled."

Kalith, too, appears uncertain, shuffling on the spot. "As soon as I retract the cages, the beasts will attack. If I were to immediately muzzle them myself—"

Malak's glare falls on him and he stops speaking.

"You know as well as I do that your metal is beneath me," Malak says with a cold stare. "I will muzzle them so I can control their leashes."

I study the two men carefully as I consider what Malak said.

Kalith has taken hold of other Blacksmiths' metal and manipulated it as if it were his own, but it occurs to me that Malak has only controlled his own black metal. He hasn't touched or changed any other metal and now it sounds like... maybe he can't.

Malak turns to me while Thoren remains stiff beside me, my brother's focus flicking to the wolves.

"You are my Vandawolf," Malak says to me. "When Kalith retracts the cages, you will stop the wolves from attacking until

I can muzzle them." He gives me a hard look. "If you do not control them, I will kill them."

A smile passes across Kalith's face, replacing his reluctance, as if he's looking forward to seeing me fail.

"Kalith," Malak says to him. "Wait for my signal and then retract the metal bars."

Closer to me, Thoren takes a step forward, as if he'll get in the way, but I snag his arm and give him a firm shake of my head.

In response, the corners of his mouth turn down and his brow furrows fiercely, but I tighten my grip on his arm.

My voice is a dry rasp, scratchier every time I speak. "I can use my Einherjar light to keep the wolves calm."

Thoren will know how impossible this is, but I hope he'll at least trust me enough to know I won't put the wolves in danger.

Once the bars are gone, I will give them the chance to escape.

CHAPTER 22

I step toward Skirra first, carefully keeping both Malak and Kalith within my sights.

Kalith positions himself at the side of Skirra's cage first, his hand hovering near the farthermost bar.

He won't be so reckless as to extend his fingers into the cage.

The way both Kori and Skirra are already growling at him indicates they won't hesitate to rip open his throat the moment they have the chance.

"Easy, Skirra," I say, slipping my hand through the bars and reaching for his snout.

I approach slowly, inch by inch, willing him to allow me to wrap my hand around his nose and hold his mouth shut.

I'm surprised when he quickly settles down onto the bottom of the cage, letting me hold him. I expected him to rage against me for trying to constrain him, since he can't read my mind to know my intentions.

With my other hand, I reach through the bars of Kori's cage.

He gnashes his teeth at me, forcing me to stop, my arm extended and fingers dangerously close to his mouth.

"Kori. Easy."

Again, he gnashes at me and I fight the instinct to withdraw my hand.

"Kori." Thoren's voice sounds behind me. "Be still."

The white wolf growls at me again, his teeth drawing back, but he slowly lowers himself to the bottom of the cage and allows me to close my hand around his snout.

Kalith watches me for another full minute as if he's waiting for one of the wolves to rebel and prove they should be killed on the spot.

When both animals remain quiet, he looks at Malak, who waits nearby.

"Do it," Malak says.

Kalith presses his hand to Skirra's cage and the bars retract, reforming a band.

Kalith steps hurriedly back, clearly expecting Skirra to attack as he slips the band onto his arm.

My heart is in my throat as I worry that Skirra might make a move before Kori is free, but the gray wolf remains quiet and still, his focus on me.

"Easy," I murmur.

As for Malak, he now prowls back and forth only a few paces away, a gleam in his eye as he waits for Kalith to step out of the way.

Kalith rounds me, but in order for him to stand close enough to Kori's cage on my other side, I have to move in front of Skirra's enclosure, blocking Malak's path.

As soon as Kalith releases Kori, I'll knock the Blacksmith aside and pray the wolves are fast enough to dart past Malak on their way to freedom.

Kalith retracts the bars from around Kori.

I barrel into Kalith, knocking him aside as I release both wolves from my hold.

At the same moment, Thoren cries from behind me. "Kori! Go!"

The white wolf leaps through the air, his claws grazing my back.

Kalith shouts and his hand shoots out—the one in which he's holding the band he just retracted, but he's too far away from Kori to cage him again.

The white wolf lands and streaks across the snow, his bloody snout a crimson blur.

Across the way, Malak drops into a crouch, both of his hands moving, palms gliding across each other so fast that it's difficult to follow.

The bow and arrow that form in his hands are frighteningly clear. The arrow is fully formed, already nocked, and the bow is already taut.

Kori hasn't made it five steps before Malak shoots.

My heart is in my throat as Kori darts to the right.

Thud.

The arrow hits the tree he passes, a mere inch from his body, cracking into the wood.

Then Kori's gone, his racing form disappearing through the trees and into the distance.

Thoren slumps at the corner of my vision, but I'm acutely aware that Skirra stayed where he is.

I'm not holding him. The moment Kori jumped up, he was free to run.

"Go, Skirra," I whisper urgently, even as Malak swivels toward us and a new arrow forms on his bow, this time pointed at the gray wolf.

Or maybe it's pointed at me.

Skirra raises his eyes to mine.

I barely make a sound as I speak, stunned by his choice. "Why?"

Why didn't he run when he had the chance?

His head turns toward Asha before he scooches forward, keeping low to the cart, and he brushes his face against my arm. The blood on his snout has dried, as has the blood splattered across my face and torso and arms and legs...

All the blood.

"Destiny," I whisper, but my voice is empty.

What will destiny cost me?

Across the way, Malak gives me a hard stare before he points the arrow at my brother instead. "It appears that your wolf will obey you, Vandawolf, but what about your brother?"

I jolt away from Skirra.

Thoren's standing only two paces behind me now, his jaw tight, his hatred for Malak written in every line of his face.

I step in front of my brother, trying to bring moisture to my mouth as I stare down the arrow Malak's holding to his bow. "My brother will do what he needs to do to stay alive."

Malak pauses, then to my relief, stands swiftly and retracts his bow and arrow, his palms cupping the metal they were formed from as if he's simply flattening pieces of parchment. "Very well."

When he separates his palms, the black band has reformed on his right hand.

He rises back to his full height and turns to Kalith, who is poised at the corner of the cart.

"Take Asha home," Malak says.

My step away from the cart has taken me closer to Asha, and I hurry to bend to her, not trusting Kalith to pull the furs over her face in a way that will ensure she can breathe.

Quickly, I turn her sleeping head so she's facing to one side before I pull the topmost fur up over her. This way, there will be a gap between her face and the pelt.

"Get out of the way, Boy," Kalith snaps at me.

"Vandawolf," I snap back, my thirst and exhaustion getting the better of me. "Do not call me 'Boy'."

My acceptance of the name Malak gave me seems only to make Malak happy, but Kalith narrows his eyes at me, his hand twitching near the copper bands resting across his bicep.

I have no doubt that Kalith would try to strike me down if Malak would let him.

I step out of his way.

He checks that Asha is fully covered before he takes hold of the sled and pulls on the straps.

"I expect a report from you tomorrow afternoon," Malak says to Kalith before he can leave. "You will give me a full account of how the families of our fallen men take the news of their deaths."

Kalith gives Malak a short nod before he draws the sled away.

I have no choice but to watch him go, even though my deep light sparks within me and the compulsion to go after Asha is strong.

I kept her alive.

I warmed her.

And now I can only watch as she returns to the people who will undoubtedly continue harming her.

Fuck.

I want to rage after Kalith, not only because Asha's disappearing from my sight, but because it means that all of this death...

My father's life... The threat to Thoren... The wolves' imprisonment...

I grind my teeth together and turn my hands into fists, promising myself that it won't be for nothing.

It can't be for nothing.

CHAPTER 23

It takes us another two hours to skirt around the city, heading north through the western mountains before we turn sharply east to cut back toward the city's northern side.

I catch glimpses of its wall in the distance, an imposing, continuous structure that follows a gentle arc, appearing broadly circular like the ring of mountains that sit around it.

Skirra stays at Malak's side, padding quietly through the snow and then the debris covering the ground as we leave the colder areas behind and the environment changes around us.

The muzzle Malak placed around his face is structured so he can pant but not bite with a collar around his neck and a leash with which Malak leads him.

We finally reach the base of the mountains, but the trees are thick enough that I can't see what the terrain ahead looks like until we step through them.

My boots crunch and I freeze on the spot.

A massive field of white stretches for miles into the distance, all the way across to the eastern mountains opposite us and all the way left to the mountains in the north.

The field appears to be covered in snow, but the flecks swirling in the air in front of me aren't cold.

They're ashen, like bones ground to powder.

Ahead of us, blackened and skeletal trees litter the field. One such tree stands only a pace away from me, its black boughs stretching toward the greener forest we came from as if it wishes for life.

Thoren's soft exclamation sounds behind me as he steps onto the field. "What hellfire burned here?"

The Einherjar would consider this a bad omen, the act of an angry god, but I am not so superstitious.

Blacksmiths happened here. I'm certain of it.

My skin prickles with an energy I can't define and an eerie clanging fills the air.

Thoren's eyes are wide as he peers at the flurries of white dust swirling in the air directly ahead of us. "The ground here is... *wrong*."

A flicker of sapphire light tinges his clothing blue around his heart, the light visible where his coat was pushed aside by the claws.

It's the first time I've seen Thoren's deep light flicker today, and I quickly catch hold of his arm, looking at his chest.

His jaw clenches visibly and his light fades.

Just in time before Malak's footfalls sound behind us.

I hurry to move onward, brushing my hand against the nearby tree. Its bark crumbles to dust at my touch and the white ash kicks up around my boots, flecks floating across our path as we move toward the city.

In the distance, only a hundred paces away, a group of people is gathered around multiple fires. I count nearly twenty people and as many fires. They're located close to the large portcullis that sits in the center of the northern wall.

Evening is falling now, the sun setting behind us, and each fire casts an unnerving, wine-red glow across the air.

A sweet and unsettling scent floats across the air, coming from the fires.

Father once described honey to me, a golden liquid from humblebees that tastes sweeter than sugar.

That is the scent I inhale now, but it comes tinged with danger.

Beside me, Skirra gives a low growl and Thoren's footsteps are cautious. We're all blood-splattered, and since I'm thirsty and my strength is waning, I know that's how Thoren will be feeling too.

As we draw nearer to the fires, it becomes clear that the people are young adults, my age or only slightly older, an equal number of males and females.

They're all standing at waist-high anvils set out in neat rows while the fires next to each of them are contained in large, black bowls that sit on pedestals to the left of each anvil.

Rhythmic clanging rings out from their hammers. With tongs, they hold chunks of metal in place on the anvil while they strike it, over and over again. Metal of all different colors: some bronze, some copper, some ruby-red, some deep amethyst, even a pale blond.

The color of the hammers they grip in their right hands matches the color of their hair as well as the color of the metal they're beating.

None of their metal is black like Malak's.

They're all breathing hard, their chests rising and falling rapidly, their expressions drawn and faces smudged with black soot.

The men are bare-chested, wearing only white pants, while the women wear strips of white material across their breasts and similar white pants. They're all bare-footed.

Sweat gleams across their bodies, the muscles in their arms honed and defined but visibly straining.

A woman dressed in intricate silver armor stands in front of them, her long, silver hair tied back and her head held high. Her figure is tall and slim, her cheekbones are high, and her eyes are the brightest green.

It's the color of the woman's hair that makes me stumble. It's just like Asha's. Except that this woman's hair is adorned with multiple hair pieces, each one intricate.

Her voice roars out in a fierce command. "*Forge!*" she cries. "You will forge until your hands bleed and your muscles break and still, you will keep on forging!"

I must have stumbled enough for Malak to catch up to me because his voice sounds in my ear. "These students are forging their first medallions."

He holds up his right hand, far too close to my face for comfort, and indicates the band resting across it. "This was my first. Forging a single medallion takes three days and two nights. They're on their first night and must not stop."

The woman continues roaring at them. "Three medallions!" she shouts. "This is your first. You will give it your blood and sweat." A hard smile forms on her face as her voice lowers. "You will give your second medallion your heart and soul. And you will give your third medallion... *fucking everything.*"

Her eyes gleam as she draws a deep breath and bellows, "*Forge!*"

As the woman's command cracks across the air, a drop of something cold lands on my cheek. It's icy as the frostiest raindrop as it travels a quick path to my chin, where I swipe at it.

My fingers come away smeared with red liquid.

But... I'm not sure where it came from.

I glance up at the clouds covering the sky above us, their crimson hue reflecting the sunset. A faint flicker of lightning passes through them as if a storm might be brewing.

At the same moment the lightning flickers, my deep light

sparks and my feet tingle. I push my light down as I refocus on the ground, unsettled by the energy I'm feeling within it. An energy that only seems to be intensifying as the clangs continue and the honeyed scent thickens in the air.

As we continue walking, Malak is a dark shadow at my side, his pace slowing now that we're closer to the group. To enter the city, we will need to pass behind them, but until then, we're in full view of them.

Multiple eyes swivel our way, but the glances are fleeting, the students quickly focusing back on their task.

I don't miss the way those brief looks take in all of us or the slight widening of eyes, particularly when they see Skirra walking beside Malak.

Given the way the forest life has mutated because of their magic, I can't imagine they regularly see a wolf like Skirra.

"That woman is Ayla Silverspun," Malak says. "She's Asha's mother and the head of the Academy."

As if she heard him, Ayla looks away from her students to send a cold glance in our direction.

The look of delight that passes across her face when she sees Skirra is chilling.

She quickly focuses back on her students, her fingers tapping her thigh as if she's counting beats before she screams again, "Heat!"

At her command, each of the students wrenches their lump of metal, still gripped in their tongs, off their anvil to ram it into the fire and hold it there.

They're all taking deep breaths and I'm certain they're making the most of the reprieve.

"Hold!" Ayla shouts, casting another delighted smile from Skirra to Malak. She tips her chin at him, her concentration on her students seeming unbroken. "Hold... hold... hold..."

Some of the students' arms are shaking, sweat pouring

down their brows. Even from this distance, I can feel the heat beating up from the coals.

The air feels thick with tension as Ayla paces in our direction, a move seemed deliberately designed to get a better look at us, before she turns sharply back to follow the next row of students, prowling between them, her eyes narrowed at each one as she passes.

Her deepening scowl lifts when she reaches the male student in the back row at the end nearest to us. She stops there, her head tilted, peering into the flames.

The fiery hue glowing from his forge is darker than the others and casts blood-red light up over her face.

"Well done, Landon," she says to that student. "Your father would be proud."

Landon is leaner than the other men and not as tall, but his muscles are far more honed. His hair is a copper color.

Ayla's expression quickly hardens before she steps away. "Do not fail him."

We've reached the back of the group now and the air is so thick with honey that it's difficult to breathe and the hum of energy buzzes in my ears.

Malak leans toward me. "Landon doesn't know it yet, but his father is dead," he whispers. "You killed him."

My eyes snap to Malak's.

He must be talking about Deron, the Blacksmith with the copper beard, which he confirms as he continues speaking.

"Deron Copperstream was the favored brother of Cohen Copperstream, who is the leader of their house." Malak inclines his head. "But of course, neither Landon nor Cohen will ever know it was you who killed Deron."

He gives me a slow smile. "Unless I choose to tell them."

CHAPTER 24

Malak's threat hangs in the air as he glides toward the gate.

He seems confident now that we won't try anything.

The wall soars up beside us, a towering structure.

Up on the ramparts, men and women in gleaming armor stand guard, the metallic color and sheen of their hair indicating that they're Blacksmiths.

The portcullis is already open and it only takes us moments to pass through the first gate, cross the width of the large opening beneath the wall, and step into the city beyond it.

A wide, cobbled path stretches ahead of us while buildings of all shapes and sizes rise up on either side of the walkway.

The hum of energy we leave behind is replaced with the drone of sound from within the city. Voices. Machines. Footfalls.

It's a wash of noises that I'm not used to and I find my ears buzzing.

Or maybe that's thirst and exhaustion. Either way, it's unpleasant.

I can't hear myself think.

People with dull, brown hair and downcast eyes hurry past us. Although they keep their heads down as they pass Malak, more than one of them glances at Skirra and then at Thoren and me, their eyes widening before they quickly look away again.

I consider the rips in their ragged clothing, the scars on their arms and legs and faces, and their thin frames.

They must be humans.

They give Malak such a wide berth that they veer to the very edge of the cobbled path and even step off it if there's space. They do so in such a way that the path simply opens up before us, the walkway clearing within seconds.

Malak strides onward, his cloak billowing in the increasing dark. A glance behind us tells me that the portcullis is already closing.

Even if we could find a way to dart back through it, we would also have to find a way to remove the claws from our chests along with the metal thread Malak shot through us.

Bells start ringing, jarring my hearing and making me jolt. I quickly locate the large, metal bells located up on the wall, set at intervals.

I'm not the only one who startles.

Skirra's ears sit flat against his head and Thoren winces with every strike of the bell.

The people around us pick up their pace.

A woman carrying a covered basket murmurs to the child beside her, "Quickly now. Back home before darkness falls and the next bells ring."

I glance at the sky. The woman didn't say as much, but I'm guessing the humans aren't allowed out after dark. The bells must tell them when they have to go indoors.

Malak pauses briefly ahead of us, waiting for us to catch up.

He gestures to the wall, seeming to ignore the bells as he

says, "If you want to survive in this city, then you must understand the hierarchy."

His tone is conversational, but all the while, the threads of tension and anxiety in the air around us only increase as humans hurry past.

"Every Blacksmith House has a role to perform," he says. "For example, House Renderbronze provides security. You will see them up on the walls and along the streets. House Silverspun is responsible for raising our children and teaching them our ways. And House Copperstream is in charge of mining and coal distribution. Come. I will show you."

Along the way, he points out the place where the Blacksmiths weave their cloth, a squat building from which emanates a hum of machines.

Next, he gestures to a forge, which he says is just one of the places where metal objects are made.

Finally, he pauses in front of a large, stone building that sits on the left-hand side of the path. The honeyed scent that was so thick around the fires at the northern gate lingers around this building, too.

Blacksmiths with the same copper hair color as Kalith are coming and going from this building, each of them bowing to Malak as they pass.

"That building there is the infirmary," Malak says, pointing to a smaller building next to the larger one. "But here is our coal house. Crimson coal is required for our forges. It's mined in the eastern mountains and must be cleaned before it can be used."

Malak continues. "It's particularly busy here today. We received a large delivery of coal early this morning, along with the return of the miners and their Blacksmith guards, in preparation for the upcoming festival."

He peers at me expectantly, as if I'm supposed to speak. So far, he has barely paid any attention to Thoren or Skirra.

I am the center of his unsettling attention.

My voice is cracked with thirst. "A festival?"

It's the last thing I care about right now.

"To celebrate our students," Malak replies. "They're given five days of rest between the forging of each medallion. Once they forge their third medallion, they will have attained their place as our next generation of Blacksmiths, and that merits a celebration. Every Blacksmith home will be bright with festivities."

He wears a smile as he turns and continues along the path.

Thoren speaks up beside me, his voice a rasp like mine, telling me he's just as thirsty as I am. "Every *Blacksmith* home," he says. "What about the humans?"

Malak spins back to us, his smile vanishing.

Thoren is nearly tall enough to meet him eye to eye and my brother doesn't look away.

"Our humans will celebrate too of course," Malak replies, peering at Thoren in the same way a predator might study his prey. "Because they live in our homes. They belong to us. They are our property. Just as you now are."

Thoren's lips draw back from his teeth, an expression that mirrors Skirra's. "Believe what you want to believe, Blacksmith."

Malak's gaze merely flicks to me. "It doesn't matter what I believe. I could happily kill *you* right now and be done with you. It's what Vandawolf chooses that matters."

Malak raises his right palm, emphasizing the presence of his black medallion. "What do you choose, Vandawolf? Do you wish for your brother to live despite his insolence?"

I reach for Thoren's arm, closing my hand around it in a hard and deliberately painful grip that forces him to look at me.

I don't say anything to him because I can't deny him his anger. But he must know that to die here, right now, inhaling the honeyed scent of Blacksmith power with our last breaths, would be fucking pointless.

Thoren wrenches out of my hold. His shoulders don't slump, his head remains high, but he takes a step back from Malak.

"Very well," Malak says, turning to the path once more. "This way."

Up ahead, still some distance away, a massive castle rises up out of the wash of buildings and structures, sitting at what could be the very center of the city.

It's a looming collection of towers along with battlements, but unlike at the wall around the city, I don't see guards patrolling them. Only one on the battlement above the gate and two more on either side of the gate down here at ground level.

Malak heads toward the castle before he veers to the left and takes us along the path around it.

Before long, we come to another stone wall, although this one is only about ten feet high.

Blacksmith guards wearing bronze armor stand guard at intervals along it. Each stone is inky black and the wall extends left and right, curving in a way that indicates it could surround a roughly circular place.

When Malak approaches the guards, one of them steps forward.

Like his brethren, he has bronze hair, but his eyes are dark brown.

"Lord Ironmeld?" There's a question in his voice as he greets Malak, briskly bowing his head before his brow furrows at Thoren, Skirra, and me.

"These are my guests, Jadiel," Malak says. "They will accompany me inside the garden today."

Jadiel's eyes widen a little. "But humans are never allowed—"

"In this case, I will make an exception," Malak says, reaching out to place his right hand, medallion and all, on Jadiel's shoulder.

Jadiel immediately freezes.

Malak lowers his voice, but not so much that we can't hear him. "These humans still have hope," he says. "I will show them that hope is futile."

CHAPTER 25

Malak lets go of Jadiel's shoulder and the guard quickly steps aside.

Moving forward, Malak presses on one of the central stones, a smaller one, at which the stones in front of him start to move.

The sound of whirring metal reaches me a moment before part of the wall slides back and to the side, creating an opening.

Malak beckons us through.

I expected to find a dark and damaged landscape, similar to the ashen field on the northern side of the city, but instead, a vast orchard sits ahead of us.

Trees bearing red fruit rise up at intervals, their branches spreading across the air so far that they touch each other and form a canopy overhead.

The path through them is lined with all kinds of beautiful plants, their leaves and flowers ranging from bright oranges to deep purples.

Living up in the mountains, I've never seen so many different kinds of plants before.

While the door slides shut behind us, sealing seamlessly

into the wall, Malak gestures to a small water fountain on our right. Clear water rushes down a stone surface into a stone bowl at its base.

"Drink," he says, retracting the leash from Skirra's collar but leaving the muzzle in place.

I don't hesitate. Thirst is dangerous, making thought difficult.

I can't assume the water isn't poisoned, but I doubt Malak would have brought us all the way into the city just to kill us now.

I'm reassured when Skirra dips his head to the bowl, licking at the surface as best he can around his muzzle. If the water were dangerous, I'm sure he would have sensed it.

Kneeling to the fountain while Thoren joins me, I scoop water into my mouth for long moments.

The hydration helps and my head clears.

As soon as we rise back to our feet, Malak resumes walking, turning his back on us, as if he has no concern that we'll attack him.

Skirra remains at my side as we follow.

Malak reaches out to brush his hands across the tree trunks, veering left to right as he follows the winding path. Right hand. Left hand. He doesn't seem to favor either.

"When I was much younger—about your age, Vandawolf— I was sent on diplomatic missions to other lands in the east and north," he says. "I learned much about other cultures during my travels. The Fae Queen has a place she calls her 'Inner Sanctuary'. Well, this is my Inner Sanctuary."

He gestures to the garden around us. "As you would have gathered from Jadiel's surprise, I don't allow anyone else in here."

"Are we supposed to be grateful?" Thoren mutters beneath his breath.

"No," Malak says, casting Thoren an uncaring glance. "But you would be wise to listen."

Malak stops in front of what appears to be the largest tree, its branches spreading all the way across the lush garden to a vine-covered structure that sits on the right.

The structure's outer walls are so heavily covered in greenery that it's hard to tell what it could be, but it's certainly at least two levels high.

Malak presses both of his hands against the tree's trunk. Then he looks skyward and says, "Wait for the darkness and you will see..."

I'm poised on the path with Thoren and Skirra on either side of me.

In the distance, the last of the sun's rays disappear and dusk creeps across the orchard, a spreading shadow.

The tree against which Malak's hands are pressed begins to sparkle. Its bark lights up from its base to its top and along its branches, an eerily beautiful sight.

All of the other trees follow, sparkling light gleaming through their trunks and boughs, leaving only their red fruit muted.

The glow breaks through the gloom around the nearby structure, making some of its parts clearer—a thatched roof, small windows, two levels, like I thought. It's some sort of cottage.

Malak doesn't look at it, remaining fixated on the tree.

"This is where my power revealed itself," he says. "I was only eight years old when I stumbled out into the darkness here, my face bruised, blood in my eyes, hammer in my hand, and I struck this tree with all my might, wishing only to break it down."

A snarl leaves his lips. "Wishing only for its destruction."

His breathing evens out again. "Instead, I made it glow. Is it not beautiful?"

Without waiting for an answer, he gestures to the garden around us. "I turned the weeds into flowers and created this oasis. With mere impulses, I painted color across a previously gray canvas. The ugly things in my life became perfect because I *made* them perfect."

I consider the trees and plants warily. "You did this?"

"Does my power surprise you, Vandawolf?" he asks. "That I can do more than turn flesh to stone?"

My jaw clenches at the memory of my father's death.

A smile flickers around his mouth. "You will have seen what other Blacksmiths can do. Using their medallions to shape and reshape metallic objects according to their will. The Copperstream Blacksmiths have learned how to turn their metal to near-liquid. Kalith was born into that house, but in accordance with our culture, he took his wife's name and transferred to her house when they married. As for Silverspun House, well, you'll see soon enough what terrible violence Ayla Silverspun is capable of."

His left hand flexes against the tree. "But I am Ironmeld. My house was the lowest of the low. So low, in fact, that we were the ones sent out on diplomatic missions to dangerous territories. We were dispensable, you see. It didn't matter if we didn't survive. Our numbers dwindled until there were only a few of us left. From my own people, I learned the power of cruelty."

He releases the tree to step closer to me. "Over time, I allowed fear and hatred to replace my hope. And I simply waited for my chance to strike." A smile grows on his face that chills me to the bone. "The perfect moment when I could slaughter those who had done me harm."

His focus flickers briefly to the cottage on the far side of the tree before he backs away. "It is all a distant memory now." He turns and leads us onward. "Come."

We follow him along the path until it opens into a small, circular clearing.

The clearing is made up of three rows of stone steps, each large enough to create seating while there is a flat area in the middle, a small courtyard with dark stones at its base.

In the open space at the very center of the courtyard is a black anvil.

"Nobody can hear what happens in this clearing," he says, stopping at the edge of it. "The placement of these trees means the acoustics stop any sound from leaving this area. You could scream as loudly as you wish, and nobody would hear you."

He smiles, and again, it chills my blood.

"Even my own people think that I forge within my castle, and sometimes I do to keep up appearances. But here is where my real work happens."

As he speaks, he reaches up to pluck one of the red fruits from the low-lying branch of the nearest tree.

"Do you see this apple?" He holds it in his right hand, his palm covering its far side while his left forefinger supports its base, the black talon at the end of his finger resting lightly against it.

"If I wish, I can reshape its entire structure."

He turns it slowly side to side so that we can see more of it while the fruit begins to change.

Shining, ruby-red liquid seeps from between Malak's knuckles, dripping down onto his left hand, the liquid taking on the appearance of glistening blood, trickling down his left forearm and dripping from his elbow.

He has already taken a step back and the bloody liquid spreads across the stone at his feet.

The apple within his fist quickly begins to shrink.

Its skin wrinkles and softens, peeling back to expose the fleshy inner that's bright red and coarsely-grained, unsettlingly similar to a slab of meat.

Thoren recoils where he stands beside me and Skirra snarls, lifting his nose to the air.

"If I wish," Malak continues, "I can take life just as easily."

The texture of the meat begins to change again, but this time, the color darkens to a putrid gray and the flesh emits a foul odor.

The scent of decay.

Malak pitches the rotting meat into the plants at the base of the nearest tree but makes no move to dry the glistening liquid from his hands or arms.

He considers us coldly, his inky-dark eyes seeming to dissect us.

"I didn't always have such full power," he says. "I had to embrace the darkness first. I had to welcome it with my whole heart." He turns to the other side of the clearing. "I had to kill the very people who gave me life."

As he steps aside, two pale, twisted tree stumps come into view on the opposite side of the clearing.

They're nothing like the glittering apple trees or the lush plants within the rest of the orchard.

Stubby branches streak out from their trunks as if lightning struck through them, sharp and violently twisted.

But amidst their wooden shapes are features belonging to people. The faint outline of a jaw, shoulders, legs, maybe cheekbones. Possibly hands.

"Don't feel sorry for them," Malak says softly. "My mother was cruel and my father was a brute. They do not merit grief."

At the sight of them, Skirra's fur stands up across his back.

Thoren takes a step back, his eyes wide.

I'm frozen to the spot. What was left of my hope has vanished. Just like Malak wanted.

What he did to my father proved he is far more dangerous than any other Blacksmith, but *this* means he has no boundaries.

Thoren's voice is strangled. "You killed your own parents?"

Malak smiles and this time, it touches his eyes. I don't miss the rage simmering beneath his calm demeanor. "Not before they taught me that the greatest power comes from pain."

He takes a step toward me and for the first time since I met him, I want to back away. As much as I try to fight the hopelessness rising within me, I can't seem to control it.

"Ah," he says, studying my face. "You understand now." His focus flickers to Thoren and back to me. "You both understand." He nods to himself. "You will hear me now and know that this is not an idle warning."

He folds his hands in front of himself. "You will do everything I want. If you disobey me, I will carve your flesh from your bodies, piece by piece, and make it rot before your eyes." He tilts his head with a brilliant smile. "And nobody will hear your screams."

CHAPTER 26

"What do you want us to do?" I ask, my throat tight with a fear I'm struggling to control.

"It's simple," he says. "Each day, you will go to work where I tell you to work. You will observe the Blacksmiths who come and go from those places and take note of everything they say and do. Then, when the first bells sound at the end of each day, you will return to this orchard and tell me what you have seen and heard."

My brow is furrowed because he's talking about Blacksmiths, not humans. "You want us to spy on your own people."

Malak doesn't deny it. "That is how you will be useful to me."

"To what end?" Thoren asks, his forehead creased.

"To whatever end I wish," Malak replies before he steps toward us. "Now, I will remove the claws from your bodies and you will go to the infirmary to have the wounds bandaged. After that, you will return to the castle, where I will have one of my human servants waiting to show you where you will eat and sleep. Tomorrow, you will go to the coal house. I've already shown you where these places are located."

That explains why he was so eager to point out particular buildings earlier. I quickly file away the places he's ordering us to go: *infirmary, castle, coal house.*

Malak advances on me, his hands brushing briefly across my shoulder.

Pain stops all further thought.

The thread he shot through me instantly retracts, tearing at my insides while the claws also recede, leaving me to lurch forward onto my knees.

Blood pools across my shoulder and I press my palm to it.

Malak already saw my father's deep light and seems to know our customs and abilities.

With a larger burst of light, I could speed up the healing process significantly, but I have to conserve what I have.

Thoren drops to his knees beside me, his face screwed up against the pain of the metal's removal, blood spreading beneath his palm where he also grips his chest.

The internal damage is too much to hope we'll heal on our own. Even though Malak has ordered us to go to the infirmary, I doubt any healer could mend the damage within our bodies.

We have to use some of our light—and quickly—a fact that Malak is probably counting on. I'm sure he knew that with our light, we could survive the claws.

And if he knows our light is finite, then he's bound to force us to use it up, bit by bit, until there isn't enough to use against him.

I give Thoren a nod before I allow the smallest spark of light to surface, aware that Thoren is doing the same.

I focus only on healing the internal damage, leaving the outer wound visible.

My light eases most of the pain and the relief forces my

eyes closed for a moment. I'll have to be careful of pulling on the wound when I move around, but it's numb for now.

Thoren watches me closely, following my lead. I know he has stopped drawing on his light when the blood flow from his wound lessens, but the outer wound remains visible through the tears in his shirt.

"This wolf will stay here, where he is free to move around," Malak says, indicating Skirra. "As long as you do what I want, he will have all the meat he needs."

At that, Malak plucks another apple from a low-lying branch, transforming the fruit.

He reaches for Skirra's muzzle, his hands moving at a blur to retract it while leaving the collar in place.

Before Skirra can snap at Malak's hand, the Blacksmith drops the slab of meat.

Skirra snatches it out of the air.

"Vandasteel," Malak says to Thoren. "You will go to the gate and wait for Vandawolf there. Pick some fruit along the way. It's all edible. Vandawolf will join you shortly."

Malak gives Thoren a hard stare. "I will know if you try to hide nearby to overhear our conversation."

Thoren gives me an alarmed look.

"It's okay," I say, although I'm just as worried as he must be.

Malak waits for Thoren to disappear along the path before he turns to me.

He gets right to the point. "You killed two Blacksmiths without using your deep light."

My wariness only increases, but I think better of correcting him. Technically, I only killed one. The first Blacksmith fell when my brother shot him with arrows.

Malak seems to read my mind. "Your brother's arrows only succeeded because you held Abdiel down. Without your savagery, Abdiel would have been able to fight back. Your brother's arrows would have hit nothing more than metal."

Malak tips his chin at me, a strange gesture of respect. "There is a violence in your soul, Vandawolf, that exceeds even the most fearsome Einherjar chief I ever beheld."

He steps closer. "You have the strength and skills to kill Blacksmiths, and I intend to put that to good use."

I can't stop myself from jolting. *He wants me to kill Blacksmiths?*

He's studying me closely. "I trust you won't have a problem with that."

I'm frozen as I fight my inner thoughts.

Fuck, no, I don't have a problem with ending Blacksmiths.

But the chances of Malak ordering me to kill Kalith are slim, and Kalith is the one I really want dead. Malak is bound to order me to kill only the Blacksmiths who may be against him.

Perhaps I should have a problem with that.

But I remind myself how I already failed to save my father.

I won't fail to save Thoren. If it means killing Blacksmiths to keep my brother alive, then so be it.

"Tell me who and it will be done," I say.

Malak smiles and steps back, his head held high. "I will tell you soon enough. In the meantime, go with your brother. Eat some fruit. Press the purple stone in the gate to leave this place. I will see you again tomorrow."

Malak's hand drops to Skirra's collar, enforcing his order that Skirra stays here.

I back away, slowly at first and then quickly.

It tears my heart apart to leave Skirra with Malak and, at the last moment, I turn. "That wolf is my brother, too."

"Don't worry, Vandawolf," Malak says. "I would sooner cut off my own arm than destroy this perfect animal."

I have no choice but to accept his word.

Turning away from him, I hurry back to Thoren.

CHAPTER 27

A second set of bells rings out as we exit the orchard through its black stone gate, each of us holding a half-eaten apple.

As we did with the water, we had to trust that the fruit wasn't poisoned and we waited after the first bite to check before devouring five each and taking the remainder of a sixth with us.

The guards on the other side of the black wall cast us narrow-eyed glances and when we step toward the path that leads back to the infirmary, the Blacksmith named Jadiel tries to grab Thoren.

"Where do you think you're going without night passes?" Jadiel asks.

Thoren lightly sidesteps him, evading Jadiel's grasping hands.

I barrel up to the Blacksmith, preparing to sweep his legs out from under him if I have to.

"Malak's orders!" I snap. "If you disagree with them, take it up with him."

Jadiel immediately steps back, but a nasty smile stretches across his face. "I believe you, but others won't."

Thoren is already backing away and I follow after him, keeping the guards within my sights until we're far enough away from them to focus on the path ahead.

"What are night passes?" Thoren whispers.

"I don't know," I murmur back. "But we need to learn everything we can about this city as quickly as we can. Malak might want us here for a purpose, but he won't make things easy for us."

Around us, the city is falling silent. In the distance, the hum of machinery starts to fade. The windows of the buildings we pass are shuttered, dim light spilling around them.

In the far distance toward the west, I make out the shapes of much grander buildings than the ones here.

Lamps are being lit along the path by human men wearing ragged clothing. Curiously, each of them has a sash of bright-white material wrapped around their right bicep. I didn't notice any humans wearing those armbands earlier.

Blacksmith guards patrol the street up ahead.

Thoren grabs my arm, tugging me to the side of the path. "This way. There's a narrow path of white stone. I saw it earlier. The same sort of path lets out beside the infirmary. If we're lucky, the paths will connect. We can avoid the Blacksmiths this way."

I give him a nod and we dart into the shadows of the unlit path, following it around until the shape of the coal house comes into view. The infirmary is tucked beside it.

We pause at the infirmary's entrance, standing at the edge of the light spilling through the door, taking in the sounds of pain coming from within it.

Unlike nearly every other building, the door here is wide open.

We can see straight through the small room at the front to

another set of doors, beyond which is a much larger room lined with beds, at least thirty on each side. A wide aisle sits between them.

More than half of the beds are filled with people: some lying on their sides, others on their backs, a few sitting on the edge of the beds, their shoulders slumped. Most of them are human men.

Women with purple streaks in their hair hurry around the room, carrying metal implements or jars or bandages and tending to the men.

It's noticeable that they're all located at the far end of the room.

There's a gap between them and a set of six visibly larger beds at this end of the room. It's harder to see because of the angle, but the flashes of metal indicate there are Blacksmiths present. I won't know for certain until I step inside if they're here as guards or as patients.

I give Thoren a nod and we pass through the small entry room.

We've barely made it to the inner doorway when a woman with a dark-purple streak in her hair intercepts us.

"Humans," she says, speaking in a way that makes it sound not like a greeting but an assessment. "You have chest wounds, but you're mobile. Petra will tend to you. Go to the empty bed at the very back of the room."

She pauses to take a breath and then lowers her voice. "Stay away from the Blacksmiths. Their own healers are all busy helping the guards that returned from the mines today, so some have been sent here instead. Pain has made them murderous tonight."

I take a moment to consider how pale she is. There's a faint splatter of blood across her cheek. It doesn't appear to be her own, but another healer in the near distance has a split across her lip.

My own blood boils. It takes a certain kind of person to hurt someone who is trying to help them.

Thoren's gaze flashes to me and I recognize the anger in his eyes before he asks the woman, quietly, "What is your name, lady?"

She blinks at him, possibly because of the honorific 'lady' that our father taught us to use when addressing women. "I'm Sybil."

"Don't worry about us, Sybil," he says, his jaw clenching. "We can take care of ourselves."

Since we left the mountain, Thoren has been withdrawn, but now I sense the increasing anger that must be writhing within him.

I reach for him, but he's already stepping into the room.

I follow closely on his heels, keeping watch and making the most of the wide aisle to steer clear of the two Blacksmiths in the beds at the front. Bandages are wrapped around various parts of their arms and legs. One of the healers—another woman with a dark-purple streak in her hair—is placing ointment across what appears to be a burn on one of the Blacksmiths' arms.

One glance at both Blacksmiths' faces tells me Sybil wasn't exaggerating.

We quickly reach the empty bed on the right hand side at the back of the room, making it past the humans and the other healers along the way.

We're still holding the apple cores and we deposit them onto a table beside our allotted bed.

Already, I'm contemplating the merits of using our deep light to fully speed up the healing process. The healers are visibly exhausted. There aren't enough of them to deal with all of the injuries I'm seeing—mostly burns, but a lot of cuts too.

A young woman kneels next to the last bed on the other side of the aisle. She's facing in our direction, but her head is down, her forehead pressed to the hand of a young man who lies, unmoving, on the bed.

She wears a pale-purple streak in her hair, fainter than those of the other healers. When she looks up, I see that her face is an oval shape with a pointed chin and her eyes are large and brown.

She can't be much older than Thoren, maybe only fourteen.

She bats at the tears trickling down her cheeks, hurrying to cross the aisle toward us, but Thoren speaks first. "Are you okay?"

She stares at the hand Thoren holds out to her, and then her eyes fill with tears again.

Her whisper is barely discernable above the sounds around us. "He was my friend."

Was.

The young man on the bed doesn't appear to have any visible wounds or broken bones, until I focus on his face.

There's a cut above his left eye and a thick streak of blood down that side of his face, partially concealed by the way his head is tilted toward the mattress.

Unbidden, I suddenly flash back to the moment I first saw Asha. The wound on her forehead. Just like this one.

Except that a small fleck of copper metal rests on this boy's forehead at the edge of his wound.

The young woman has taken Thoren's hand and he steadies her, but her eyes widen when she focuses on the blood on his shirt. "That's a bad wound."

She gestures to the empty bed. "I'm Petra. I can help you."

I can't stop myself from stepping into her path. "How did your friend die?"

She tenses and I recognize the flood of intense fear that washes over her, as well as the sudden stillness of the nearest healer and the men in the beds closest to us.

Regret fills me. I didn't mean to frighten her or draw attention to us.

I take an immediate step back, but then I choose to move to where she will be blocked from the sight of the Blacksmiths at the front end of the room—if they look this way.

I expect her to dart toward the empty bed now that I'm not in her way, but she pauses, her voice incredibly low.

"Landon Copperstream killed him," she says. "A single punch with a fist covered in metal."

CHAPTER 28

Landon Copperstream is the student Ayla Silverspun was gloating over when we first arrived at the city.

I killed his father, the Blacksmith named Deron, but Landon doesn't know that.

Chances are he won't even know his father's dead until the students have finished forging their first medallions.

If Kalith follows Malak's orders, Landon will hear that wild beasts killed his father.

Petra pulls herself upright, clears her throat, and becomes matter-of-fact.

"Shirts off," she says. "Sit on the side of the bed. I need to see your wounds."

The hubbub near us resumes, but I'm conscious of the continued scrutiny from a human man in the bed next to ours.

A healer tends to what looks like burns across his hands and lower forearms. He's sitting propped up on his bed, but I estimate he's nearly as tall as me. He's bulky through his chest, arms, and legs, and like many of the humans I've observed so far, he has brown eyes and brown hair, although he wears a short beard.

He's bare-chested and there are many scars across his chest and shoulders.

It's easy to keep an eye on him and the rest of the room when we sit, side by side, facing forward on the edge of the bed.

When we remove our shirts, placing the bloody material to the side, Petra pauses again.

"I've seen these marks before," she whispers, keeping her voice below the hum within the room. "The central wound and the claw marks. This is Malak's work. Isn't it?"

At our nods, she swallows. "I've only seen these marks on dead bodies. How did you survive?"

Her question seems aimed at Thoren.

His jaw clenches, but he gives nothing away. "We've survived worse."

Thoren has never been injured this badly before. Father and I made sure of that. But I understand what he means. There isn't any physical wound that compares with the pain of losing our father.

Petra's eyes are wide, but she seems to quickly gather herself together, reaching for the tray of bandages and the salve from the table where we put our apple cores.

When she reaches for me, I stop her. "My brother first."

She nods and sets to work.

Thoren follows her movements as she quickly sets about tending to his wound. The salve she uses smells like some of the plants we would gather on the mountain.

"What happened to everyone else here?" Thoren asks.

"These men all work with crimson coal," she replies. "It's dangerous to handle. Most of them are miners who've returned from the mines this afternoon. Braddock hauls coal within the city."

She indicates the man in the bed next to ours—the one who hasn't stopped scrutinizing us, even though he hides it well.

Thoren considers her a little longer, leaning toward her. "What does the streak in your hair mean?"

A smile glimmers around her mouth. "It means I'm training to be a healer. The women with dark-purple streaks are senior healers, like Sybil."

But she tilts her head, her hands pausing. "Why don't you know that already?"

Anyone who grew up in this city wouldn't have to ask these questions.

I give Thoren a warning glance before he can answer truthfully. This city is vast enough that the humans can't possibly all know each other. There's no reason to tell her where we came from.

"We're Malak's property," I say gruffly before Thoren can reply. "That's all we can tell you."

Thoren's expression hardens and now his anger is directed toward me.

I'm prepared to bear the weight of it. Thoren has always been truthful. Honest. Loyal. Lies don't sit well with him.

A commotion at the front end of the room draws our attention.

Kalith Silverspun stands in the far doorway, his chest heaving, and suddenly, all of the healers are standing to attention.

The blood on his face and clothing has dried, but his expression is dark.

"They told me I had to come to this fucking place," he snaps into the silence. "So here I am."

His surly tone and expression are nothing like the regal façade he presented on the mountain when Malak was around.

Sybil hovers near to him. "Lord Silverspun, how can we help you?"

Kalith advances on her. "Isn't it fucking obvious? My nose is broken."

I'm surprised he went all afternoon without setting it back into place, but then, Malak was clear about his instructions. Kalith was responsible for speaking with the families of the dead men. I'm sure it would have helped with his story that Kalith was also visibly wounded.

But now, it seems, his rage has boiled to the surface.

Sybil darts away from Kalith, her eyes wide as she heads straight for us.

Petra is frozen where she stands beside Thoren. "Oh, no."

Sybil's voice is already snapping across the distance. "Petra! You're the best with broken bones. See to Lord Silverspun."

"I'm not the best," Petra whispers beneath her breath, her hands shaking as she stares at the approaching healer.

"Then why is she asking for you?" Thoren hurries to ask, leaning toward Petra.

"Because she's too afraid to do it herself." Petra's face is deathly pale as she steps away from us and into the aisle.

"Quickly, girl!" Sybil calls, gesturing firmly.

Thoren slips off the edge of the bed, as if he would follow Petra, but he stops when he reaches the aisle.

Kalith seems so self-absorbed that he doesn't appear to have noticed us here, let alone recognize us.

I slip off the bed, too, watching Petra's back while Sybil follows her to the front of the room and then hovers nearby.

The older healer keeps enough distance between herself and Kalith that he won't be able to grab her quickly.

The other healers all appear to be holding their breath, but they're visibly trembling—one of them so much that she puts down the tray that was audibly rattling in her hold.

Petra speaks softly, but the room is so quiet that we can hear her. "Lord Silverspun, if you would kindly take a seat."

She keeps her eyes lowered as he perches on the edge of the bed she indicated.

After moving to stand in front of him, she reaches for his

face. She must have set a few noses before because she positions her hands just right, the way Father once showed us.

Her hands move, exactly as we were taught, a perfect maneuver.

But if our Father's warning was correct, it hurts like hell.

Kalith shouts. His fist shoots out, punching into Petra's chest so hard that she gains air before she crashes across the room, hitting the end of the bed opposite him—*smack!*—and collapses at the base of it.

"Little bitch!" Kalith shouts, lurching after her. "That fucking hurt!"

Thoren is already sprinting toward them.

I'm aware of Braddock heaving himself out of his bed before I also break into a run.

I quickly catch up to my brother. Chasing after monsters in the forest has given me strength and speed and the floor in this place is far easier to run across than snow.

Up ahead, Petra has curled into a ball on the floor and Kalith is drawing back his boot, preparing to kick her. I have no doubt he'll break her ribs.

I overtake my brother and throw myself into Kalith before his boot can connect with Petra's chest.

Oomph! The force of my hit propels us far enough across the room that we reach the doorway.

I catch a brief glance of Thoren skidding to a stop beside Petra and hooking his arms beneath hers. I'm certain he'll drag her out of the way now.

That's all I see before the two Blacksmiths in the nearby beds launch themselves at me.

Kalith shouts from where he's sprawled on the floor.

My father must have really hurt him during their fight because he's slow to get up.

I've ended up on my knees on the floor, but I regain my balance fast enough to knock my elbow back into the face of one oncoming Blacksmith before I swing to the other, grabbing his wrist before he can slash a bronze dagger down my back.

Jumping to my feet in the same move, I use my upward momentum to shove him backward, my boot connecting with his stomach a second later, ramming him into the nearby wall.

The first man has recovered from my hit to his face and a thick thread of ruby-red metal shrieks across the space between him and me, twining around my neck before I can get my hands up.

If only I was as fast as they are.

"Back to your knees," the Blacksmith snarls at me as the metal tightens around my throat.

I try to see his features. Metallic-red hair and eyes with unnatural red flecks in them.

He kicks at the back of my legs, forcing me onto my knees.

Desperately, I try to push my fingers between my throat and the rope to give myself enough space to breathe, even though the metal will likely chop my fingers off.

I'm kneeling side-on to the room and I can see that Thoren is now halfway down the aisle, crouched there, his arms around Petra. He's looking around. If he had his bow and arrow, he'd be firing it already.

All of the other patients and the healers have remained where they were, their eyes wide. Sybil is pressed hard up against the nearby wall.

Only Braddock has taken a step toward me.

My attention returns to Kalith, who has risen to his feet and now looms over me.

I'm gratified when he stays a full three paces away from me. Far enough to remain out of reach of my fists.

"*You*," he snarls, seeming to finally recognize me.

The corners of his mouth twitch upward as he glances at the ruby-haired Blacksmith. Kalith takes a step back toward the door. And then another. Easing toward the darkness in the street.

To the ruby-haired Blacksmith, he says, "Finish the human if you wish." His smile grows. "But I was never here."

With that, he slips away into the night.

If Malak ever asks, Kalith will deny any knowledge of what happened.

"Gladly," the ruby-haired Blacksmith says as his rope cuts across my throat.

CHAPTER 29

My eyes are watering so badly that I can't see properly.

The ruby-haired Blacksmith stands right where I can't punch him without turning in such a way that I'll cause the rope to slice through my neck.

Just as the first drop of blood slides down my throat, Braddock shouts. "That human is Lord Ironmeld's property!"

I blink hard, trying to clear my vision.

Braddock now stands near Petra and Thoren, his hand raised toward me.

"Malak's property," he repeats, pointing at me.

"Fuck." The ruby-haired Blacksmith gives an unhappy snarl before his metal rope whips away from my neck.

The other Blacksmith glowers nearby. "They could be lying."

"Can't risk it," the first one mutters.

Both men seem to make a decision at the same time, backing away toward the doorway while the ruby-haired man continues to mutter beneath his breath, "Fucking Kalith nearly got us killed."

I rise back to my feet as they disappear into the darkness beyond the infirmary doors.

As relieved as I am, I'm a little stunned. And worried about why they backed off so quickly.

I turn to Braddock, who stumbles back to the edge of his bed.

"You look surprised, Boy," he says gruffly.

"I am," I say into the silence while the healers and patients all stare at me, even the ones who look like they can barely lift their heads off their beds. "I'm surprised you put yourself in harm's way to help us. Even more surprised that they abandoned the kill so quickly."

"Don't you know?" Braddock scoffs, ramming a finger against the largest scar across his chest. "Only Malak gets to damage his property."

I guess this explains why Braddock was scrutinizing us so closely, since his words imply that he, too, belongs to House Ironmeld.

He saved us from a hard fight. I'm grateful for that. But we'll have to be careful what we say around him.

If Malak wants Thoren and me to spy on Blacksmiths, who knows what Malak might force other humans to do?

Petra is nestled into Thoren's side, but one of her arms is clutched around her ribs. I didn't hear her bones break when Kalith shoved her, but I'm sure she's badly bruised. Not as badly, though, as she would have been if Kalith had kicked her.

Sybil peels herself off the wall and steps forward, softly clapping her hands. "Back to work."

At her command, the tension breaks.

I return to my brother, the healers get back to work, and the sounds resume around us.

Petra's eyes are wide when I reach her. "Nobody fights Blacksmiths."

"We do," Thoren says.

It's a dangerous statement to make, but I can't exactly refute it after what we did.

She hobbles to her feet, her free hand wrapped in Thoren's. "I didn't finish bandaging your wound."

He doesn't let her go and she doesn't tug away.

"It's okay," he says.

I clear my throat. "It might be best if we leave as soon as possible. I don't want those Blacksmiths to target any of you because we're here."

My reasons aren't completely altruistic. The longer we stay, the more questions we'll be asked. We did what Malak asked us to—we came here. He didn't specify how long we had to remain or if we needed to have our wounds fully tended to.

"Could we take a small pot of salve and some bandages?" I ask. "We can deal with the wounds ourselves."

After all, we know how to tend our own wounds. We only came here under orders. Just as we'll return to the castle tonight and then tomorrow we'll go to the coal house. Again, because Malak ordered it.

Petra gives a quick nod. "Of course, but..." She glances at Thoren. "I work here at nights and if your wounds don't heal... and if you're permitted... I'll be here."

In the course of gathering supplies, she lifts Thoren's coat off the bed, pausing as her hands brush the warm fur on its inner side.

"Is this fur?" she asks at a whisper.

Thoren has stayed close to her side while I wait in the aisle, keeping the rest of the room within my sights.

"Only Blacksmiths have fur." She lifts the material to her cheek before she turns her questioning eyes on Thoren. "How do you have this?"

"It's yours if you want it," he replies, his head tilted to hers.

She presses her lips together but gives back the coat,

shaking her head. "The Blacksmiths would kill me if they saw me with it. They'd think I stole it."

Is she now wondering if we stole the coat? Along with our fur-lined pants and boots?

Thinking quickly, I say, "Malak gave us these clothes."

She nods, but worry floods her eyes as she turns back to Thoren. "Whatever Malak made you promise in exchange for this clothing, be careful."

Thoren is tense, but he doesn't correct her assumption that Malak gave us the clothing as some sort of incentive. I'm sure my brother realizes it's far safer for us if we accept whatever conclusions these humans draw that fit within the workings of their world.

After Thoren pulls the coat back on, Petra hands him the supplies, along with the two apple cores.

"Don't waste these," she says. "It's rare to have fresh fruit here. The Blacksmiths keep it for themselves."

"You can have them," Thoren says before he grimaces. "I mean what's left of them."

This time, Petra doesn't immediately say *no*.

Thoren reaches for her hand, lowering his voice. "I can bring you more." A crooked smile grows on his face. "Fresh ones. Not half-eaten."

She worries at her bottom lip. "Only if you won't get into trouble."

He nods. Then pauses again. "I'm sorry about your friend."

She blinks away fresh tears as her focus shifts to the bed where her friend lies. "Maybe one day we'll be strong enough to fight back."

Dangerous words.

She must realize it because she glances at the rest of the room before she speaks again, clearing her throat, but this time with a little hope in her eyes. "I don't know your names."

Thoren hesitates. "I'm..."

He looks at me, but I won't deny him the right to choose what others call him.

"I'm Thoren," he says, a steely glint in his eyes.

"And you?" Petra asks me.

It's unsettlingly clear that the room has quieted down again.

There are many listening ears.

Malak calls me 'Vandawolf'. He chose that name because it means 'of the wolves', but in the Einherjar language, *Vanda* means *vicious*.

I make myself a vow: I won't reclaim my real name—the name my father gave me—until I'm free again.

Until then, when it comes to the Blacksmiths, I will be the vicious wolf.

To Petra, I say, "You can call me 'the Vandawolf'."

CHAPTER 30

My brother and I keep to the shadows and make it back to the castle without being stopped.

A woman we haven't met before waits in front of the half-lowered portcullis; the handle of a basket hooked over her arm.

She clutches two sashes of white material in one hand and a lamp in the other. Her focus flits between the Blacksmith guards who stand on either side of her and back to us.

One of the guards gives her a nod and she steps toward us.

Like the other humans, her hair is brown and her frame is thin. But her eyes are soft and more sad than angry as she gestures us forward. "Quickly now. Follow me. Before the gate closes."

We've barely passed through the large, arched opening when the portcullis slams down behind us.

The woman continues speaking at a rapid pace. "I'm Maybelle. Whatever you did to be assigned to House Ironmeld, do not speak of it. Every part of this castle has ears." She flashes me a haunted look. "We all do what we must to survive."

Ahead of us is a wide courtyard. Around it on three sides are dark corridors with tall, black pillars.

In the courtyard's center is a large, black table made of what looks like the same metal that Malak's hammer and medallion are made of. It's the same metal from which his anvil in the orchard appears to be constructed.

On one side of the table are two large, metal cages, both big enough for a bear to stand up in. Or a human.

On the other side of the table is a large, titanium bowl, waist-height, and glowing with wine-red flame. As we approach, I make out the crimson-colored rocks within it.

The honeyed scent filters through the air, but this time, it carries a chill with it, a malevolence that makes the hairs on the back of my neck and my arms stand up.

"That is Lord Ironmeld's forge," Maybelle says. "It is always lit. Do not go near the fire. Those flames are—" She shudders as she walks. "They are hungry. They will destroy your body. Likewise, do not touch any part of that table."

She veers wide of it, the basket she's holding knocking violently against her thighs, and I realize it's because she's shaking.

"That metal has soaked up too many screams," she says, her voice strangled. "Most recently the cries of two innocent children."

Children.

Thoren is tense beside me and I feel his anger.

Maybelle takes a shuddering breath and repeats her warning. "Do not touch it. Or any of Lord Ironmeld's metal, for that matter. You may be able to risk contact with another Blacksmith's hammer or even their medallions, but not Lord Ironmeld's."

Hurrying onward, she leads us toward a tower that sits in the southeast corner.

On the way, she points out a place from which comes the

faint smell of food. "That is the kitchen. There will be food there twice a day—between the first and second bells in the morning and again in the evening. I have some bread for you to eat now." She pats the basket. "Also your night passes."

When she stops in front of an ornate, wooden door, she hands us the sashes of white material. Unlike the plain, white sashes we saw on other humans, these have black hammers embroidered along their length.

"You don't need to give these passes back in the morning like humans in other Houses do," Maybelle says. "Lord Ironmeld expects us to do what he wants at all times of day. The guards may dislike having to raise the gate in the middle of the night, but they will do it."

She nods and taps the sash around her own arm. "With these passes, you can move about the city freely. I suggest you wear them during the day, too. The other Blacksmiths will know whose property you are and leave you alone."

She grabs my hand as I study the material. "Do not share these passes with anyone else thinking to help them move freely. Lord Ironmeld will find out and he will cut off your arm."

She swings away from me, heaving a sigh as she pushes on the door with her free hand, holding the lamp high as she leads us along another corridor to another ornate door.

Within the room beyond it is a surprisingly opulent-looking bed with embroidered blankets and pillows and wooden furniture around the walls, all beautifully carved.

"What is this?" I ask warily. "This is not a room for the likes of us."

"You're right," Maybelle says, handing the lamp to Thoren, who takes it and steps into the room, his expression wary. "I don't expect you to know this, because few humans have seen inside these castle walls, but this tower belonged to Malak's sister. This room is where her friends would stay. Until now, we've been forbidden from coming anywhere near this tower."

"Yet he assigned this room to us," I say carefully, meeting my brother's eyes.

I want to ask Maybelle more questions, but once again, we're in danger of revealing that we haven't been in the city long enough to know what might have happened with Malak's sister. He said that there were only a few Ironmeld Blacksmiths left, but he never mentioned her specifically.

Maybelle wrings her hands. "When Milena died, Lord Ironmeld lost all reason."

She steps away from the room as if she's having trouble breathing. "You'll have to forgive the dust."

She seems to have forgotten the basket of bread in her arms —and only remembers it now—pushing it toward me.

"Thank you," I say.

Despite the way she's poised outside the door, as if she would like nothing more than to leave this place, she pauses. "I do not wish to know what you did to be brought to this House, but... may I ask which House you belonged to before this?"

This time, Thoren is the one who appears cautious. "Why do you want to know?"

She worries at her bottom lip. "Only that my husband, Kedric, belongs to House Silverspun and it's been years since I saw him. Or heard news of him. And if that's where you're from...?"

"I'm sorry," Thoren says. "We don't have news of him."

The hope fades from her eyes. "Oh."

I step toward her, suddenly the one who might ask dangerous questions. "If your husband belongs to House Silverspun, can you tell us anything about that House?"

She shakes her head. "I'm sorry. I know only what you must surely already know. Ayla Silverspun's cruelty matches Lord

Ironmeld's. It was her own children whose screams fed his anvil while she stood by and watched."

Ayla's children. My eyes widen. Asha is her child—or one of them, as it turns out. "Was Asha one of those children?"

I immediately regret my question. It was too direct to ask about Asha by name.

Maybelle's forehead creases and she leans back a little.

I don't blame her for being cautious.

I expect her to refuse to answer, but she surprises me. "No," she says. "It was the twins. Gallium and Tamra." Her expression softens as she speaks of them. "Beautiful children. Kind and gentle. Nothing like the other Blacksmiths. It's beyond my understanding how two such vicious Blacksmiths had kind children—"

She jolts when there's a faint clatter in the distance.

Quickly, she backs away from us. "I have to go now."

"Thank you for the food," I say.

She nods and hurries away into the dark corridor.

I turn to find Thoren standing in the middle of the room, the lamp lowered, shadows casting across his face.

"This city is as fucked up as Father warned us," he says.

"We need to survive it and we need to escape," I say.

His lips press into an angry line. "What about Asha?" he asks. "Since she's so important to you. Will you risk our lives again trying to free her too?"

His voice is angrier than I ever heard it and I wish I could see his eyes, but he's lowered the lamp even further.

"You're worried about a Blacksmith woman," he says, "but what about all of the humans imprisoned in this city?" He spits my name. "Would you leave them here to suffer while you save one of their oppressors?"

Did he not hear the way Maybelle spoke about Asha?

My shoulders are tense, my chest aching.

I can't answer him because I know it's *yes*.

If the only way to escape this city is with my brother and Asha, I would leave the humans behind.

CHAPTER 31

The tense silence between Thoren and me stretches through the following morning. From the time when the first bells ring, through a hurried breakfast, and during the walk to the coal house.

Our night passes seem to not only keep Blacksmiths away from us, but other humans too, passersby avoiding coming too close to us.

When we reach the building, there's a line of human men making their way inside. They're all taller and bulkier than the humans we passed along the way. I catch sight of burn scars across their arms where their sleeves are rolled up.

Braddock is among them, ahead of us in the line. He's pulling off the bandage that the healer wrapped around his hand and wrist last night, even though his burns clearly haven't healed.

I'm surprised to see a human standing just inside the door, counting heads and noting the names of the men who file inside.

Like the other men, he's heavily built but has a shaved head and sharp eyes.

"Next!" he shouts before I step up.

He glares at me. "I don't know you, Boy."

I lift my arm, ensuring he can clearly see the night pass before I incline my head at Thoren. "Lord Ironmeld sent us."

The man's jaw clenches and his brow furrows. "Did he now?"

His gaze rakes over Thoren, pausing for a moment on my brother before settling back on me. "My name is Nero. I work for Lord Cohen Copperstream. He's in a particularly bad mood this morning after he learned of the death of his beloved brother yesterday."

Nero rams a finger against the red sash wrapped around his bicep. "Do you see this sash, Boy? There's only one like it. It's granted to the foreman of the mines and gives me responsibility for protecting the coal."

He shoves his face into mine and lowers his voice. "Which means I don't give a fuck who sent you. Give me any trouble and I'll kill you. Do you understand?"

There's a look in his eyes that tells me he isn't bluffing.

"Understood," I say.

He steps back. "Go to the third table. There are three empty spaces there to choose from. Men who died in the mine." The corners of his mouth turn down. "Braddock will show you what to do."

With that, Nero is already focused on the man waiting behind Thoren. "Next!"

Inside, the coal house is a square shape. Three rows of long tables line the room from one end to the other, leaving only enough space at the far end for three large crates that are as high as my chest.

At this end of the room, there's a larger space where three Blacksmiths stand—all Copperstream, judging by their hair color.

The man in the middle is the shortest, has a round face, and wears a copper-colored beard. He stands a step in front of the others, his hand twitching near the copper hammer that sits in a harness at his waist while the medallion in his right palm swirls across his skin like water.

On either side of the Blacksmiths are many smaller metal crates, each with wheels on the bottom and straps at their sides.

As I pass by the first of them, I see that it's empty.

We hurry to the far table, where Braddock stands at the farthest end. Tools are set up at intervals along the table—a chisel and hammer, along with a clamping device that appears to be attached to the table.

Many of the other human men have already taken up position at the tables and the remainder hurry to do so.

Nero follows the last human into the room but remains at the door. "All miners are accounted for, Lord Copperstream," he calls.

The shortest Blacksmith standing in the middle of the three gives a sneer, his hand resting down on his hammer. "Then get the fuck to work already."

He must be Cohen. Uncle to Landon. Brother to Deron.

Thoren and I will need to be particularly careful around him.

Nero reaches for the door, sealing it shut with a *clang*.

We're dropped into near-darkness, the only light coming from several small openings in the roof.

"Get to work!" Nero bellows.

Braddock casts me a glance, murmuring, "Do what I do."

That's all he says as he steps away from the table toward the nearest crate at the end of the room, reaching in to pull out a misshapen, gray stone, which he carries back to his place at the table.

Thoren and I do the same while the men farther along the table shuffle past us, each choosing a stone one by one.

I watch Braddock carefully, mimicking his actions when he

clamps the stone to the table and starts chipping away at the outside of it.

The purpose of our actions becomes clear when he chips away a piece to reveal the bright coal hidden beneath it.

The surface sparks at the next impact of his chisel.

A flash of heat.

A spark of flame.

Fuck! I fight my instinct to leap away from it.

No wonder these men all have burn scars.

I quickly roll up my sleeves in case the material catches fire. It certainly explains why Braddock was removing his bandages.

Along the table, small pinpricks of light illuminate the workers' faces until there's a haze of crimson throughout the room.

We work for hours, chipping the stone away from around the coal, using tongs to carry the clean chunks up to the empty crates near the Blacksmiths.

They patrol around us and, given the cruel expression on Cohen's face and the way his metal swirls across his powered hand, I expect violence at any moment.

But it seems that the Blacksmiths respect the coal's volatility and don't get too close to us.

Thoren is quick to clean multiple pieces, but when I follow him up to the crates with my own clean piece—a moment when all three Blacksmiths are at the other end of the room—Nero grabs his arm.

"You're working too fast, Boy," he mutters beneath his breath, his demeanor not as hostile as it was before. "You don't want to draw attention to yourself."

Thoren narrows his eyes. "Why would you warn me?"

Nero's expression gives nothing away. "Because my daughter told me what you did for her last night and—"

"Petra?" The furrow in Thoren's brow clears.

"She won't forgive me if you die on my watch."

Cohen is turning back in our direction.

I softly clear my throat, at which Nero bellows into Thoren's face. "Hurry up, you useless scum!"

We head back to our positions and Thoren slows down after that.

Halfway through the day, Nero stops us to bring in water and we're allowed to use the bathroom at the back of the room.

Then we're back to work.

By the time the first bell of the evening rings, my arms are aching.

Thoren and I have worked long days before, spent hours chopping wood or forging metal in the little forge beside our cabin, so our exhaustion isn't as bad as it would have been otherwise.

Thoren and I trudge back to the castle, veer around it to the orchard, and wait for the guards to allow us inside.

Jadiel scowls at us before he presses the stone that opens the door.

Once inside, we drink our fill from the fountain and devour several apples.

When we reach the clearing, Malak is standing behind his anvil. A bowl of crimson coal glows beside him. He's gently tapping away at a tiny piece of black metal with a much smaller chisel than the ones we used all day.

Skirra isn't muzzled, but he's chained to the side of the anvil. He looks well-rested and unharmed and I hope he was allowed to roam around the orchard while we were away, only chained up now that we've returned.

The hairs on the back of my neck rise as we approach Malak's anvil. It's hard to tell from this distance, but it looks like he's carving the shape of a wolf's snout.

He doesn't look up. "Report."

I speak before Thoren can, recounting everything that happened between leaving the orchard last night and returning here now. I describe what happened at the infirmary and even our conversation with Maybelle and Nero's warning to Thoren at the coal house.

I only skip two details: Thoren revealing his true name at the infirmary and his offer to bring Petra apples. They feel like small omissions that can't cause any harm, and they're easy to move past since I focus instead on Thoren's offer to give Petra his coat.

It takes a long time to tell Malak everything, and when I finally fall silent, he doesn't look up.

"Good," he says as he peers more closely at his creation.

I wait for him to say more.

He merely smiles, but I'm not sure if he's pleased with his work or with my report. "You didn't lie to me."

Thoren steps forward, his brow furrowed. "How would you know?"

Malak looks up, his expression suddenly sharp, his smile vanishing. "Because you're not my only eyes and ears." He tilts his head, as if once more he is dissecting us—my brother this time. "You would do well to remember that, *Thoren*."

My brother stiffens and so do I.

The only time Thoren spoke his real name was at the infirmary last night. He didn't even use his name at the coal house.

There were a lot of listening ears last night. Of course, Petra might have mentioned it to her father, who might have used it today at some point. Completely innocent. Even if Malak is trying to make us feel unsettled by it.

Malak casts his steely-eyed gaze at me. "An omission I'm sure you were about to correct, Vandawolf. Since your report was otherwise so thorough."

I have no choice but to nod.

"Very well," Malak says. "You will work at the coal house

again tomorrow and for the next four days after that. That is all."

He focuses back on his task and we step away.

Skirra rises to his feet and I want nothing more than to go to him, but my instincts tell me not to.

Thoren picks two apples on the way out, holding one in each hand as he walks ahead of me.

By the time we reach our room, night has well and truly fallen. Last night, we dragged the blankets off the bed and onto the floor, because the mattress was too soft for us. We're used to sleeping on furs on the ground.

Thoren collapses onto his rug on the floor without speaking.

My head hits my rug and sleep claims me within seconds.

The next day passes much the same.

We chip away at the coal all day, during which time Thoren openly uses his real name and Nero takes to bellowing it loudly.

That evening, I give my report to Malak, skipping nothing.

He dismisses us without any significant remark.

Thoren picks two more apples from the orchard on our way out, and as soon as we reach our room, we collapse onto our rugs and fall asleep.

But tonight, it feels like only moments later that I awake with a jolt, lurching upright.

The room is still pitch dark. It must be the middle of the night, but something woke me...

My focus flies to Thoren's spot on the floor only a few paces away.

It's empty.

He's gone.

CHAPTER 32

My heart is in my throat and panic threatens to swallow me.

Anything could have happened to Thoren. Anyone could have harmed him. Malak. Another Blacksmith. A human.

I find myself reaching for the hunting knives that aren't there. The bow and arrow I would normally scoop up.

I force myself to breathe and focus, quickly crossing the floor to his bed.

The rug he was lying on is neatly folded. There are no signs of a struggle within the room and a fight would have surely woken me.

The tidy state of his bed indicates that he got up of his own accord and took a moment to fold the bedclothes.

Or someone folded them for him.

But again, a struggle would have woken me.

Father drilled into us that we should never leave any place without telling each other.

He also taught me to assume the worst.

My thoughts keep splitting between the possibility that

someone dragged Thoren out of here and that he crept out on his own.

Then my focus passes across the space on the floor where he left the apples before he lay on his rug.

They're gone.

So is his night pass.

Petra told Thoren that she works at the infirmary at night and Thoren offered to bring her more apples.

Some of my panic calms, but not all of it.

For him to choose to go out at night without me—and without telling me—is a reckless thing to do.

Reaching for my night pass, I tie it on quickly and step silently out into the empty corridor beyond our room.

Within minutes, I've checked the walkways and the courtyard, listening carefully.

The silence within the castle grounds is heavy.

The only sounds are coming from the city outside the castle gates.

Heading out to the courtyard, I cross to the gate. The lone guard up on the wall opens it for me.

Then I set off at a quick run, my bare feet silent. I'm risking cuts and bruises, but I don't want to draw attention to myself as I race along the stony pathway.

By the time I reach the infirmary, my heart is racing with worry.

I dart through the shadows outside the door and into the entry room, praying I'll see Thoren inside.

My brother stands halfway along the room beside a patient's bed, his head close to Petra's.

She's stirring a pot of salve, her expression animated.

Thoren nods as she speaks, seeming intent on listening to what she's saying.

Before I lean back into the empty space behind me, I also catch sight of Nero stepping toward them. He gives his daughter a smile before he grips Thoren's shoulder briefly. It's a fatherly gesture. The kind our own father would make.

I step out of sight without making a sound.

My chest feels empty.

I'm relieved that my brother is safe. Angry that he didn't tell me where he was going. Fearful that he's forming connections with people whose lives are fragile and whom we have no ability to help.

I slink back into the darkness of the street, studying the boarded-up windows opposite the infirmary before casting my gaze skyward.

Clouds have gathered in the distance again, seeming centered over the northern field. They are the same strangely crimson clouds that boiled above the field when we first arrived.

A drop of cold liquid hits my cheek and when I brush it away, once more it looks like blood.

The intense silence from the north suddenly hits me.

While the city around me carries a soft hum, much softer than during the day, the northern field is silent.

The constant clanging of students hammering their medallions has stopped.

They must have finished forging their first medallions.

I teeter on the edge of stepping back into the light and letting my brother know I'm here.

But he chose not to tell me he was coming here.

He didn't want me to know.

As quickly as I can, I make my way back to the castle, back to the room belonging to Malak's dead sister, and I try to sleep.

I wake before the first bells.

I tossed and turned during the night but must have fallen

asleep at some point because I didn't hear Thoren creep back into the room.

He's still fast asleep and I don't wake him. He needs as much sleep as he can get or he'll make mistakes with the coal today.

When the morning bell rings and he finally stirs, I say, "You should have told me where you were going last night."

There's a pause before he sits up with his back to me.

"Why, Erik?" he asks. "So you could report it to Malak?" He turns to pin me with a hard stare. "It's better that you don't know where I go or what I do."

He isn't wrong.

But we've never withheld information from each other before. It worries me that Thoren is willing to do that now.

"Thoren—"

He's already heading to the small bathroom at the side of the room and I have no choice but to let him go.

When we reach the coal house that morning, Nero is waiting for us.

"Vandawolf! Thoren!" he bellows at me and my brother. "You're hauling coal today."

Nero gestures to two of the crates at the front of the room, where Braddock also waits. The crates are large enough that they're like small carts, each one waist-height and on wheels with straps at the front.

"Vandawolf, you're to take this crate to the Academy." Nero points to the first crate before indicating the second one. "Thoren, this crate is to go to House Copperstream. Braddock will clear the path for you both and show you where to go."

At a glance, I can see that my crate is full while Thoren's is only filled to the half line.

I'm happy to carry the heavier load, but I'm unsettled that Thoren could be forced out of my sight today and especially if he has to attend House Copperstream, where Landon could be now that the first medallion-forging is finished.

I'm conscious that Cohen Copperstream is watching us from the far side of the room, his arms folded across his chest and his eyes sharp. A line of copper twines around his right arm, extending from a ring on his right thumb.

Braddock steps to my side, keeping his voice low. "Don't worry about your brother," he says to me. "We'll go to the Academy together first and then I'll go with your brother to House Copperstream. I won't leave Thoren alone."

I give Braddock a nod of acknowledgement before I take the straps attached to the crate and slip them over my shoulders.

All it takes is a single tug to know that the crate is fucking heavy.

Worse, the moment I take a step toward the door, the coal within the crate sparks violently.

The heat at my back is immediate.

My heart kicks in my chest.

Every step I take between here and the Academy will be fraught with the danger of catching fire.

I'm conscious of the way the other workers are watching me —and Thoren too.

Nobody wants a fire in here.

I grit my teeth and make it through the door without any mishaps, my muscles bunching.

Once we're outside, Braddock gives me a grimace.

He points to a burn scar partially visible up the back of his neck. "I can't say I'm sorry it's you and not me today. You'd think there'd be a safer way to haul this fucking stuff, but wrapping each piece in soft material to try to stop the pieces knocking against each other only increases the chances of fire."

He suddenly grins at me. "Apparently, the Blacksmiths once tried to encase a crate in metal so the sparks wouldn't fly out during transport, but when they opened the metal box at the other end of its journey, it exploded in their fucking faces."

I'm conscious of Thoren drawing to a halt beside me while Braddock leans a little closer. "I once heard a whisper that the coal is volatile because it doesn't want to be disturbed. These rocks have a soul. A soul filled with fire and it wants to punish us for digging it up."

Behind us, Nero has stepped up into the doorway and glares at us.

Braddock takes a quick step away from me. "Let's go."

With that, he strides ahead of us, shouting, "Clear the path! Coal coming through!"

The people on the walkway ahead of us instantly make themselves scarce.

My muscles continue to bunch as I pull the crate as smoothly as I can.

I fight my fear with every step.

Thoren keeps pace on my right, his muscles visibly straining, especially on the upward slopes.

By the time we navigate off the main path and into the western part of the city, my muscles are stretched and sweat pours down my face, chest, and back.

Braddock calls quietly to us. "Go carefully now. We're entering the residential sector. The Academy is located beside House Silverspun while House Copperstream is farther west."

It's impossible to miss House Silverspun. It's a large building that appears to be made from white stone and stretches several hundred paces in each direction. The placement of the windows indicates that it's as many as three stories high.

A smaller building rests beside it, but it reminds me of a lesser version of Malak's castle with towers at each corner.

Braddock gestures to the wide-open doors into the smaller building. "Right through there, you'll find the courtyard, where the students train. You'll see an empty crate on the right side. Replace it with this one."

"Okay."

He catches my arm. "There's more. You'll be expected to fill their bowls with coal—three pieces each. You'll find a pair of tongs hanging over the side of the empty crate and a bowl to carry chunks of coal. Be careful about it."

He doesn't have to tell me twice.

As quietly as I can, I pull the crate through the doors and take stock of the white, pebbled courtyard.

The layout of the anvils is very similar to how they were placed in the northern field: all waist-height and set out in neat rows with large, black bowls that sit on pedestals to the left of each anvil.

These bowls are cold and empty, waiting for coal.

I recognize many of the students from the field, nearly twenty of them, all milling about the courtyard, many standing in groups.

They all appear to be my age or slightly older and wear their hammers like I would wear a dagger, in a sheath at their waist.

But unlike before, they're also now wearing a band of metal on their left biceps. Their first medallions.

I'm unhappy to see Landon Copperstream with two other students, all leaning against the empty crate I'm headed toward. One is a young man with an amethyst-colored hammer that matches his hair and the other is a young woman with ruby-red hair.

Their focus is immediately on me.

If I thought for a moment that Landon knew I killed his father, I'd be significantly worried.

I take a chance to check Landon's expression. No sign of tears or mourning.

Landon lifts himself off the crate, his lips stretching into a grin. "Well, fuck," he says loudly to the other two. "Looks like we have a strong one."

"He's sweaty," the girl replies, her mouth tugging up at the corners as she looks me up and down. "He could be fun, Landon."

The boy with the amethyst hammer also sizes me up. "He might actually put up a fight."

Landon narrows his eyes at me, his focus falling on my night pass. "Maybe."

I'm not as thin or as frail-looking as the other humans. Even the miners are more wiry than well-muscled. I used to fear running out of food on the mountains, but my family ate well compared to the humans here.

"Way more fun than that piss-weak runt the other night." The girl scoffs.

Landon grins as he rubs his fist. "Down in one strike." But he follows up with a huff. "Except that this one's Malak's property."

The girl rolls her eyes and leans in close to Landon, rubbing his arm. "Since when has that stopped you? You got away with dragging Asha out into the snow. Nobody fucking cares—"

Landon grabs the girl so hard that she winces. "Because nobody fucking knows it was us."

He casts a rapid glance around them before he focuses back on the girl. "And we're not going to fucking mention it again, are we?"

"No," she gasps. "Of course not."

He lets her go and all three of them step away from the crate.

They don't give me a backward glance.

I am nobody to them.

A haze of anger has descended over my vision, a rage that makes my blood pound in my ears.

These three students are the ones who took Asha out into the snow and left her there to die.

If they hadn't hurt her, she wouldn't have needed help, and my father would still be alive.

My father is dead because of them.

I can barely see through my rage.

I slide my arms free of the crate's straps and take a step after them, calculating how fast I can snatch a hammer from one of them and what it will take to crush in their skulls.

That's when a door on the right-hand side of the courtyard opens and Ayla Silverspun glides through it.

"Darlings!" She claps her hands. "Take your places! Today is a momentous day."

Her presence is as glittering as the white stone around us. She wears a silver pants suit that hangs on her lithe frame, seeming to make her green eyes even brighter. She carries a silver hammer at her waist and, just like the other night, her hair is adorned with multiple metallic hair pieces.

But it's the young woman who follows behind her who draws my attention.

Her head is down, her silver hair tangled down her back and hanging across her face. Her shoulders are hunched and her posture is drawn and tense.

Her footfalls are silent, her presence a mere shadow compared to Ayla's and yet she is all I see.

Asha.

CHAPTER 33

Asha doesn't look up.

I hover only a single step away from the crate, waiting for her to raise her eyes, trying to see her face and if the wound on her forehead is healing, but she moves like a wraith, slipping toward the anvils.

Her arms are bare. She doesn't carry a medallion or a hammer.

I remember the way Malak spoke about Asha up on the mountain. The way he described the shame her parents feel about her powerlessness.

I didn't know what to think of that at the time, but now the absence of metal around her body confirms what Maybelle said about her: She is not like other Blacksmiths.

And yet Malak has ordered that she be kept alive.

He took his Blacksmiths out into the snow to find her and bring her back. He told Kalith it was a test of loyalty, a burden Kalith has to bear to prove his allegiance to Malak.

Asha takes up position behind one of the anvils at the center of the courtyard, her head still down and her back now to me.

There she stands, arms hanging at her sides, not touching anything.

My eyes narrow to see Landon take up position at the anvil directly behind Asha while his two friends position themselves on either side of him, all three of them now at her back.

I'm supposed to dish out the coal to them, so that's what I set about doing.

At the head of the class, Ayla Silverspun demands their attention. "Now that you have medallions of your own, you can decide how you carry them on your body."

She taps her hairpieces. "You can compel them to take any shape you like. Even change them daily according to your mood."

She holds up a finger. "But always remember that if you revert them to their medallion shape and put them away from your body, they will become inert. You will have to waken them again by tapping them with your hammer. For that reason, it is best to always keep them in contact with your body. Now, let's begin!"

As the students start experimenting with their medallions, I move quickly and efficiently, making it across the back row, moving back and forth between the crate and the bowls beside the anvils.

Given that the students don't seem to need fire today, it feels like a meaningless task.

But it gets me closer to Asha with every step.

When I approach Landon's redheaded friend, I watch my path, well aware of her suddenly outstretched foot, as if she thought to trip me.

I then deftly avoid her spinning metal as she whips it back so fast that it would have sliced across my arm without my evasion.

I'm not sure if she has considered who will handle the coal if I'm too injured to do it.

Still, it's easy to dodge her.

Far harder to hide my scorn.

Her tactics are those of a child.

I'm warier as I approach Landon, remaining conscious of his posture and balance, ready for any small change that will indicate he's about to strike out. I expect him to be far less obvious about his intentions.

But I make it to his bowl and carefully slide three chunks of coal into it without incident.

He narrows his eyes at me as I pass him by.

I bring coal to his other friend and then the rest of that row and finally, I'm at Asha's row.

Two anvils away from her. And then one.

Then, finally, I pause beside her, close enough to brush her arm with mine.

The air around her is still and calm.

Her breathing is soft.

I force myself to remain conscious of the rest of the room, including Landon and the metal he's shaping so close by, even though Asha's presence threatens to make everything else disappear.

When I found her in the snow I felt a terrible peace. A calm that, even now, rises within me.

Terrible, because it feels like the quiet before a storm. The waiting for my peace to shatter.

Within my mind, I will her to look up at me.

I need to understand her thoughts.

I need her... to see me.

She doesn't move, even though I've paused beside her for several seconds longer than I should have, the coal gripped in the tongs I hold above her bowl.

Maybe if I could somehow free one of my hands from my task to touch the back of her hand...

I edge closer, only to finally glimpse enough of her face

between the strands of her hair to understand that her eyes are far away. Her mind isn't here.

She is somewhere else.

"Silly boy!" Ayla calls out and I stiffen to find myself the center of her attention—and everyone else's. "Don't waste coal on my useless daughter."

She laughs, a melodic sound, and the entire class laughs with her. Their ridicule washes over me as I wait for Asha to respond to her mother's cruelty.

Nothing.

Wherever she is within her mind, it's a long way from here.

Or so it seems. Until her palm presses to her thigh and her fingernails curl inward.

She doesn't otherwise move. She certainly doesn't look at me, but her whisper sounds softly beneath the loud laughter. "Please don't risk burns for me."

Her voice is so quiet that I could believe I imagined she spoke. That is, if my deep light didn't spark and my heart didn't kick.

I raise myself upright beside her, needing only to hear her voice again.

I need it as badly as I need air.

My heart is pounding and my deep light is threatening to glow.

I'm about to speak, preparing a whisper when the door at the side of the courtyard opens again, loudly enough to draw everyone's attention away from me.

Two small children, a boy and a girl, both with silver-blond hair like Asha's, stand in the doorway, while a human man hovers behind them.

They can't be more than nine years old, possibly younger, judging by how small they are.

Even from this distance, I can see the dark rings around the children's eyes and the haunted looks on their faces as they shrink back from the courtyard.

"My little tributes!" Ayla throws her arms open and crouches to the ground. "Come to your mother!"

She called them *tributes*. Maybelle told me that Asha's twin siblings had suffered Malak's power while their mother looked on.

Asha's head snaps up, her eyes suddenly acutely present and her focus on the children as they cross the courtyard to their mother.

Asha jolts forward, well and truly out of eyeline with me now, and then stops, her palms pressing to the edge of her anvil, as if she would push the damn thing out of her path.

Across the way, the children look to her, their faces ashen, their pale-green eyes pleading, and their expressions beseeching.

Asha's palms press so hard to the edge of her anvil that the blood leaves her hands while her mother embraces each of the children and draws them away from the human man, even as they edge back toward him.

It stuns me that Blacksmith children would rather stay with a human than go to their own mother.

"Thank you, Kedric," Ayla snaps at the man, prying Tamra's hand from his arm. "You can leave now. Tamra and Gallium will watch the lesson today."

Kedric. I'm sure that's the name of Maybelle's husband. I study the man more carefully. He looks gaunt, wiry, but he's alive and I'm certain that Maybelle will be relieved to hear it.

He retreats slowly, darting glances back at the children.

Ayla ignores him, clapping her hands for attention once more.

"Darlings!" she calls to her students. "Continue your creations. Show me how far your imaginations can reach."

She's smiling, but her focus suddenly turns to me and a crease forms in her forehead.

I've paused here for too long.

I have no choice but to keep moving away from Asha.

I'm reluctant to leave her back exposed, especially now that I'm stepping away from her and not toward her like I was before. I no longer have an easy line of sight to Landon and his friends.

I work as quickly as I can so that I can approach from the other side and see her again, but I'm not fast enough.

I'm at the end of the row when metal glints in the distance.

Landon's medallion has taken on the form of a web of fine copper strings, each edge appearing razor-sharp as it unfurls and spins toward Asha's back.

My hand dips to the coal, my fingers closing around it, ready to pitch it as hard as I can across the distance to knock the web off course, but the web reaches Asha within the blink of an eye.

It slices through her hair where it hangs down her back.

Silver strands fall to the ground.

For a moment, I think that's the only damage, but then the material at the back of her shirt opens.

Blood blooms across her skin.

She gasps and jolts forward.

I'm gripping the burning coal and I don't care that my palm is burning.

Landon is a dead man.

I'll fucking kill him.

My jaw clenches so hard that my teeth clack together.

In that instant, I plot a path to Landon's anvil and calculate the strength it will take to throw myself across it and knock him onto his back, anticipating the blade he'll no doubt swing at me before I can ram the coal down his throat.

I will make him scream as he burns from the inside out.

But I'm also aware of something else in that moment: Asha's brother and sister at the head of the room.

Tamra's eyes have filled with tears. She gives her brother a nod.

Gallium darts toward his mother, snatches her hammer right off her waist, and runs toward the first row of students.

Ayla Silverspun has barely turned and doesn't even seem to realize that her hammer's missing before Gallium throws it with a strength that defies his age.

The hammer spins through the air, its metal shrieking and humming, before it crashes into a bowl of coal—the one at the anvil on Asha's right that I already filled.

Clang!

The sound bites the air, but it's the explosion as the bowl flies right off its pedestal that takes my breath away.

CHAPTER 34

Three pieces of coal knock into each other as they shoot out of the bowl.

One hits an anvil and the second strikes the white stone ground. Both explode, sending flames in all directions, blowing several students backward.

The final piece ricochets toward the ruby-haired girl, hitting her squarely on the chest.

She screams as her hair and clothing catch fire while Landon leaps clear of her.

I dart toward Asha, preparing to snatch her up and get her and her siblings out of here. I have Malak's pass. The other Blacksmiths won't touch me, not even Ayla.

But Asha's already moving.

She launches herself toward her brother and sister, darting around her anvil, her arms and legs pumping as she navigates the other anvils, throwing herself over two of them, her ragged, silver hair flying behind her.

I skid to a stop in the middle of the chaos...

The fire burns behind me. The white stone alight with

flames. The students scream as they try to put out the flames biting at their clothing.

Despite it all, I can't help smiling as Asha shoots forward, deftly evading her mother's grasping hands to scoop up Tamra and Gallium into her arms and run with them.

The determination on her face, the way she moves like a warrior, intent only on protecting her brother and sister...

Fuck, she's beautiful.

And then she's gone, sprinting through the door at the side of the courtyard while Ayla has no choice but to rush back to her students, screaming at them to get to the side of the room where it's safe.

Landon is the first to run there while Ayla leaps through the fire to drag the redhead away from the worst of the flames.

The ruby-haired girl appears unconscious, the skin across her face and neck burned, but not so badly as I thought it might be.

I'm now the only one left standing near the flames, practically within them, the wine-red fire flickering across the stone around my feet in a vicious burn.

One of the pieces of coal rests only a few paces away from me. The ones in the bowl I'm holding seem to glow even more brightly.

Braddock said this fire has a soul. He said it seeks retribution.

Somehow, I believe him.

My deep light sparks again, the sapphire glow tinting my skin and playing around my hands in a way that feels like it's drawn to the coal.

Maybe that's why I don't feel the heat even as the fire licks toward me.

Ayla Silverspun lifts herself up to her full height where she stands in front of her students, glaring at me across the flames.

She lifts her arm and points at me.

"Lord Ironmeld will hear of this!" she screams. "He will hear of the mess you made here, Boy. Spilling the coal. Causing a fire. Hurting a student."

Ah, so I'm the scapegoat.

Better me than Asha or her little brother.

"As you like, Lady Silverspun," I say, finally stepping away from the flames and into the clear space behind me.

I bow without taking my eyes off her.

In that moment, I wonder how much Kalith told her about what happened on the mountain.

The way she looks at me without recognition, even if it's with anger, makes me wonder if he kept it all to himself like Malak ordered him to.

After all, the first Ayla Silverspun saw of me was in the northern field when Malak brought me and Thoren to the city. There was no obvious connection between us and her husband's journey into the snow to retrieve Asha.

I'm just another human to live and die at her whim.

As I continue to meet her eyes, she falters back a step, her focus flickering from the flames to where I remain so close to them.

And then to the night pass that marks me as Malak's property.

Her face turns red as she shrieks, "Go! Get out of my sight!"

Gladly.

Malak's orchard is as quiet as always as Thoren and I make our way toward its center.

Thoren casts me worried glances as we approach, a far cry from the way he would arch his eyebrows at me on the hunt and tell me not to worry.

He and Braddock had already heard about the fire at the Academy by the time I returned to the coal house. The other miners all avoided coming anywhere near me—even more than they normally did—and Nero steered well clear of me.

All he grumbled was, "Malak's decision."

Now, I'm about to face the consequences.

Malak works at his anvil, his black hammer tapping at another fine chisel, his head bent to the small piece of black metal he's working on. It's in the shape of a tooth, but it's too tiny to really tell, especially against the backdrop of the black anvil it rests on.

Skirra rests on the ground beside the anvil as he usually does when we come to give our report, but he still looks well-fed and his eyes are bright, his breathing normal.

He gives a yip when he sees us.

I marvel at his calmness the same way I marveled at his resolution to stay with us when he could have escaped with the white wolf Kori. Not for the first time, I wish I could know Skirra's mind.

We stop a few paces from Malak's anvil, and I hold my breath, waiting for an instant reprimand or worse, but he doesn't look up.

"Report," he says.

I begin, as I always do, with the start of the day and work forward in time. I describe how we were assigned to haul coal and briefly mention the crates and how much coal there was in each.

I'm about to move on to the trip through the city when Malak raises his hand. "Stop." His dark eyes meet mine as he looks up. "You took a full crate to the Academy while Thoren took half a crate to House Copperstream?"

I nod. "That's correct."

A dark cloud descends over Malak's face and the tools in his hands seem suddenly forgotten.

I haven't told him about the fire and yet something has clearly angered him.

"I've heard enough." His lips twist. "Vandawolf, you will stay. Thoren, you will leave. Be sure to take three apples to your sweetheart tonight—I've heard she enjoys them."

Thoren stiffens before he backs away, but he's slow to obey.

"Go!" Malak roars at him.

The worry in Thoren's eyes increases a thousand-fold, but I give him a nod. If he stays, I'll be concerned about protecting him. This way, I only have Skirra and myself to worry about.

Thoren has barely disappeared along the path when Malak snaps. "A full crate to the Academy? Did they think I wouldn't notice?"

He smacks his right fist down onto the anvil, his teeth visibly gritted before he looks up at me again.

"Do you know the beauty of this place, Vandawolf?" he asks, raising his fist to our surroundings.

Blood drips down the back of his hand from the knuckles he split open.

I don't think he wants me to answer, so I stay quiet.

He smiles, but it looks like a grimace. "The beauty of this place is that nobody can hear me."

He tips his head back and roars up at the darkening sky and the stars that are starting to appear within it. "*Fucking traitors!*"

His hand drops to his side and his grin is dangerous as he steps out from behind the anvil.

I fight my instinct to move back.

"Fucking betrayal," he says, no longer shouting. "They smile in your face, they pledge their allegiance, and all the while, they scheme and conspire against you. It is only fear that slows them down. Never forget that, Vandawolf."

My father's own warning echoes back within my mind, and I speak before I can stop myself. "Be careful of the enemies you keep close."

Malak stops moving. He gives me a nod. "Yes."

But now his dark gaze is turned on me.

I am also his enemy kept close.

"I have known for some time that Cohen Copperstream has been amassing power and support to overthrow me," he says. "His house controls the crimson coal, without which we cannot forge. He has been restricting coal supply to other houses."

I catch on quickly. "But not the Academy."

"The Academy, run by Silverspun House." Malak tilts his head. "To them, it seems he is now giving an abundant supply of coal. Of course, it looks like it's for the students, but it is not. Other than the bare amount needed for the students to forge, the rest of that coal will have already disappeared into House Silverspun."

Malak's gaze becomes far away. "Until now, I didn't know which house was supporting him. I didn't think it would be the one closest to me." His jaw clenches. "With all that coal, they will be forging something to bring me down... A weapon. A monster. Something strong enough to kill me..." His focus snaps back to me. "But I will send them a message written in blood."

He takes a deep breath and his expression becomes serene again. "You will kill Cohen Copperstream for me."

CHAPTER 35

My thoughts churn.

Not because I object to the task, but because, of all the targets Malak could have given me, Cohen Copperstream will be one of the hardest.

All of the times I've seen him, he hasn't been alone. He's always flanked by at least two other Blacksmiths from his house.

"I know you can do it," Malak says. "You sliced up his brother as if he were nothing more than an animal."

I don't deny it. "I'll need time to plan."

"You will kill him at a time of my choosing. No sooner and no later," Malak says firmly. "Do not squander your time over the coming days. My command could come at any moment."

I take a breath, already contemplating how I might study House Copperstream for weaknesses.

"There's one more thing you must do," Malak says.

I'm more wary now. "What is that?"

"You will make it look like the human foreman, Nero, did it."

"What?" I take a step back before I can stop myself. Nero is

Petra's father. If he's accused, the Blacksmiths will kill him for a crime he didn't commit. "Why?"

"Because Nero is Cohen's faithful servant. He knows how to run the mine and the coal house. He has worked hard to gain a position of trust within House Copperstream. With both him and Cohen out of the picture, House Copperstream's hold over coal supply will be fragile. I will replace Nero will someone I can control."

Braddock. I'm sure Malak must be thinking of Braddock because until we arrived, Braddock was the only other human working in the coal house who is also Malak's property.

But no. I can't do this.

I will gladly kill Cohen Copperstream, but I can't implicate Nero in Cohen's death. I don't know if Nero has a wife or other children, but Petra could also be killed because of it, and Thoren...

My brother would never forgive me.

I grasp at reasons to convince Malak to take another path. "Nobody would believe it was Nero. Like you said, he's a faithful servant."

Malak laughs. "No, Vandawolf, by the time I give you the order to kill Cohen Copperstream, nobody in this city will doubt that Nero wanted him dead."

A cold chill runs the length of my spine. "Why?"

Malak clicks his tongue at me and doesn't answer my question. "Be sure to wrap Nero's red sash around Cohen's neck so there's no doubt who killed him."

Malak steps back with a dismissive wave. "Go now. Continue working at the coal house. Report back to me at sunset each day. We will keep up the routine. But otherwise, you are free to do whatever you must to succeed." He narrows his eyes at me. "Remember what you will lose if you fail."

My brother.

Whose trust I will lose if I succeed.

My heart is heavy as I retreat through the orchard.

Halfway along the path, I stumble and reach out to steady myself against the nearest glittering tree, this thing of beauty.

Malak has given me a task, but I also have time to plan and permission to roam. While I shadow Cohen Copperstream, I can find out more about the city's weaknesses. I can study House Silverspun too.

I can find a way out of here.

A way to get Asha and her siblings out, along with my brother and Skirra, and get us all to safety.

By the time I reach the gate, my mind is calm, but my brother's agitation is clear.

"What happened?" he asks as we make our way to the kitchen.

I cast a glance around. "Not here."

By the time we've eaten and finally reach our room, Thoren is beyond agitated.

"What happened?" he asks again.

I choose my speech carefully, focusing on what's important. "I'm going to get us out of here."

He takes a step back from me. "Who is 'us,' Erik?"

I know he won't like my answer. "You, me, Asha, her siblings—"

"What about Petra and her family? What about Maybelle and the husband she mentioned? What about all the other humans?"

My heart is heavy again. "I can't save them all, Thoren."

"No, you can't," my brother whispers. "But *I* can."

I consider him with wary surprise. "What are you talking about?"

He pauses before he gestures to the fresh apples he placed on the floor beside his rug. "Do you remember when we left those apple cores for Petra? Well, as a healer, she studies the properties of plants, so she tested grinding parts of the apple and combining them with different substances to see what would happen."

He steps toward me, his voice lowered. "She discovered that by grinding the seeds into the salve and then applying it to your skin, it causes the salve to form a protective layer."

I remember the way Petra and Thoren had their heads together over a pot of salve the night I followed him to the infirmary. Petra was explaining something and Thoren was nodding.

"It helps heal burns in a fraction of the time, but that's not all. It stops the burns altogether."

My forehead creases. "What do you mean?"

"I mean that you can smear the salve on your hands and safely handle the coal."

"Okay, that's great for those of us who work with coal, but—"

"No, you're not hearing me, Erik." He peers at me in the gloom and his voice lowers even further. "The coal is explosive. Everyone heard what happened at the Academy. If we can safely handle the coal, we can use it to attack our enemies."

I take a sharp breath. "Wait... Thoren... You're talking about—"

"I'm talking about an uprising." He nods. "On the night of the celebration, all of the high-ranking Blacksmiths will be gathered at House Copperstream. Cohen Copperstream has been stockpiling coal. Nero knows where it is. The Blacksmiths will be gathered in an open courtyard with ramparts on every side from which we can target them. We can take out all of the high-ranking Blacksmiths at once."

I'm cold because I'm certain Malak must know about this plan.

He wants me to take out Nero as well as Cohen. He made it sound like it was about disrupting House Copperstream's hold on coal supply, but Nero is also the architect of this uprising.

I shake my head. "Thoren, this is dangerous. Malak has too many eyes in this city. He told you to take more apples to Petra. Why would he say that unless he knows what you're doing?"

"Maybe he does know," Thoren says, giving me a stubborn look. "But it's still our best chance."

"Certain death is not a chance—"

Thoren's snarl cuts me off. "Why would you care?"

I'm struck silent by his fury.

"I don't understand your choices, Erik." His voice lowers, but the corners of his mouth turn down as he glares at me. "No, you know what? I fucking *hate* your choices."

I take a step back at the anger in his voice.

"You *chose* to bring a Blacksmith into our lives," he says. "You brought death to our door. You made the choices that killed our father. And now you're telling me not to make the choices that I know are right."

My hands are suddenly shaking. "I can't lose you, too."

He scoops up the apples and heads to the door, but he pauses there. "These people need us, Erik. We have strength and skills they don't have. We know how to fight." He presses the heel of his hand to his heart. "I can't turn my back on them. The only way you'll lose me is if you refuse to fight beside me."

The door closes behind him.

Fear threatens to crush me, but regret is the weight that drives me down where I crouch, gripping my knees.

Destiny, my father said. But fate can only be a fucking lie, a construct to hold the weight of my guilt and culpability.

I chose to save a woman I didn't know and in doing so, I forfeited my father's life.

I can't be the reason my brother dies too.

CHAPTER 36

For the next four days, I work at the coal house during the day, report to Malak at the evening bell, and then I step out into the darkness of the city, learning its pathways and vulnerabilities, assessing the security around both House Copperstream and Silverspun.

Each day, I expect Malak to command me to act. He listens intently, tapping away at his creation, before he dismisses me.

Every night that I prowl through the city, a part of me hopes I might catch a glimpse of Asha, maybe steal some of the calm her presence brings me, but I don't.

As soon as I have the chance, I tell Maybelle that I saw her husband. Her eyes fill with tears and she shocks me by hugging me before she hurries away.

As for my brother, I watch and listen, shadowing his footsteps, learning his plans without committing to them because I know that if it comes to it, I won't let him risk his life.

I convince myself I'll have time to find a way. A better way forward.

I'm surprised when, in the afternoon of the day before the students are to forge their second medallions, Nero tells me I'm to haul the coal out to the northern field for the forging the next morning.

When I question why it should be me, given what happened last time I hauled coal, he snaps at me.

"Malak's orders!" He sticks his face into mine. "Count yourself lucky, Boy. For some star-forsaken reason, Malak refused to kill you even after Lady Silverspun demanded your head."

I'm unsettled, but I have no choice but to obey.

I don't have any trouble waking before first light because the bells ring out early to ensure everything is ready for the students at dawn.

Luckily, that also means that when I exit through the northern gate, none of the students have arrived yet.

I hurry to haul the crate as close to the anvils as I can and fill each bowl with three pieces of coal.

I've only just finished filling the last bowl when Lady Silverspun and the students file out onto the field. The students are wearing their white forging clothes. Lady Silverspun is once again dressed in ornate silver armor.

Nobody speaks as the students take their places.

All around us, it's eerily quiet before dawn. A silence before the darkness will break and the first light of day will shine across the horizon.

I step away from the anvils, aware of Landon Copperstream's dark glare and the way Lady Silverspun's lips pinch when she sees me, but my attention is drawn skyward when a cold droplet falls onto my forehead.

It's another drop of crimson liquid. A color that rain shouldn't be.

Only moments before, dawn seemed close, but now dark clouds are gathering above me.

Lightning flickers through the clouds and my skin prickles with an energy I still can't define.

When Thoren and I first stepped onto this field, he described the ground here as *wrong*.

I sense the strangeness again now as I study the sky and then the ash beneath my boots.

As quickly as I can, I step away from the field, glancing back only once when the second bells ring and the first hammers sound.

There are two empty spots among the rows of students.

One in the same place where the redheaded student stood at the Academy. Another in Asha's spot.

As I turn my back on them, the horizon in the far distance beckons to me, the snow-capped mountains and all their freedom.

I miss a step as I wonder if Malak deliberately sent me out here this morning, not to unsettle Lady Silverspun or the students, but to remind me that freedom is not mine to take.

A strangled laugh rests on my tongue as I realize that I spent the last hour dishing out coal on an empty field with only the guards up on the wall to watch me and not once did I think of running.

Not once did I contemplate saving myself.

My jaw clenches as I turn back to the city.

I tell myself I can stay on the path I've chosen, that freedom will be mine and my brother's.

I will find a way.

I reach the coal house at the same time that Thoren does, but for the first time since we started working here, Nero isn't standing at the door. It's closed and appears locked.

The other workers are milling around, more than one of them shuffling and mumbling. I look for Braddock among them but don't see him.

"Nero should be here by now," one of the men says.

"Why is the door closed?" another asks.

I take a step back, a chill settling at the base of my spine.

"No," I whisper, turning to Thoren, whose shoulders are tense, his quick gaze clearly assessing the group. "That isn't the important question."

Thoren's face is pale as he asks what the others should be asking. "Where is Cohen Copperstream?"

As he speaks, a shout sounds behind us and three Blacksmith guards rush past, heading west toward the residential sector.

I step in that direction just as I recognize Maybelle racing toward us along the path.

She's out of breath, trembling so hard that she shakes in my arms as I catch her.

"Vandawolf! Thoren!" She gasps for air. "It's a flogging. At Copperstream House." Her eyes fill with tears as she looks at Thoren. "They say it's Petra."

"What?" Thoren's eyes are wide as he grabs Maybelle. "Why?"

"She's accused of stealing apples from Malak's orchard." Maybelle's face is ashen. "The penalty is death by lashing."

"No!" Thoren tears away from Maybelle, darting away down the path.

I spin to Maybelle. "Get back to the castle. Stay hidden. Don't come out."

She rushes away from me, and I sprint after Thoren.

I know the way to Copperstream House now, having scoped out the quickest paths to it, but there are too many people in my way, too many humans rushing in that direction and slowing me down.

Thoren is quick and agile and he stays in front of me, darting between the humans and Blacksmiths.

He's ten paces ahead of me when I finally race along the path that leads directly to the front of Copperstream House.

A wall surrounds the grounds, a wide opening in the middle that leads into a vast courtyard.

Up on the ramparts, Blacksmith guards stand at intervals, while on the ground, they line the wall, each of them holding a pole weapon with a single-edged blade at the end. I recognize these weapons as glaives, which are good for keeping an opponent at bay while you gut them.

In front of the Blacksmiths on the ground is a row of copper spikes, all pointed outward, their sharp ends positioned at varying heights between stomach and eye level.

A roar of sound fills my ears as humans—many humans—are gathered in front of the spikes, all of them shouting.

All of them are protesting, even as the guards up on the battlements form bows and arrows with their metal and threaten to shoot.

One of the humans sees Thoren, shouts to the others nearby, and instantly, a path through the crowd opens up between us and the spikes.

I don't have time to be astonished at the way the humans recognize my brother, the way his name is called, or the overwhelming trust that fills their faces as he sprints past.

"Thoren is here!"

What kind of affinity has my brother forged with these people in such a short time? Gaining their trust and their faith like this?

In my heart, I know it's the kind of kinship that I could never attain.

Thoren leaps at the top of the spikes, taking hold of the nearest sharp end, even though it could impale him, before he vaults smoothly over it.

The Blacksmith guards directly in front of him move to intercept him, but he feints left and then right, slipping through the gap between them with all the agility that hunting in the mountains has given him.

I'm now only five paces behind him, catching up along the path the humans cleared.

I follow my brother, vaulting over the spikes and barreling into the Blacksmith guards, taking advantage of the way they were already unbalanced to get past them. The guards up on the wall shout, but I'm too close to their brethren for them to shoot their arrows at me.

As I sprint through the opening in the wall, the vast courtyard beyond it becomes fully visible to me.

A whipping post rests in the center of the space.

Petra is chained to it, facing away from me, her hands secured high above her head.

Her shirt has been ripped open to expose her back. The storm of noise prevents me from hearing if she's shouting or crying, but the way she struggles tells me she's fully conscious.

Because of the way she's chained to the post, she won't be able to see what's happening behind her.

Cohen Copperstream stands near the post at her back, a metal whip in his hand that has three sharp-looking tails. They drag along the yellow cobblestones as he takes a step toward her.

It will only take a few strikes for those lashes to cut through her body.

Nero is only five paces away from Cohen, shouting and thrashing while three armored Blacksmiths attempt to subdue him.

He knocks one of them to the side, punches the second, and nearly makes it a step in Cohen's direction before the third Blacksmith strikes the back of Nero's head and knocks him to the ground.

As Nero falls forward, metal spreads out from the Blacksmith's palm, a chain whipping outward. It wraps around Nero's neck and spears into the courtyard on either side, acting like a noose that pins his head to the stone.

"Not my daughter!" he shouts.

My mind flies back to the moment when I, too, was anchored to the ground, unable to stop my father's death.

Malak promised me that Nero would have a very believable reason to want to kill Cohen, and it looks like this will be it.

I assess all of this within the few seconds it takes me to sprint toward a second row of guards, who stand in a wide ring around the whipping post. They're also holding glaives.

Still five paces ahead of me, Thoren remains quick and agile, running faster than I've ever seen him move.

The second row of Blacksmiths appears to see him coming, turning their weapons in his direction moments before an arrow flies from the ramparts, hitting the ground behind his feet.

The nearest guard on the ground moves to intercept Thoren, his weapon glinting in the dim light, but Thoren quickly changes course. Darting around the man, my brother charges through the gap the guard left behind himself, narrowly avoiding the blade of the next Blacksmith.

Thoren's movements are so fast, they're hard to follow, but I catch the moment he snatches a dagger from the hilt of the first Blacksmith's belt as he darts past.

And then he's through.

He doesn't stop. Doesn't falter. Doesn't shout.

He runs straight for Cohen Copperstream, whose eyes have widened.

Thoren's muscles bunch visibly as he leaps from the ground toward Cohen.

My brother's body is a blur, the dagger gripped in his hand, the blade flashing across the air as he aims it for Cohen's face.

The breath leaves my chest as Thoren arcs through the air, stronger and more determined than I've ever seen him.

But my brother is used to fighting from afar. He doesn't have experience with close combat and my heart is in my throat.

Cohen draws back his whip arm, clearly intending to strike the lashes across Thoren's body, but Thoren has already reached him.

At the last moment, Cohen turns his head.

Thoren's blade slashes across his cheek and nose but doesn't impale him.

As Thoren's blade arcs down toward the left, his momentum takes him in that direction.

Cohen's whip handle turns to liquid in an instant, covering his right fist, which he rams upward.

Thoren's flight takes him right into the punch.

Crack!

A roar tears from my mouth as the sound of breaking bone sends a shock of fear through me.

Please, no.

Thoren sails backward. His head hits the ground first, and there's another sickening *crunch*, before his body follows.

Arrows fly into the ground around me, one of them narrowly missing my legs as I storm through a gap between the guards and throw myself across the stone to reach my brother.

I'm aware that Cohen is raising his whip as if he'll use it on me, but several Blacksmiths are pointing and shouting, "Malak's property!"

Cohen's arm falters and that's all I'm conscious of before I pull Thoren into my arms.

He's so heavy and his body is so hard to lift, his arms sliding outward as I try to pull him close, desperately trying to see his eyes.

"Thoren?"

I can't breathe. I can't breathe.

"Look at me, brother. Please. Look at me."

He doesn't move. Warm liquid fills my palms where I cradle his head, blood dripping between my fingertips.

His skull is crushed.

His kind, gentle eyes hold no light.

"Thoren!"

A roar builds within my chest, a terrible, horrible roar. *"Thoren!"*

Cohen Copperstream's shadow drops over me as he takes an angry step in my direction. "I don't care whose property they are. I am Lord Copperstream. This is my house!"

He raises his whip again. He'll cleave my body apart, but I'm barely aware of the danger because my brother's blood is pooling around my knees and covering my hands.

Thoren was already gone before I pulled him into my arms and now my heart... My heart...

My brother was my heart. He was my compassion. He was the one who told me to care, the one who told me not to be afraid.

Now he's gone.

What am I now except the one who does the cutting?

Cohen's whip descends toward me but I'm already moving.

I rise to my feet while, high above me in the sky, the darkness finally breaks.

CHAPTER 37

Rage clouds my mind as the first rays of sunlight shine down onto the bloody courtyard.

In the distance, I can see that the humans have fallen silent, a sea of tear-filled eyes, an ocean of sadness that will never belong to me.

Cohen's whip shrieks in the air as the lashes whip toward me.

My hand snaps out, closing around Cohen's right wrist, clamping so tightly that, in that brief moment, his bones shift beneath my hold and a flicker of fear crosses his face.

I am oblivious to the whip's lashes and their sharp edges as I use his downward momentum against him, just as he used Thoren's.

I drop my weight and yank Cohen's arm forward into the space beside Thoren's body.

Cohen's shoulder *pops*.

Calling on my deep light, I reach for the strength I need to wrench Cohen down toward the ground while I continue to drop my full weight at the same time.

He loses his balance, only for a moment, but it's long enough.

A shout strangles in his throat as my left hand closes around the back of his exposed neck.

The whip's lashes spiral through the air, slashing toward my face, turning to liquid that will surely form blades, but I don't care how many cuts I suffer now that my brother is dead.

I smash Cohen's head, face first, into the stone.

Again and again.

Vicious, merciless hits.

Breaking his skull like he broke my brother's.

Blood splatters up across my face and that's when the silence around me breaks.

Chaos erupts as Blacksmiths shout and storm in my direction.

Leaping away from Cohen, I meet the nearest man head on, inviting the cut of his glaive as I dart to my right, my left hand snaking out and bending his wrist back, breaking the bones and forcing him to drop his weapon into my other hand.

His glaive is now mine.

I spin, twist, and strike back at the next man.

I hardly know what I'm doing as I slash and cut and punch and kick, stealing another glaive so that now I have two while I drop the men who come at me.

Then I'm beside Nero.

Blood covers the back of his neck where he has strained to raise his head and get free of the noose that pins him to the ground.

He's breathing heavily, his voice seething. "My daughter."

"My brother," I snarl at him before I swing one of the glaives at his head.

The blade slices through the chains pinning him down, freeing him.

I drop the glaive beside him before I spin to face the next Blacksmith.

Nero jolts forward, snatching up the blade I gave him before launching himself up from his knees. He sprints toward Petra, swings the blade at the pole, and cuts through her chains.

She slides to the ground, her legs clearly giving way, but he catches her.

Pulling her into his arms, he runs for the gap between the guards that I'm creating for them.

"Go!" I roar.

But now Petra is facing the courtyard and she has seen Thoren.

"Thoren! No!" She screams and struggles, trying to free herself from her father's hold, crying my brother's name over and over again.

Nero's arms clamp around her as he pulls her away from danger, running with her through the opening in the wall, darting left and right to avoid the arrows raining down on them from above.

Outside the wall, fighting has erupted. Humans are battling Blacksmiths, and part of the spiked barrier has been torn apart...

That's all I see before the Blacksmith guards within the courtyard close ranks around me.

Half of the Blacksmiths on the ramparts point their arrows at me while the other half fire into the crowd outside.

I'm acutely conscious then of the many opening doors on three sides of the courtyard and the new stream of Blacksmiths taking up position behind the circle of guards.

All of their hatred is directed at me.

Ten Blacksmiths lie dead on the stone around me.

Blood drips down my hands, but too much of it belongs to my brother.

I snarl at my captors. "I will kill you all."

When nobody moves, I roar at them. "Are you afraid of death? Are you fucking cowards?"

At my shout, the inertia breaks.

They come at me all at once, too many of them.

An arrow slices across my arm and a blade cuts my cheek, but I welcome the pain as I drive myself forward, slashing and fighting until—

A heavy object smacks into me from the side and drives me to my knees.

The swarm of Blacksmiths suddenly parts.

Malak steps through the opening they create, his black cloak swishing and swirling.

I look down to discover that once again, a black thread has pierced my chest and dark claws clamp across my torso.

But this time, I keep fighting, striking at the claws with the glaive in my hand, trying to cut through them, not caring that I'm cutting myself.

Malak's face is dark with fury as he strides toward me, the thread that has pierced my chest extending from both of his hands.

With a single tug, he yanks me to the ground, his strength far beyond that of any other Blacksmith I've fought today.

The metal tears through my shoulder but I keep thrashing against it, roaring at him. "You'd better kill me, Malak!" My voice tears out of my throat. "You'd better kill me!"

He launches himself forward, his right hand wrapping around my forehead, the fingernails of his left hand and his black metal talon digging into my shoulder.

I wait for him to utter the whisper that will turn me to stone, or shadow, or dust, or ash...

I scream at him, tears of rage choking me. *"Just kill me!"*

Instead, my heart slows beneath Malak's clawed fingers and my head swims, and before I pass out, all I see are his inky-dark, furious eyes.

CHAPTER 38

I wake with a shout on my lips.

Chains bite my wrists, ankles, chest, and neck.

A cold surface rests beneath my back while I face the open sky. I recognize the castle courtyard and the glowing metal bowl filled with wine-red coal on my right-hand side.

As my consciousness sharpens, a deep terror replaces my rage.

The metal I'm lying on...

It must be Malak's table. The one that Maybelle warned me never to touch.

Sound strangles in my throat as cold malice strikes through me. All I can hear is screams, but they aren't coming from outside me, not from other people, because the courtyard and even the ramparts are completely deserted.

Horror floods through me from the surface I'm lying on.

A shadow passes at my back and Malak's furious face comes into view.

"It was not my plan to do this so soon!" he snaps. "Your brother was not supposed to die today."

He steps to my left and I follow his movements, finally seeing what lies beside me.

A cry rises into my throat.

Skirra rests on the table to my left, his body chained to the surface, but he isn't moving.

My heart slowly cracks. "Skirra?"

Malak raises his left hand for me to see that in it he holds a small object, rounded at the edges and no bigger than his thumb.

It's made of finely interconnected parts, but I recognize some of them—a wolf's snout and teeth. I watched him carve them while I gave my daily reports.

Now it seems he has brought them together into a design of two wolf heads on their sides with their teeth interlinked between them.

Malak leans toward me as his voice whispers over me. "Skirra's soul is already mine."

Tears burn down my cheeks as I try to stretch beyond my chains and reach Skirra with the tips of my fingers. "Have you not taken enough from me?"

Malak is quiet for a moment before he replies. "Nothing will ever be enough."

He climbs up onto the table and kneels beside me, gripping his hammer in his left hand before he turns the small device onto its side, its sharp edge pressed against my skin above the location of my heart.

A shudder runs through me as I sense the power in his creation, the cold darkness that feels vast and empty and hungry.

He positions his hammer above it, ready to strike. "You may not survive this. But if you do, you will be my greatest creation. You will stand at my right hand while Asha stands at my left and nobody will dare betray me again."

Without another word, he drives the hammer down.

The device strikes into my chest, its edge cutting through my flesh and bone, and all I know is pain.

I thrash against the restraints that pin me in place, desperately needing to fight back, to live, but my hope is crushed.

I'm roaring with agony, a sound that echoes around me as if it's made by someone else, while much farther into the distance, the faint sound of hammering floats through the air. The students are still forging their medallions out in the northern field.

A cold breeze brings the scent of rain, but my throat is filled with the taste of copper, my own blood filling my mouth.

I have only one path left.

In that moment, I make the same decision my father made.

Death is inevitable.

There is no other way.

My deep light bursts around me, striking up across Malak's face and body, turning the air around me sapphire blue.

I will burn out my light and take Malak with me.

But even as I thrash and struggle, even with this new strength beyond any I've had before, I can't break through the chains that hold me down.

The darkness in Malak's power drags at my light, seeming to feed off it, only growing stronger as he cuts open my chest and hammers his metal into my heart.

Deep within my mind, I'm running through the snow beneath a sapphire sky.

I'm chasing a leopard I won't catch, not this time.

The beast has the taste of my blood and he'll come back for me and my family.

He will strike in the dark of night with claws and teeth, and my family will die because of me.

Deep in the mire of fear is the faintest light.

Strands of silver. Snowflakes caught on eyelashes. A soft hand, icy cold.

Asha.

Her scent draws me from the darkness to the tree, where her hair is caught and her body is half-covered in snow.

I inhale the air around her and my chest fills with power. Her power, rising from a spark that glows across her left side.

She is ours.

We must save her.

I scratch at the snow with my claws, determined to free her, slowly becoming aware that...

I don't have claws and I'm much closer to the ground than I ever was on two feet, and that I can smell and hear everything around me. The falling snow. The rustle of the leaves. Her quiet breathing.

She is ours.

We must keep her alive.

With a strike of clarity, I recognize that these memories and these impulses aren't mine.

Skirra?

His instincts resonate through me, and I understand him as clearly as if he spoke to me.

Stop burning your light and wake up, Vandawolf, he snarls into my mind. *You have work to do.*

I open my eyes.

CHAPTER 39

The screaming has stopped, but the air still smells like blood.

Raindrops patter across my body, while the sounds around me are amplified within my ears. I hear every scrape and scuttle, every scamper and thud.

There are rats in the courtyard walls.

A human woman hides in the back of a room within the maze of corridors. Her heartbeats hammer in my hearing while she sobs quietly.

There are more humans underground somewhere close by, their heartbeats slow, their breathing labored.

But closer to me is a presence so dark that it rends the very air apart.

I slide off the table and onto the ground, landing lightly on the cobbled stone before I draw myself upright.

My point of view has changed from before Malak chained me to the table. It's higher now as if I've grown taller. The weight of my body has also altered. Heavier, but stronger.

My tattered shirt slips away from my torso and slaps the ground, sodden with blood.

Within my heart is a single spark of deep light. The final spark that, if I draw on it, will force my death, but I tuck it away, committing it to Skirra's care. He will ensure I never access it.

My light is no longer available to me, but a new power has replaced it.

I draw my lips back in a quiet snarl, a wolf's growl, and that's when I become aware of the cutting sensation across the left side of my bottom lip.

I run my tongue across my upper teeth to discover one sharp tooth protruding on my left side. My hair at the corners of my vision is now the color of Skirra's dark-gray fur.

The hole in my chest has closed. Malak's dark device must be part of me now, but so is Skirra's soul.

Malak stands, half-crouched opposite me. He grips his hammer in his left hand while his black medallion is wrapped around his right palm. His dark-colored clothing can't hide my blood. It's splattered across his face and neck and hands.

I speak and my voice is a growl that rumbles through me, guttural in a way it never was before. "You should have kept me chained, Malak."

He's tense, his chest rising and falling, his heartbeat drumming in my hearing as he watches me with wary eyes. "I did."

He did?

I glance back at the table to see the mangled chains strewn across it. Also Skirra's body, now chain-free and curled up as if he's sleeping peacefully.

Did I place him like that before I slid off the table?

I'm not sure if I did, but I quietly make him a vow. When this is over, I will bury his body wherever he wants.

I turn back to Malak, but that's when I realize that something isn't right about him. His hand is upraised, his

"No matter what I can achieve and create, my people hate what they can't understand."

Again, I shake my head at him. "So you left her to a life of pain."

"Pain is all we are given," he snarls. "Anything more must be taken. She has proven she will not take what she deserves."

She is ours.

She must live.

As Skirra's impulses wash through me, I exhale quietly into the air that reeks of blood.

"If she will not take power for herself," I say, "I will take it for her."

With that, I leap toward Malak, strength exploding through my legs, carrying me farther and faster than I could have ever jumped before.

He swings his hammer at me, a forceful hit with his non-powered hand, while energy flows visibly through the medallion on his left palm.

But a wolf's strength and speed are now mine to use.

I grab his right wrist, deflect the hammer's blow, and punch my free hand toward his chest to propel him away from me before he can touch his medallion to my skin.

As he skids backward, his medallion transforms into a black shield, but I'm just as fast, following him as quickly as he tries to retreat, punching through the metal.

It caves and tears, and Malak's wide eyes come into view behind it.

He gasps. "I made you too strong."

It seems he did.

With a cry, he throws himself farther backward, retracting his metal while both of his arms swing forward. His sleeves pull upward and that's when I glimpse all the medallions lining his arms. Ten of them. Maybe more.

He snatches up a new one and throws it at the ground, a

thin thread forming to maintain the connection between the band and his powered hand.

The medallion expands across the courtyard, metal spikes forming in an instant, their sharp tips shooting up around me so quickly that I'm forced to jump back to avoid them.

Another three bands streak from his hand, this time in the form of spears. I dodge the first two and catch the third, crouching in the clear space I jumped into before I throw it right back at him.

He pitches himself to his left, narrowly evading the spear, which thumps into the courtyard wall and *twangs* in the air.

Before I can rise, more of his metal comes at me, this time forming two ropes that lash around my chest like vines. Thorns form along their edges, piercing my outer arms and my chest. My arms are pinned to my chest, but with my new strength, all I have to do is open them to snap the metal.

I take the cuts across my torso as I rip the ropes apart.

Before Malak can retract them all, I snatch at the end of one, pulling the strand sharply toward me.

Malak is wrenched forward, nearly impaling himself on the spikes that remain across the courtyard between him and me before he's forced to let the vine go.

With a grunt, I snap off a portion of the rope's tip, keeping a length of jagged black metal in my hand. A makeshift dagger with a sharp tip.

My father's command echoes back to me: *"Let Erik do the cutting."*

An eerie calm fills my heart while Malak regains his balance opposite me, his wide eyes meeting mine across the sharp, waist-height forest of metal that lies between us.

"My father trained me to hunt monsters," I say.

He taught me to navigate danger and strike when it's time to strike.

Malak is now the beast that has the taste of my blood, and I must end him.

I crouch again to gain momentum and use the new strength in my legs to easily leap over the spikes and land lightly on the other side.

He backs away from me, plucking more medallions off his arms and stepping to my right.

I prowl after him, suddenly aware of an influx of shimmering power around me—not from Malak but within the air.

A moment later, a cold raindrop falls on my cheek. I don't need to swipe at it to know that it will be blood-red like the other droplets that have fallen from the sky.

Malak fixates on the liquid that's sliding down my cheek as he continues to back away from me.

"I am not the only monster," he says. "There will be more."

"There are already more," I say, thinking of the other Blacksmiths.

"Not my people." A sneer rests on his lips. "We created our own doom."

His answer makes me pause because I'm not sure what he means, but even so, his statement rings of truth.

"What are you talking about?"

"Our creation magic has seeped into the soil beneath our feet," he says. "All the dead creatures, the failed manipulations, the experiments, we buried them in the northern field and thought nothing of it, but power now gathers within the wasteland we created." He nods. "Monsters will rise. You will see."

He isn't making a lot of sense, but the pitch of his voice and his heartbeat tell me he believes what he's saying.

A flash of lightning sparks across the sky and a patter of rain falls across the courtyard, stopping again just as suddenly as it started, but not before Malak holds out his hand and catches some of the droplets.

"Do you know what's wonderful about blood, Vandawolf?" he asks, letting the crimson liquid seep through his fingers.

I give a shake of my head.

"It has iron in it." He smiles softly as he turns his gaze upward. "A storm of iron."

At that moment, sharp needles of rain fall where we stand.

He snatches them from the air and flings them at me.

Chains of blood-red rain extend from his palm, each one with a dagger at the end, and at first I think they will remain liquid, but then they solidify, cutting through the air as they shoot toward me.

I dart left and right to avoid each one, the hairs on my arms and the back of my neck rising as the liquid streams around me, its sharp edges gleaming.

But it's the power within it, the charge of magic, that truly triggers my fear.

Blood rain. It makes sight difficult and weighs heavily across my back and shoulders.

I fight against it, throwing myself forward into danger.

Malak moves fast, his hands and arms swaying through the liquid, sending chain after chain at me as I dodge each one to make it closer to him.

I'm only five paces away when he drops to the ground and flicks his hand through the puddle at his feet.

A cascade of what looks like red icicles pours toward me, each spoke sharp and deadly.

But by crouching, he has paused in one place for a moment too long and what's more, he's now backed up close to the courtyard wall.

The cascade of bloody spikes arcs toward me in a spiral and with my quick reflexes, I identify the clear spot right in front of Malak.

My leg muscles bunch before I leap toward him, clearing the top of the spikes, my makeshift dagger raised as I fly through the air.

His eyes widen—he must know I'm about to land right in front of him—and he rushes to get back to his feet while at the same time, his left hand swishes through the rain and pulls the wash across his body. The crimson liquid solidifies like bloody armor around his form.

It can't protect him from me.

I punch my free hand into his armored chest, using the full momentum of my jump to knock him back against the courtyard wall.

I don't stop, following him there, ramming my left shoulder into his chest before his body can rebound off the stone.

I'm now facing his left arm and it only takes me a split second to focus on the power that streams from his left palm—the power that gives him strength and speed and the ability to kill me.

He's already whipping his arm toward me, his powered hand closing in.

I've put myself in the most dangerous position possibly and if he touches me with his power, it will be my end.

But I know my prey.

I push hard into his chest with my shoulder and catch his left forearm with my left hand, my fingers so strong that his bones break beneath them.

He screams, roaring unintelligible words, as if he's trying to command me to turn to stone and ash and dirt and blood, and for the smallest moment, deep fear floods his face, draining it of color.

With my right hand, I swing my makeshift dagger, a blade made from his own metal, and slice through his wrist, tearing through sinew and bone.

Let Erik do the cutting.

A trail of blood remains on the wall behind him, quickly washed away in a final splatter of rain.

His severed hand falls to the sodden ground and his knees buckle so fast that I'm now holding him up.

"My power," he gasps, his dark eyes instantly dull, his skin no longer luminously white. "Where is my power?"

As I continue to pin him to the wall with my shoulder, I consider the dullness of his skin and then the hand I cut from him.

How fucking simple.

I growl at him, letting Skirra's visceral impulses take over. "I will not kill you quickly. You must have trained the guards well to ignore all screams from this castle, but you will regret that now."

I step back from him, allowing him to fall to the ground where he clutches his arm.

He roars at me, but his power is gone.

Nearby, the spikes that were formed from rain suddenly melt and flow back to the ground. The metal spokes he created remain.

Above us, the clouds clear.

He grins up at me now, a deranged twist on his lips. "Was saving Asha from the snow worth losing *everything*?"

My heart is nothing more than broken pieces, but I mean my answer with every remaining shred of conviction left within me. "Yes."

Blood drips down my hands. It's caught in my hair. I can taste it in my mouth. A terrible copper tang.

"Now," I say, as I take hold of his arm and drag him toward the table. "You will tell me everything I want to know."

CHAPTER 40

I drag Malak's lifeless body across the courtyard and toward the spot where I sense men breathing underground.

It doesn't take me long to find the hidden stairs down into a dungeon where the scent of fear is thick in my chest. Malak told me all about the secret passageways throughout this castle.

There are cells on both sides of the walkway, constructed of thick, steel bars that appear to have been driven up into the rock ceiling and down into the floor.

Multiple human men, including Braddock, sit shackled within the cells.

They watch me with wide eyes as I drag Malak's corpse to the far end and drop it to the floor beneath a wall of glittering weapons made of all different-colored metal.

When I turn back to them, Braddock has wobbled upward, leaning against the back of the cell, since his shackles won't allow him to stand up fully.

His voice is a bare whisper. "Vandawolf?"

"Malak is dead," I growl, even though it's obvious. "I will free you, but in return, you will do something for me."

Malak made a deal with me and now I will make deals to ensure that I can control every outcome of this day.

"Name it," Braddock says while the other men nod.

I wait a moment, assessing each of them and their fearful heartbeats. None of them is quite looking at me, somehow finding a spot right past my face to focus on.

I don't know what I look like now. I don't care, as long as it gets me what I need.

"You are all Malak's spies," I say. "So you must know how to move about this city unseen. You will use those skills for me today."

The men shuffle a little, but none of them deny it.

"You will spread a message to every human who is willing to listen," I continue. "Tell them to stay inside and remain hidden. Tell them to stay out of my way. No humans need to die today. Do you understand?"

They stare at me, their lips parted and eyes wide.

Braddock is the first to nod and the others follow.

I reach for the steel bars, intending to bend them, only to find that I can't.

Huh.

But the lock on the door is easy to break, as are the shackles holding each of the men, and I quickly free them.

They keep clear of me before hurrying away, but I snag Braddock's arm before he can pass.

"Make sure Petra's safe. My brother's death will be meaningless if she loses her life today."

Braddock gives me a solemn nod. "I'll make sure of it."

"And Braddock?" My grip on his arm tightens. "I know it was you who told Malak about the apples."

He freezes. "I had no choice."

"Didn't you?"

He's silent opposite me, his focus on the ground.

I let him go and he races away.

My gaze passes across the weapons on the wall. Before he died, Malak told me many things, including that these weapons were forged by Blacksmiths who would not bend to his will.

My gaze stops on two silver daggers. They belonged to Asha's grandmother. She was one of the Blacksmiths who attempted to defy Malak and stop him from rising to power.

They aren't hunting knives, but they'll do.

Emerging into the courtyard once more, I make my way to the only other human presence I now detect within the castle walls.

I find Maybelle crouched in the corner of the kitchen, her arms wrapped around her knees.

She startles at my approach and I quickly put the daggers down onto the floor before I crouch to her. "Maybelle? It's me. The Vandawolf."

She peers at me with tear-filled eyes. "You're alive?"

All I can do is nod.

She wipes her eyes, but I don't miss the way she, too, doesn't quite look at me, her focus slightly wide of my face.

"How did you survive what Malak did to you?" she asks. "Nobody could have—"

"He made me strong," I reply, avoiding answering her question as I reach for her hand and help her stand. "Maybelle, there's something I need you to do for me."

"What is it?"

My second deal.

"I need you to find Kedric and make sure that Asha Silverspun and her brother and sister remain safe. In return, I promise you, you will both have your freedom today. Can you do that for me?"

Her eyes are wide. "I'm not sure how I can make that happen."

It's an honest response. *How can a powerless human protect Asha and her siblings?*

"Malak told me that when there was a human uprising once before, he called his favored Blacksmiths to the throne room and promised they would be safe there."

Maybelle nods. "That's right. It was the uprising when his sister was killed."

Supposedly killed, but I don't say that.

"Can you get that message to Kedric so he can spread it through the Silverspun household?" I ask.

"But—"

"Soon, there will be chaos, Maybelle," I say. "Nobody will know for sure if Malak is alive or dead. The Blacksmiths will be fearful for the first time in many years. They will cling to any promise of safety. If you can make sure the high-ranking Blacksmiths believe they're supposed to come here, I will deal with them at this end. That is, once the rest of the city is purged."

Her voice is a strangled whisper. "'Purged'?"

My lips set into a line. "The bells won't ring tonight. By the end of this day, there won't be a Blacksmith alive who will ring them."

I rise to my feet. There's a silver tray on the counter Maybelle was huddled beside and I catch sight of my reflection in it.

I freeze at what I see.

I'd already glimpsed the difference in my hair at the sides of my face, but now I see that my features have changed too. My left eye is amber and almond-shaped like Skirra's eyes were. The sharp canine tooth at the left side of my mouth protrudes when I draw back my lips.

I hunch my shoulders, allowing my hair to fall across that side of my face before I quickly look away.

No wonder the men couldn't look at me.

"Vandawolf?" Maybelle asks. And then she calls me something I never expected to hear. "Lord? What's wrong?"

I press my fist to my heart, where it hurts. "Thoren should be the one about to fight for your people."

She doesn't refute it, a soft exhale passing her lips.

"Yes," she says, looking up at me. "But now it must be you."

CHAPTER 41

Many hours later, blood drips down my blades as I stand at the northern gate.

In the distance, the sun has descended below the horizon.

The northern field is quiet. The students are no longer forging their medallions. I'm not sure exactly when they scattered from this field, but it didn't do them any good.

Bowls of coal still burn wine-red while unforged metal lies abandoned on the anvils.

Up on the wall, the guards are dead.

Within the city, bodies lie in streets and alleys and within buildings, all of them Blacksmiths.

Maybelle succeeded in her task—I know this because when I reached Silverspun House, Ayla and Kalith and their children were gone. So were Landon Copperstream and several of the other high-ranking Blacksmiths when I reached the other houses.

The humans are not unscathed, but I helped them where I could and by some miracle, none have died.

They gather now behind me, carrying makeshift weapons and quieting down as I remain standing, unmoving, my focus on the ashen field.

With my new power, what I see before me sends a chill to my bones. When I stepped onto this field the first time, my skin had prickled at how *wrong* it felt.

Now I can see the swirls of energy snaking through the ash, spots where power gathers and boils, creation magic that even now is still creating.

Malak spoke of monsters rising from this soil and I have no doubt they will. Above me, the sky is already dark again.

"The Blacksmiths are not all you have to fear," I say as I turn away from the field. "They've scorched the earth and their magic hasn't finished its work. We will have new monsters to fight soon."

The crowd of humans is deathly quiet as my words seem to sink in.

Braddock pushes through them, carrying a bloodied axe. He approaches me slowly, quietly murmuring. "Your brother's body is safe with Petra."

My throat constricts and all I can do is nod.

Braddock is an enemy I will need to keep close. I will never be able to trust him.

As I turn back to the humans... my people... it once again strikes me that it should be Thoren standing here.

Thoren, whom these people trusted because somehow, he'd gained their faith and belief.

He would have told them not to be afraid. He would have told them that we will face the coming battles together, and together, we will win.

But I can't force words from my tongue that don't come from my heart.

I will keep the humans safe and honor Thoren that way.

But they will never come to think of me as their friend, not when they can't even look me in the eye.

I am a beast to them and that is how I will remain.

"Do *not* come near the castle until it is done," I say, at which the crowd parts to let me through.

My mind is filled with resolve as I make my way back to the castle, prowling along the city streets as I go, using my heightened senses and my ability to identify Blacksmith power to determine that there are no more Blacksmiths alive outside the castle's walls. Only within it.

Near to the castle, Maybelle waits in the shadows, embraced in her husband's arms. They both have tears in their eyes.

"Maybelle?"

"Ayla and Kalith took their children to the castle like you wanted," she says.

I give her and her husband a nod. "Thank you."

That's all I need to know before I continue on.

I watch the ramparts carefully as I approach, sensing the immense power within these walls.

The strongest living Blacksmiths now stand between me and Asha.

I count the heartbeats from a distance, sensing the power attached to each one. Skirra's senses confirm that Asha is not among the eight Blacksmiths standing guard within the courtyard itself.

Farther back are two more Blacksmiths, both waiting in a corridor beyond the courtyard. The power emanating from those two is the strongest of all.

They must be Ayla and Kalith Silverspun.

I close my eyes and stretch my senses, seeking the fainter heartbeats farther back still. The ones I care about. They sound different in my ears than the other Blacksmiths' heartbeats.

It is Asha, Skirra confirms, and I trust that he would recognize her heartbeat. *The other heartbeats belong to children.*

Skirra didn't have the chance to interact with Tamra and Gallium, but it has to be them. The protectiveness Asha showed her brother and sister at the Academy means she wouldn't let them out of her sight.

Steadying my breathing, I stretch out my shoulders and neck, and then I grip my daggers, turning them back and forth through the air, clearing my mind of all doubt.

I remind myself of the cut of blood across Asha's back, the fall of her hair, and the ice in her fingers, and I fill my thoughts only with rage.

She is the reason I'm here.

She is the reason I won't fail.

With a snarl, I leap forward, sprinting toward the gate.

The portcullis is closed, but it doesn't stop me.

I turn my shoulder, absorbing the impact as I smash through it, sending pieces of metal and splinters of wood flying across the courtyard.

Eight Blacksmiths are waiting for me. One of them is Landon Copperstream, although I already dealt with his friends.

He sneers at me. "Well, it looks like it's true. Malak turned you into a dog."

None of the other Blacksmiths echo Landon's laughter. I suppose they're smart enough to acknowledge all of the screaming they must have heard today. My ears are still ringing with the death I brought.

All the blood is on my hands now.

Several of the others dart toward me, but I duck between their blades, moving faster than they can as I head straight for Landon.

He extends his right hand but a sword hasn't even finished

manifesting before I sever his outstretched hand from his body and slice through his throat. Two quick cuts with my daggers.

Shock fills his eyes as he falls to his feet.

Immediately, I spin to the next attacker and ram my dagger through their heart.

Clangs ring out and strength thrums around me as the Blacksmiths fight back, but within seconds, all eight of them lie dead around me.

My chest heaves, but I allow myself only a moment before I continue on.

I step into the mouth of the wide corridor that sits at the head of the courtyard.

Kalith and Ayla stand in the shadows, their metal glinting.

"You will suffer for what you've done this day," Ayla says to me, her voice cold. "I will cut you apart, piece by piece, and I will enjoy your screams."

Beside her, Kalith scoops multiple medallions from his left arm and presses them all against his chest, liquid copper rushing out from around his palm and covering his torso with armored plates.

Without another word, Ayla takes a step toward me, plucking a hairpiece from her hair, her hands moving as she spins a web of fine, silver threads.

Before today, I would not have been able to follow her quick movements, but now, I make out every detail.

There's fresh blood under her fingernails and the scent of it tells me it isn't her own.

I brace for her attack as she thrusts her arms forward, releasing the web of threads. They billow out from her hands toward me, a deadly lace made of razor-sharp strings.

There are so many of them that they will slice right through my hands and arms if I try to grab them or even strike at them with my daggers. My only option is to dodge and dart as she continues to spin more wire and fling it at me.

Kalith turns my evasive maneuvers to his advantage, transforming another medallion into an axe and swinging it at my neck.

I manage to evade the blow while dodging the next thread Ayla shoots at me, but I don't miss the triumph on Kalith's face.

"I should have killed you in the mountains, Boy. A mistake I will rectify today."

Only then do I realize that Ayla was not just throwing her metal at me randomly, she was setting up a deadly web around me.

The end of each thread has attached to one of the walls on either side of me, weaving a maze of razor-sharp threads that will cut me to pieces once retracted.

Kalith was the distraction to make me step right into the center of it.

All Ayla has to do is pull back her hands and the threads will constrict and slice me to pieces.

Ayla's arm muscles tense, a cruel smile on her face, as if she will revel in the blood that is about to be spilled.

Her hands move.

But my strength has increased a hundred-fold.

With a burst of energy, I harness the power in my legs and leap upward to the wall on my right, my dagger outstretched.

My leap takes me parallel to her position.

I ram one blade into the wall, using it as an anchor to spin before I rip it out of the wall again and drop right behind her.

She tries to turn toward me, but she doesn't let her metal go in time and it slows her down.

I ram my blades into both sides of her neck, the metal slashing through bone and clashing as it meets in the middle.

"Ayla!" Kalith's roar of rage washes over me as I wrench my blades from Ayla's neck.

She drops to the ground, her threads twisting and their tension tightening as she falls to her side.

Kalith has frozen for a moment, his heartbeats betraying his shock and the press of his lips revealing a hint of despair, which is soon replaced with pure anger.

He knocks his right fist against the side of his neck and his metal extends up over his face to form a helmet. He's now covered in full body armor that doesn't seem to impede his movements.

A copper sword forms in each of his hands as he charges at me, driving me back into the clear end of the corridor.

The door to the throne room is only a few steps away.

Kalith slashes with his swords, one after the other, cuts I have no hope of defending with my much shorter daggers. So I duck and dart once more, narrowly evading his lightning-fast attacks, waiting for the moment to strike back.

And then, there it is.

I let him force me into a crouch, his left arm rising to gain the speed he needs to slice off my head. Instead of throwing myself backward, I launch myself up and forward.

With all my strength, I strike with my dagger at the location of his heart.

I remember the way that my father's blades crashed and slid off Kalith's armor when they fought in the mountains.

But now, my strength takes the blade right through.

It's a seamless strike, rending apart Kalith's metal and descending into his chest.

I hear his breath catch, feel the thump of the beating organ through my blade. And then I twist the blade and wrench the metal out.

Before he can fall, I take hold of the back of Kalith's head.

"For my father," I growl, ramming the dagger through the metal at his throat and tearing his neck apart.

I stand over his body, my chest heaving, my own heart torn apart, listening for the echoes of my father's voice, as if my vengeance could somehow bring him back.

There is only silence.

A roar tears out of me, all of my pain rising to the surface, tears flooding my eyes. And still I roar until I have no air left in my chest and I'm forced to stop.

I want to believe my fight is over now, but it isn't.

My greatest battle will be the quiet one I have with Asha.

CHAPTER 42

The door into the throne room is only a few steps away, but I can't go through it yet.

I don't want Asha and her siblings to see all of this death when they come out, so I quickly cut down Ayla's metal, using my silver daggers like spindles to wrap the thread around before I ram the daggers safely into the wall.

Then I drag the bodies from the corridor and the courtyard, four at a time, and pile them outside the wall next to the gate.

I already put Skirra's body away safely in the orchard before I left the courtyard this morning, and I returned Malak's tools to his table—his hammer and three medallions—knowing no other Blacksmith would go near them. I also broke apart the metal spikes he created and piled them in one of the secret rooms he told me about.

When this is over, I will have all Blacksmith metal brought to me and destroyed, except the metal I still need.

A heavy exhale rests on my lips as I consider the courtyard now. There isn't much I can do about the blood all over the ground.

I head once more to the other side and along the corridor to the door beyond which three heartbeats continue to sound.

There I stop, my shoulders hunched, my palms pressed to the wood, my chest heaving.

Asha will know that I've slaughtered her people.

She will believe I've come to kill her too.

From inside the room, a little boy's whisper reaches me through the wood. "I'll fight beside you, Asha."

That must be Gallium. My lips tug in a brief smile, because I believe he would.

Asha replies, so softly that I can barely make out her words even with my enhanced hearing. "Quiet now."

I press my forehead against the wood. For a wild moment, I consider scooping them all up and following one of the hidden passageways and disappearing into the mountains with Asha and her siblings.

I nearly do it. I'm prepared to do it, but then reality stops me.

She won't come with me willingly. She'll think I'm dragging her out into the wasteland to kill her and her family. To protect her brother and sister, she'll fight me as hard as she can.

I'm covered in the blood of her people and there's nothing I could say that would make her believe my purpose is to keep her alive.

Without the option of escape, there are no good choices open to me.

Malak told me how he drained her siblings' power, so I know I can convince the humans that the twins are harmless, but Asha is another Blacksmith in their eyes. They will fear her and want her dead, and if I try to stop them, if I fight them...

The taste of death fills my mouth and I fucking hate it.

I can't stomach even one more death today.

The only way I can bring peace to this city while keeping Asha alive is for her to choose to be my captive.

I will do whatever it takes to force that choice, even if I have to threaten to cut off the hand I once saved.

I hang my head for a moment before I take a deep breath and tell myself I will be nothing more than a beast to her and that is what I must continue to be.

Pushing away my doubts, I ram my fists against the door, knocking it off its hinges and cracking through the wood. The door crashes across the room and I sense all three heartbeats jumping and thudding.

The broken door slides to a slow stop halfway along the black marble floor that stretches out ahead of me.

It's a cold, empty room, at the end of which sits a silver throne. The malice radiating from the throne is as chilling as the cruelty in Malak's table.

My new weight makes my footsteps heavy, thudding across the floor as I approach the thin strip of white material protruding from behind the throne.

I round the seat, prepared to meet Asha's eyes for the first time, prepared to face her hatred, but instead, she huddles there with her head down.

She's holding Tamra and Gallium to her chest, her hands across their ears as if she was trying to block out the screams.

Tamra's hair is matted with blood, her scalp is bleeding, and her shoulders and arms are scratched. Gallium, too, is bruised and has a cut across his cheekbone.

I remember the blood beneath Ayla's fingernails and I can't stop my growl of anger. Can't calm the breath seething in and out of my mouth. Even though all it does is frighten them.

It's just as well. Asha must fear me if she is to surrender.

As soon as my shadow falls over them, Tamra starts crying, her quiet sobs tightening like claws around my chest, but I force myself to harden my heart.

"Fear," I snarl, low and soft, trying to ignore how much I hate that I'm the cause of their dread.

But then my senses alert me to the absence of the emotion I expected most.

I'm surprised. And confused.

"But not hatred," I say.

Asha's chest rises and falls rapidly while her heartbeat pounds in my hearing. "I can't hate you."

But she must.

She *must* hate me or my walls will crumble.

"Then you pity me," I snap.

Her denial is a shout, clear and certain. "No!"

That's when she looks up.

For the first time since I found her in the snow, she looks at me.

Finally, she sees me and her gaze nearly drives me to my knees.

Her eyes are the palest green, but the life within them, the hope and desperation, steals the breath from my chest. I know without a doubt that if my deep light was not burned out, it would be spilling around me now.

I wait for a hint of recognition on her face, searching her eyes, unable to deny my hope that maybe she remembers me. Maybe she woke up, even for a small time in the mountains and she knows I kept her warm.

My hope fades when she looks at me without recognition.

She doesn't know me.

She doesn't know the price I paid for her life.

I expect her to quickly look away, to focus past my face like everyone else does, but...

She doesn't.

Her gaze passes briefly across the splattered blood and gore on my bare chest before returning to my face, where she peers intently at me.

Her eyes widen as if something has surprised her.

Am I not what she expected?

Am I not furious enough? Vicious enough? Hateful enough?

I give her a dangerous grin, baring my sharp, canine tooth.

"I have no pity for you," she says, her gaze impossibly unwavering.

"Then give me your hand," I challenge her, certain that this will ensure she hates me because by now, she must have heard how I went about killing her people today.

"No."

She defies us.

Skirra's response is delighted.

But maybe I can use her defiance. Maybe I can find the words to tell her to come with me…

At that moment, the sound of the mob of humans converging on the castle reaches me.

I'm running out of time. I snarl at her instead of reasoning with her. "Give me. Your fucking. Hand."

She won't give it to me. I know it.

I will have to take it.

I'm reaching for her as she says, "Only if you let them live—"

My hand is already closing around her right wrist, wrenching her upward, harder than I intended—*damn this new strength*—but there is nothing gentle about me now.

She tries to hold on to her siblings, but they tumble from her arms and land on the floor. They're reaching for her, crying for her, but it only takes me seconds to pull her away from them.

She's shouting, screaming, but not to save herself. "These children have no power. Let them live!"

I pull her to a stop, hardening my heart against the terror I've caused them.

"These children can't hurt anyone," she pleads, her eyes raised to mine as she continues searching, searching between the bloodied strands of my hair, as if she's desperate to read my thoughts. "Please. Let them live."

On the floor behind her, Gallium and Tamra have reached for each other and are huddled together once more, their sobbing painful to hear.

"No power?" I narrow my eyes at them, reconsidering their hands.

Malak confessed to draining their power but... *No.*

There is a spark in both of their right hands. It's a small spark, certainly, but it's there.

Perhaps he didn't take all of their power or perhaps, more dangerously, they're already recovering from the ordeal.

My fear rises that one day they will regain their full power —not because it will allow them to challenge me, but because if the humans catch even a hint of it, they will lash out and kill these innocent children. The pain of the humans' history will ensure it.

I take a deep breath, promising myself I will plan for that day and I will keep the twins alive despite it.

Even though I'm resolved, I question Asha's assertion, because from now on, I must be careful about revealing what I already know.

"You are the children of Kalith and Ayla Silverspun," I snarl. "Your parents were two of the most powerful Blacksmiths to stand at Malak's side. How is it possible that your brother and sister are powerless?"

"My parents gave them as a gift to Malak," she says, a painful hope rising in her eyes, and I suppose it's because I'm listening to her. "He drained their power for his own purposes."

"What of *your* power?" I ask, wondering if she has any knowledge at all about how much power she wields—a power Malak said she isn't aware of.

Her shoulders sink. "Malak didn't want mine."

Oh, but he did.

He craved Asha's power.

"I sense your hatred now," I say.

Anger flashes in her eyes. "Malak was a monster. So were my parents."

"As am I!" I roar, needing her to believe it. "Do not forget it."

I'm running out of time. I pull her toward me, hoping to make her believe that I will cut her power from her body, even though I came here without a knife.

Her left hand shoots forward, her palm landing flat against my bare chest.

Within my mind, I'm suddenly transported back to those fearless moments in the cabin when she rested her hand against my heart beneath a warm fur. The fine strands of her hair tickled my chin and my cheek. Her head fit perfectly in the crook of my neck.

Her scent, even now, speaks to me of peace.

I fold up the memories and put them away.

They are no help to me now.

Outside the castle, a cheer goes up, cries of jubilation coming closer. The humans will have seen the final bodies outside the castle walls.

Asha's face falls and her heart thuds in my hearing. "Please," she whispers. "Have mercy for these children."

My father's voice echoes back to me. *"They will have no mercy for us."*

A roar tears from me. "You beg for mercy, but where was the mercy for my family?" My grip on her tightens. "When I fought to save my father's life and my brother's life, where was mercy then?"

Her heartbeat tells me she's terrified, but it's the compassion in her eyes that tears me apart.

"Then take *my* life," she whispers, her face pale, her heart a slow, heavy beat. "Take my life in front of your people so they can be done with their vengeance. Let your justice end with me. Not with these children."

My shoulders slump. She has offered me her life and given me what I need to keep her alive.

At my command, she will fight the monsters that rise in the wasteland and make herself indispensable to the humans. I will give her Malak's tools for this task. She will wield his hammer and all his terrible power. She will defend the humans and they will need her even if they hate her.

One day, I will find a way to secure her freedom.

Until then, she is mine to command.

Quietly, I say, "I accept."

PART TWO
THE WOLF IN THE FLAMES

PRESENT DAY

CHAPTER 43
PRESENT DAY

My back is broken.

I'm lying on my side in a circular clearing that, until minutes ago, was covered in snow. Dragon fire has turned the snow into a wash of melting ice that now laps at my body, freezing and hot in turns.

The *crack* my spine made when I hit the ground echoes through me, along with the shriek of searing flames that raged after us, the popping of leaves on the lone tree nearby as they burst into flames, and the hiss of burning sap within the tree's bark.

Asha created that tree.

She knelt in the snow, touched the darkness, and turned it into something beautiful and alive.

Now, there's silence around me.

A thick, unnatural silence that tells me my hearing is dangerously impaired. My right ear is underwater, but the intense pain in my neck is stopping me from lifting my head.

My left ear...

I sense warm blood trickling from it and sliding down my

jaw. That was the side where the dragon's paw hit me when he knocked us to the ground.

Agony thrums through my head and down the top of my spine, but it stops at my shoulder blades. It's the complete absence of feeling below that point, the nothingness where I know I should be able to feel my arms and legs, that concerns me.

My spine must be broken in multiple places.

Panic pushes at me.

Without my hearing, I can't sense Asha.

Without my legs, I can't run to her.

My deep light is no longer available to me to help heal myself.

All I can see is the side of the clearing I'm facing, and she isn't within my field of view. We're high up in the mountains and there's nothing but sharp drops on every side of this clearing except the one in the direction of my feet, where a forest extends back across the mountain range.

It took us five days to reach this clearing in our search for Milena Ironmeld, the lost sister of Malak Ironmeld, whose thirty-year reign over the humans in the south brought terror to their lives and mine.

We thought our search would begin here, in the west, at a supposed outpost belonging to the human army with which Milena is aligned.

Instead, we found Milena trapped within the trunk of a monstrous tree, guarded by a fierce bear.

Her power was gone, her mind was broken, and she couldn't remember the man who had trapped her here.

We soon learned it was Malak's son.

The deliverer of that news was Graviter Rex, the dragon king, whose child had been murdered by Malak's son. As retribution for the death of his child, Graviter has vowed to end all Blacksmiths.

I know his pain.

I've felt it.

I know what it will have done to his mind and his reason.

The air above me shimmers with heat and the vibrations through the stone tell me that Graviter is close.

I can't do a damn thing to protect myself or Asha—wherever she is—except silently roar at my body to move.

Fucking move!

My body fails to respond.

Directly in front of me, a jagged, white bone is caught on the rocky ground, resisting the shallow flow of water.

A blue leaf, burned at the edges, is trapped beside it.

The leaf brushes my outstretched hand and then... *finally*...

My fingers twitch in the freezing water.

It's the first movement my body has made and it sends a shock of hope through me.

At the same moment, the heaviness of the burning smoke lifts. A fresh breeze fills my chest.

It brings Asha's scent.

I taste fear, anger, and desperation, but also life, and that's what matters most.

My fingers twitch again.

A painful flood of feeling suddenly rushes through my left arm, so agonizing that I grit my teeth to stifle my groan and hide my wakefulness.

I can't pinpoint Graviter's exact location, but if he thinks I'm completely immobilized—if he thinks the threat I pose to him has been neutralized—I'm not going to enlighten him until I'm certain I can fight back, at least with my arms.

Assuming my other arm regains feeling—

Fuck!

The rush of pain through my chest and right arm—the return of feeling—is searing, hotter than the dragon's fire that burned across my back.

Far worse is the agony that tears through my stomach, hips, thighs, and calves only seconds later.

The pain lasts so long that I'm screaming within my mind, my fingers clawing the ground.

I focus on the dark metal that protrudes from my fingertips and cuts into the rock beside me. These claws are as unnatural as the changes Malak forced on me and Skirra. They're long and sharp and appear as if they're fashioned from the same titanium alloy that comprises Asha's hammer—the same alloy that she used to plug my wounds when I was bleeding out.

I woke up with these claws after she pulled the device that Malak used to transform me from my heart.

Malak didn't give me these claws.

Asha did. Along with the ability to sharpen both of my canine teeth and transform both of my eyes. My eyesight was already enhanced, but my new wolf's eyes allow me to see much more clearly at night.

At the same time, I lost Skirra from my mind. His impulses no longer fill my mind or influence my actions, and while I miss his directness, it doesn't feel as if he's gone. We've fully merged and now my thoughts and instincts are complete.

Asha made me whole.

I'm not sure exactly how she did it. She seems to use her power instinctively, which makes it equal parts breathtaking and terrifying.

I squeeze my eyes shut now, fighting the pain and pushing back against my increasing panic.

I can smell Asha's blood, fresh and new, and it's driving me to desperation that I can't do a fucking thing to help her.

Taking another long breath, I wait.

Wait...

The pain in my upper back begins to ease.

I take the chance to test my arms, using my claws where they're impaled in the ground as leverage to ease myself upward a bare inch off the ground. Hopefully not so much that I'll draw attention. Just enough to lift my right ear out of the water. Once I've done so, sounds rush in.

First, I hear the water running over the edges of the clearing as the icy deluge drains away.

Then Asha's furious voice reaches me from somewhere at my back, her tone filled with all the brutality she carries in the palm of her hand. A malice she fights with every beat of her heart. Even so, she sounds winded, as if she can't breathe properly.

"Why do you think I know where Malak's son is?" she asks, and I can only assume she's speaking to Graviter Rex since the shimmers of heat through the air above me are growing more intense.

Malak's son orchestrated this whole situation.

He murdered this dragon's child but made it look like his aunt, Milena Ironmeld, had been behind the murder. Then he imprisoned Milena on this mountaintop and left her here for us to find, knowing that the Graviter would seek revenge for his child's death.

It was a trap.

The fact that I didn't see it coming has shaken me.

I made Malak tell me everything before he died. I'm certain he never knew he had a son.

Right now, my focus is on surviving the fight with this dragon, but if we get out of this alive, we'll need to know everything we can about Malak's son and what he wants—other than wanting us dead.

I take a moment to test my toes, then my calves and stomach muscles, clenching and unclenching them. They're finally responding to my commands.

The pain has eased.

I'm not sure how I've recovered so quickly. Perhaps my

bones weren't broken, after all. Maybe the paralysis was only temporary.

I don't have time to second-guess it.

Behind me, Graviter Rex has continued to speak, and Asha's response is even more breathless.

He can only be seconds away from killing her.

As fast as I can, I shove at the ground where my claws are driven into it, pushing myself upright.

In the seconds it takes me to rise into a crouch and get my feet under me, I take in the entire half of the clearing that was behind me.

The tree that Asha transformed comes into view first.

Milena Ironmeld has remained sitting propped up against its trunk. Scorched leaves float around her and blood trickles down the side of her nose from a cut in her forehead.

Countless large bones litter the ground around her. Any one of them could have struck Milena when the dragon's fire blasted through the snow.

Then I take in Asha.

She lies on her back in the now-shallow water only ten paces away from me. Her hair was once silver, her skin once pale, but both were tarnished in forge fire, and now a dark sheen covers her skin and her hair is nearly black.

Graviter Rex, the dragon king, looms over her, his large body extending back across the clearing, his tail nearly touching the trees.

He pins Asha to the ground with a paw pressed onto her torso. One of his talons is rammed into the ground beside her shoulder, but the others appear to be impaling her sides.

She was already bleeding from the fight with the monsters that guarded this clearing.

Fresh blood swirls in the water around her.

I take it all in within a heartbeat, and my vision instantly clouds with rage. He's hurting her.

For that, he'll pay.

A savage growl builds in my throat and my muscles bunch.

I've already left the ground, leaping the distance to him, when Graviter utters a final threat to her.

"Blacksmith, with your last breath, you will tell me: Where is Thaden Kane Ironmeld?"

The world spins.

Shock floods my body.

Thaden Kane is Malak's son?

CHAPTER 44

H*ow did Thaden Kane deceive me?*

The ramifications are sickening. The consequences, disturbing.

But in that split second as I fly toward the dragon's shoulder with my claws outstretched, all I care about is keeping Asha safe from the threat that's right in front of her.

Graviter flinches, becoming aware of my attack too late.

I register Asha's cry and the way her eyes fill with hope and a rush of tears. "Erik!"

Her left hand flies to the side of Graviter's paw, as if she would try to use her power on him, even though his scales will protect him.

At the same moment her palm lands on his paw, my claws rip across his shoulder.

It's a far more savage cut than I would have delivered when I still believed we could reason with this dragon without causing him serious harm first. Even when I stabbed his back during our earlier fight, I caused only shallow puncture wounds.

His scales tear open in long gashes, and he roars with pain, releasing Asha and leaping backward, his head lowering, his fire only moments away.

I drop to the ground between Asha and him, my right hand upraised and claws fully extended.

I let my teeth sharpen and my eyes change, calling on my wolfish nature. Skirra's soul used to influence my thoughts, his wildness dominating parts of my life, but no more.

Since Asha removed the device from my chest, my thoughts are wholly my own.

I growl with all the ferocity of the primal predator that I have become. "Graviter Rex!"

Graviter's ears prick up, a wary light entering his eyes. He remains hunched as he backs away another step, heat continuing to radiate from his mouth while blood gushes from the cuts in his shoulder.

"I could have killed you," I snarl. "I didn't have to stop."

"Then why did you?" he roars at me, waves of heat gushing from his mouth.

"Because you're in pain," I say, at which he jolts. "Your pain is driving you to self-destruction. You wish for death, but death is not the way."

Graviter shakes his head, swaying back and forth and pawing the ground, edging forward, then back again, as if he can't decide whether or not to attack me.

Behind me, Asha has jumped to her feet, but I sense her crouching again briefly before she rises once more.

The water swishes, as if she scooped something out of it, although I can't see what.

I want to check that she's okay, but I can't take my eyes off Graviter. I have to make do with knowing that her heartbeat is strong and steady.

"Blacksmiths killed my family," I say to Graviter, letting my pain rise to the surface. Against my will, my eyes fill with tears of rage, but I force myself to continue. "My brother was good. Kind. Innocent of all this. Just like your son."

Graviter rakes his talons across the stone at his feet, causing the rock to spark. The heat from his body is drying out the ground and I worry about the little flames that seethe from between his lips.

Still, I continue, my voice filled with a wolfish growl. "If you want revenge against Thaden Kane, then you will need our help. You need my claws, and you need Asha's power—"

Graviter gives a howl. "I don't need her darkness. It's the same malice that doomed my son."

"She is not darkness!" I roar, my control finally snapping. "Asha is the only light in my world."

I sense her stillness at my words. The sudden jump in her heartbeat.

Without taking my eyes off Graviter, I point to the tree behind me. "Do you see what your fire has burned, dragon?"

His wild eyes focus beyond me for a second. Then back to me.

"Take a longer look, Dragon King." I lower my voice. "Look at what Asha created from the monster Malak's son left here to kill us. Look at the beautiful thing she made from such ugliness and hatred. Now, tell me again how you don't need her help."

The dragon hunches low to the ground, his snarls coming thick and fast, but it's Asha's voice that cuts across the mess of sound.

"The dragon's right," she whispers, and her voice sounds far too hollow. "I can't fight Thaden Kane."

I risk a glance at her, surprised to see that she's gripping the dragon-imprinted medallion in her right hand. Her other medallion is still in the form of a chain and lies a mere five paces away, where Graviter threw it off his neck.

Of course, the medallion that's fused to her hand has remained exactly where it is.

Blood drips from cuts across her shoulders, arms, and thighs. Her clothing is torn. There's more blood in her hair, clumping the strands.

Her cheeks are deathly pale. She's trembling hard.

She could be freezing from the icy water dripping off her body or going into shock or shaking with rage. Or all of these things at once.

"My power is useless against him." Despite the danger right in front of her, she squeezes her eyes shut as she continues to shake. "Thaden made sure I knew it. Again and again. He stopped me from hurting you that time in the prison. He used his father's own medallion to forge weapons that nearly killed you. He even hugged me when I was at my most dangerous."

She opens her eyes and her expression is bleak. "When I arrived at the fae castle, he saw this medallion fused to my hand, and unlike everyone else, he wasn't afraid. He looked *pleased*, Erik. As if the thing I feared most gave him comfort."

Her shoulders hunch and her fists clench, and she suddenly gives an icy laugh, so chilling that it makes me shiver.

"He used the dragon to change his appearance." She nods her head. "Graviter said he was a child with eyes and hair as dark as night. Just like Malak. But if he'd looked like his father, we might have noticed the resemblance. Instead, he came to us with bronzed hair and fiery eyes and the scales of a dragon.

"He used the lie about being transformed to explain the Blacksmith magic he must have known I'd sense within him and... Oh!"

Her hand flies to her mouth. It's the hand clutching the dragon-imprinted medallion and despite the pain it must be causing her, she presses it to her lips.

"Oh, he was clever," she whispers. "He covered his powered hand—his right hand—in dragon scales so that no ordinary blade could sever his hand from his body."

Her gaze quickly slips to Milena, whose own hand is

missing, cut from her, leaving her unable to access her power ever again.

But then Asha's focus slips to me.

To my claws.

The weapons she gave me that sliced through Graviter's scales only moments ago.

She nods again, then takes a deep breath, her heart calming a little. "You're right, Erik. Graviter needs your strength. The question is whether or not he'll accept it."

I've kept my focus on Asha for dangerously-long seconds, and I'm somewhat surprised that Graviter Rex has stayed where he is. More surprised to recognize that with every word Asha has spoken, the dragon's heartbeats have become more regulated and less frenzied.

When I glance at him, I find him considering Asha with an expression that's unreadable, although the fury in his eyes has abated and the fire around his mouth has receded. Not much, just a little. Enough to give me hope that he's listening to her now, just as she tried to make him listen before he blasted us with his fire and knocked us to the ground.

"Thaden Kane has my family." Asha clutches her stomach, rocking forward on the spot, her lips twisting. "He told me he would 'take care of them'. And I trusted him! How could I have trusted him?"

In the last few stomach-churning minutes, I've wondered how he managed to deceive me.

I, too, sensed the Blacksmith magic within him, but like Asha, it was explained by the fact that he was changed by it, his appearance taking on the qualities of a dragon just as I'd become wolfish.

I never imagined that a Blacksmith would willingly put themselves through the extreme pain and torture I endured when I became the wolf. Or risk the high likelihood of death that comes with it.

Tears streak down Asha's cheeks as she lifts her eyes, but this time to Graviter Rex. "What darkness gave him the power to engender such trust?"

Graviter's eyes slowly widen. His response is a bare whisper in the air. "A darkness that is like a breeze, cooling your fears before it burgeons into a storm that tears apart what you love most."

"Yes." Asha pulls herself upright, swiping at her cheeks with one hand after the other, the medallions she's holding sliding across her skin.

I know her expressions well enough to recognize when she's made a decision that will endanger her own life for the sake of protecting someone she loves.

Hell, I've seen her stand up from her death bed because she wanted to protect Tamra and Gallium.

I see that look on her face now.

Whatever she's decided, I won't be able to change her mind —although until I hear what she has to say, I'm not sure if I'll want to.

All I can do is stand aside and pray she'll trust me to ask for help if she needs it.

She wipes her face clean of every emotion except pure, fucking determination as she steps slowly toward the chain that Graviter Rex threw off his neck.

He watches her warily, but I step between them, making it clear I will protect her.

She bends to scoop up the chain with her left hand, instantly transforming it into a band, which she continues to grip. The ends of it poke out of her fist next to the medallion that's fused there.

Then she steps directly toward Graviter Rex, casting me a long glance as she passes me by.

I read a warning in that glance: *Stay back. Stay safe. Be ready.*

"Graviter Rex," she says to the dragon, giving him her full attention. "You've lost your child and succumbed to grief, but my family is still alive. They're in terrible danger and I will do anything to keep them safe."

A hum sounds deep in the dragon king's throat, but he doesn't surge forward and the flames don't increase around his mouth.

With slow, deliberate movements, Asha presses the dragon-imprinted medallion to her left hand, aligning it with the black band melded to her palm.

All three bands are now gripped in her palm.

She shakes with the power that must be thrumming through her.

Then she delivers a veiled threat. "Even without Erik's claws, know this, Graviter Rex: Thaden Kane found a way to use his power to kill a dragon, which means I can find a way, too."

Her heartbeat remains calm as she continues. "I don't want to harm you. You aren't my enemy. But if you stop me from protecting my family, then believe me... Not only will I kill you, but I will seek revenge against all dragons. I will tear your people apart until they're nothing but blood and bones on thirsty ash."

Graviter's focus flickers to the medallions and for the first time since he arrived, he seems more wary than wrathful.

Still, he's yet to respond, and his silence unsettles me more than if he'd raged at her.

"We will have a war," Asha says, her eyes narrowing at him. "Is that what you want, Dragon King? Because if it is, then let it begin here and now. With you and me."

CHAPTER 45

Graviter Rex takes a slow step toward Asha.

The tip of his tail swishes against the remaining snowdrifts near the trees at the edge of the forest. The wounds in his side are healing much faster than I thought they would, but I've proven I can do serious damage to him if I want.

My claws remain out.

As the heavy silence between us extends, snowflakes begin to float once more through the air, a sign of the receding heat.

Graviter's lips finally part with a low rumble, but his request is unexpected.

"Wolf," he says, addressing me, although he doesn't take his eyes off Asha. "Bring me a leaf from that tree. The one beneath which Milena Ironmeld now lies."

I don't want to move too far away from Asha, let alone step all the way back to the tree, which is a good thirty paces behind us.

What's more, I'm not sure what Graviter's purpose could be right now.

I expected violence.

Instead, he's unnervingly subdued. I can't assume he isn't trying to lure me into a false sense of peace.

Before I can object, he says, "I give you my word I will not harm Asha Silverspun while you do as I ask."

I consider him carefully. *How can I tell if he's lying?*

His heartbeat is steady, his body language is relaxed.

Fuck. The answer is: I can't.

Asha gives me a little nod. I don't miss the way her fist closes around the two black medallions now pressed to her left palm.

I'm also conscious of how bloodless her lips and cheeks are.

The longer she holds that metal, the longer the pain the medallions cause her continues.

I hurry toward the tree but don't turn my back completely, keeping Graviter within my sights and my claws extended, prepared to use all my speed to sprint back to Asha at a moment's notice if I need to.

There are many leaves strewn on the ground along the way, caught on the rocky surface, but they're burned. Some are so blackened that they're curled into the shapes of cocoons.

I head for the bough that was farthest from the fire where the tree's bark is un-scorched and a few glistening, blue leaves still hang.

Quickly plucking a single one, I veer toward the trunk and to Milena, where she has remained sitting.

So far, Graviter has been true to his word and hasn't lashed out at Asha. They aren't speaking to each other. I'd be able to hear them if they were. But the fragile truce between them gives me the chance to check on the Blacksmith woman.

Crouching to her, I quickly check the cut on her forehead, finding her skin cold.

She's alive—her heartbeats tell me so. But the beats are weak and stuttering.

She may not be long for this world.

Before the fight with Graviter Rex, it became apparent that Milena's mind was broken. We have no way of knowing how long she was encased in the monstrous tree. Long enough that it would have killed a human, but Blacksmiths are stronger than both human and fae.

When we freed Milena, which was only moments before Graviter stormed upon us, she struggled to remain lucid.

It seemed that she couldn't remember anything about how she'd gotten here—or about the Blacksmith who'd put her here.

She wasn't even able to speak Thaden's name.

In fact, it seemed that every time she tried to remember him, the effort would trigger her to slip into a momentarily unresponsive state. I'm not sure if that's because of something he did to her, or because the loss of her power traumatized her, or because she spent so long encased in the tree that its darkness had consumed some of her memories.

No matter the reason, if there's a chance we can revive her, we need to take it. We can't afford to lose her knowledge of Thaden Kane.

Of course, keeping her alive in the longer term could be problematic since Asha vowed to end her. It was part of the bargain Asha made with the Fae Queen to keep me alive. But, as I tried to convince Asha, she didn't promise *when* she would fulfill her vow.

Rapidly retracting my claws, I scoop Milena up out of the clumped ice that has remained around the base of the tree.

In the distance, Asha doesn't look surprised by my action.

She gives me the briefest smile that quickly fades as she refocuses on the dragon.

Graviter, on the other hand, appears wary, tilting his head and narrowing his eyes at me. I guess it doesn't make a lot of sense that I would fill my hands with this woman and hinder my ability to fight him.

I don't plan to hold her for long.

She's icy cold in my arms, so I take the chance to sidestep toward one of the pelts resting on the ground. Asha and I wore them to stay warm on our journey here. This one must have floated on the water's surface instead of sinking because it's mostly dry.

I wrap it around Milena, its dry side toward her skin, and place her on a bare patch of rock where the dragon's heat has kept the stone warm.

There isn't much more I can do for her until we resolve the situation with Graviter.

Carefully making my way back to him, I hold out the leaf I plucked from the tree.

Graviter sweeps a single claw across the air, impales the leaf on its tip, and holds the frond to his nose.

He gives a little huff.

Then he pops the leaf into his mouth and chews.

My eyebrows have risen. So have Asha's.

His behavior is baffling now.

In the next moment, his irises dilate so fully, they seem to be defying the afternoon sunlight reflected off the snow-capped peaks around us.

Then he exhales and I'm dismayed by the flames curling once more around his mouth.

Then I'm startled to see that they're a burning-blue color, and that, once again, the dragon seems fixated on Asha.

I quickly prepare to step between them.

"Asha Silverspun." Graviter growls, emitting sapphire flames as he speaks.

She throws her head back and stands her ground. "Have you chosen war, Dragon King?"

"Yes," he says, his voice heavy. "There will be a war. I see it now. I see it all."

He takes a step toward her and still, she stands her ground.

"A war in which dragons, humans, Blacksmiths, and fae

will stand across a battlefield and be tested," he continues, his head lowering to the ground, his eyes nearly in line with hers. "A war that will only be the beginning of other wars. But without a beginning, there can't be an end."

Asha's left hand rises. Her stance shifts. It's a fighting pose I saw her take a hundred times when she faced a monster. In those moments, she was single-minded. Nothing could stop her.

Nothing could distract her.

I crouch to the ground, ready to spring at the dragon, but Asha's right hand flies out toward me as if to command me: *Stop.*

My eyes widen at her gesture.

Damn. Maybe she won't ask for help, after all.

"A war that begins with the purest flame and an impossible choice," Graviter rumbles. "*Your* choice."

"What choice?" she asks, a demand for an answer.

Graviter doesn't give it.

Flames as blue as the purest sunlit sky burst from his mouth, rushing across the short distance between him and Asha.

My shout of fear is drowned in the shrieking fire. "*Asha! No!*"

I leap forward, but so does Asha.

She throws herself into the flames, her left hand outstretched toward the dragon's face.

The blue flame engulfs her, filling the air with light so bright that it blasts me backward.

CHAPTER 46

I find myself lying on the stony ground, unable to understand why I can't get up until I realize there's an immense pressure on my chest.

When the light burst toward me, so, too, did the dragon's paw strike me, but not with talons extended.

I recall the *thump* of the dragon's paw against my torso as it drove me to the rocky surface and now pins me there.

I can't see anything through the brightness in the air except the paw that restrains me.

An icy heat is cracking my heart. "Asha!"

I'm ready to stab and slice at the dragon's leg to free myself from his hold when a heartbeat later, the flames stop.

The light clears a little. Not completely, but enough to allow me to see through it to Asha.

She has remained standing, now very close to Graviter's face.

Both of her hands are turned, palms up.

Blue light pulses around her, swishing across her legs, torso, arms, and head. It plays most intensely across her arms, where she appears transfixed by it, her gaze following its ebbs and flows up and down her forearm.

"What have you done to her?" I growl at the dragon. My claws are drawing his blood, but I don't care. "What are you doing to Asha?"

His focus swings to me and he rumbles back at me, "Be calm, Wolf. You can't help her. She has to make her choice."

Be calm? Easier to command than to obey. It's impossible to feel anything but fear right now. I only snarl harder, my claws pressing into his paw.

"Be calm, Wolf," the dragon says more forcefully, giving me his full attention. "Your fear won't help her."

I force myself to retract my claws—a move that makes the dragon wince when the sharp edges glide across his skin.

"I'm calm," I snap. "Let me up."

He arches an eyebrow at me.

I wouldn't believe me, either.

Still, his hold on me eases. As soon as it does, I jump to my feet.

Within the circle of light, Asha continues to appear transfixed, and I'm not sure she can even hear us.

"Keep your distance," Graviter warns with a low voice. "It's up to Asha whether or not she accepts the gift of light magic that I'm offering her."

"Light magic?"

"Every dragon is a creature of light magic," Graviter says. "But not every dragon is born with the ability to share their light. Only fire dragons have that ability, and even then, not all of them. There is one of us in every generation, and sometimes not even that. *My* fire can fill a receptive heart with light."

I remember how the fae healer, Gliss, described dragons. She said they aren't like other creatures, that their thoughts are complex and concealed with magic: *light* magic. The purest kind.

At the time, I recognized what she said about light magic. It's the same deep light that my father's people revered—the same light that I burned to stay alive when Malak transformed me.

"You were right, Wolf." Graviter's expression is solemn now. "Asha Silverspun has the power to alter the nature of darkness itself. The composition of the leaf proved it to me. But if she wishes to save her family, she must be prepared to accept my gift of light and its consequences."

He calls it a 'gift'.

But all I can see is the deep light bursting from my father's body when his own light magic gave him the strength to fight the Blacksmiths.

The final burst before his death became inevitable.

The dragon isn't lying. I recognize now that these sapphire flames are pure light magic.

But Asha's death is what I fear.

It's what I've fought against since the moment I found her in the snow all those years ago.

I can't stop my savage snarl. "You would give her the gift of death?"

Graviter shakes his head. "I would give her the ability to fight the war she needs to fight. But to face it as she truly is, not as she was made to be."

I'm not sure what he means.

For once, *I'm* on the receiving end of ambiguous answers and hidden meanings and I don't like it.

But I take his warning seriously. Every instinct in my body is telling me to stay clear of Asha right now.

Her chest is rising and falling rapidly. She continues to stare at her palms, her forehead creasing, her lips pressing together.

Her hair and skin were tarnished by forge fire when the

humans ground up crimson coal and created an explosion that was intended to kill her.

That fire permanently melded one of Malak's medallions to her left hand and it's been part of her for over a week now.

It changed her, but not in my eyes.

When I look at her, I see her as she was: kind, determined, beautiful.

Graviter focuses back on her and it's clear he's speaking to Asha when he says, "Who are you?"

I wasn't sure if she could hear anything outside the light, but it seems she can. Without looking up, she replies softly, "I don't know anymore."

He exhales softly and little tendrils of blue light waft across the space between them. "I have eaten the memories you poured into that tree, Asha Silverspun. You don't have to confess anything to me. I know it all."

She finally looks up at him, tipping her head back, and even though she is so much smaller in stature than he is, her presence is somehow more powerful.

She's barely tested the limits of the magic she controls and for the first time... that scares the fuck out of me.

How far can her power reach? How much more can she do?

"Are you a beast?" the dragon asks her.

"I can be," she says.

He nods. Pauses. "Are you a killer?"

She doesn't look away. "I have been."

Again, the dragon nods. "Are you a sister?"

This time, she's slower to answer. "I was."

Her answer makes my forehead crease because I was sure she'd say *yes*.

She continues quietly. "I was a sister for the first nine years of my siblings' lives. After that, I was a stranger."

Fuck.

I did that to her.

I convinced myself it was the only way to keep them all alive, to separate them and ensure that the human community saw Tamra and Gallium as powerless. I told myself it would only be for a short time and that I'd soon find a way to make them safe and get them all to the mountains.

Soon. But that day didn't come soon.

Over time, I justified my inaction and my failure, telling myself that Tamra and Gallium weren't strong enough yet, reassuring myself with the knowledge that their power hadn't yet returned. Convincing myself there wasn't a safe way to free them.

But all the time, I knew the truth: Asha was my last connection with the family I lost.

She was my last reason for living.

I didn't want to let her go.

It was fucking selfish.

I made her a stranger to her family. I tore them apart.

There is nothing I can ever do to atone for that.

The dragon king asks her, "If you have become a stranger to your brother and sister, why would you risk your life to save them?"

Immediately, she says, "Because I love them."

Love is powerful.

But it doesn't always drive us to goodness. *This* I know.

Graviter edges toward her. "I'm offering you the gift of my light magic, Asha Silverspun. I've breathed it from my soul into the air around you, but it's up to you if you will accept the help it can give you. So I ask you: What would you do to keep your family safe?"

She holds his gaze. "Anything."

"Then make your choice, Asha Silverspun."

He steps back, and it seems he's done talking.

Asha lowers her eyes from the dragon and across to me, and now I can see that there's a battle raging within her mind.

I don't know what choice she's making, and my inability to help her draws growls of frustration to my lips.

All I can do is wait.

She exhales, a soft sound that reaches me beneath the humming light.

"I have to try," she whispers, as if she's trying to explain her reasons to me, even though I don't know what she's deciding.

Without another moment's pause, she slips her hammer from the belt at her waist and drops it to the ground, where it lands with a *clang*.

Then she turns her left hand over, palm down.

The dragon-imprinted medallion and the plain, black band fall together to the stone, clattering and landing near the hammer.

But the medallion fused to her palm stays where it is. It's part of her and would never simply fall off...

Her chest is rising and falling rapidly as she uses her free hand to press against the end of the band where it wraps beneath her left thumb.

Her face fills with pain, strain in the lines around her mouth and eyes, as she rams her fingernail under the medallion's edge.

With a scream, she rips the metal upward.

CHAPTER 47

The muscles in Asha's arms bulge as she tears the black medallion off her palm.

The band must be fighting her because she's gripping it hard enough to turn her knuckles white, straining against it, her body shaking and her teeth gritted.

"Let me go!" she screams at it, tears spilling down her cheeks. "I don't want this. I never wanted this!"

Her pain and anguish force me back a step.

I was the one who made her pick up the hammer. I forced her to connect with the darkness. I told myself it was the only way to keep her alive, to make her into something the humans needed and couldn't do without.

The final edge of the medallion lifts up. The brilliant-blue light immediately washes down her forearm and converges on her palm.

She drops the medallion and it hits the stone beside the other two with a heavy *thud*.

I catch a glimpse of her palm where her flesh is red and raw.

Then the sapphire light bursts into a renewed flame, billowing and rushing over her entire body. It forms a tornado that buffets her, plucking at her torn clothing and her hair, once again too bright to look at.

The way her silhouette moves tells me her knees are buckling.

This time, the dragon doesn't make a move to push me away. Maybe he will, but I can't stay back.

I launch myself into the brightness, reaching Asha just as her legs give way.

"Asha!" I catch her before she falls to the ground, both of us enveloped in the light.

She rests in my arms, her face turned up to mine, a soft exhalation on her lips.

I thought the light might burn me, since it wasn't intended for me, but it's soft, brushing my skin like feathers.

It flows across Asha's hair and skin in waves, and my eyes widen when it seems to draw out the tarnish as it goes, leaving her skin pale and new, stripping the darkness from her eyes and hair.

As the energy finally recedes and silence falls, she is, once again, silver-haired and her eyes seem to shift between blue and green and even violet.

"The light allowed me to lift the medallion from my hand," she whispers. "It gave me the strength to fight back. I'm me again."

But then she slumps in my arms. Her eyes flood with new tears and she lets them fall. "I'm powerless again."

I shake my head, my voice sticking in my throat. "You were never powerless."

As I speak, Graviter Rex shifts closer so that he towers over us, his body blocking out the late afternoon light. His voice breaks the hush that has fallen over us.

"Asha Silverspun, do not pick up that hammer or touch those medallions again," he says. "The dark magic within them is unforgiving. If you touch them again, you will never rid yourself of them."

Asha's response is heavy with frustration, her luminous eyes seeking the dragon's. "I may not have a choice. Milena Ironmeld is the last hammer-maker and she's lost her power. I will never have tools of my own. Without tools, I can't fight Thaden Kane."

Graviter takes a deep breath, strong enough to pull at the air around us as he nods. "It's true that Milena is the last hammer-maker, but Blacksmith hammers were not always made this way."

"What?" She sits a little straighter in my arms. "What do you mean?"

He lowers his face to hers, his deadly teeth far too close to her for my liking. "I mean there may be another way. It's very dangerous, but it's possible."

"Dangerous," she whispers, some of the light leaving her eyes before it surges again, her lips pressing in a determined line. "Nothing is too dangerous if it means protecting my family."

But the protest is already leaving my mouth. "What other way?" I demand to know. "If there was another way, Malak would have used it. He wanted nothing more than to give Asha a hammer so he could access her power and use it for his own purposes."

The dragon's lips stretch back. "This is a way known only to dragons."

"And it's dangerous." My brow furrows and my arms tighten around her. "Asha—"

All she has to do is turn her gaze to mine and I know that arguing is pointless. I exhale my concern. I can't help the small smile touching my lips. "I will help you. Whatever it takes."

She gives me a nod.

The dragon casts me a solemn look. "First, we need a forge."

Asha chews her lip for a moment. "We were led to believe that dragons are aligned with the human army in the west," she says. "Is that true?"

"It is." The dragon growls. "Humans have always been our allies. Sometimes, we even allow them to ride us."

"Can we seek shelter with those humans?" she asks, then adds, "Because they must have forges."

Graviter appears to ponder this before he shakes his head. "It would not be wise. Thaden knows where they're located. He grew up in their villages and has been inside their stronghold. If he seeks to find you, Asha Silverspun, then it will put the last free humans in danger. They're already under attack from the fae."

The fae have battled their way across the west to escape the dark rot that has taken hold of their land in the east. It's a rot that spread from the wasteland the Blacksmiths created.

The Fae Queen Karasi claimed that the humans in the west had rejected every peace treaty she offered, but it's far from clear that she truly wants peace.

Graviter continues. "Milena has her own personal forge, but likewise, Thaden knows its location, so we can't go there, either." He huffs. "But it may be our only option."

I'm very still now. My chest feels like it's constricting.

I know of a forge. One I haven't been back to in ten years because I could never revisit the place where my father died.

When I speak, my voice is wooden. "There is a forge that Thaden Kane won't know about. It's only small and simple and there's a possibility that it may no longer be intact."

"We need only the basics: an anvil, a human hammer, a pair of tongs, and a fireplace that can contain the hottest flame," Graviter says. "Can the place you speak of provide that?"

My arms feel numb where they rest around Asha. "It can."

Heat licks around Graviter's sharp teeth. "Then it will suffice."

"What of the raw metal we'll need?" Asha asks, a sound question since a hammer can't be made out of air.

"Don't worry about the rest," Graviter replies with a confident smile. "I will provide it."

The numbness in my body only spreads. "I can take us there."

Asha's forehead is lightly creased. Despite the possibility that she might finally have a hammer, she seems focused entirely on me now.

"Erik?" Her hands press against my chest before she reaches up to cup my cheek with her left hand—the hand I saved all those years ago. "What is it?"

I can't answer her question. She's resting within the circle of my arms, wide awake while snowflakes drift around us. White flecks that take me back to places I haven't visited in my mind for a long time.

For the last ten years, I couldn't stand to set foot on snow, to feel it crunch beneath my boots, to be reminded of the cold and the fresh mountain breeze and the hunting knives I once held in my hands. And the faces of my father and brother as they stood beside me on the hunt.

For years, Skirra's wolfish mind and his wild nature kept the memories at bay, but now I have to fight to stop them flooding back.

"Erik." Her voice is soft. "Whatever it is, wherever this forge is, if going there will cause you pain, we will find another way. We can find another place."

I close my eyes, needing to block out the concern in her eyes because she has the power to break the boundaries around the memories and set them free.

Shaking my head, I say, "This forge is our best option. It's hidden and nobody knows about it."

Nobody still living.

Her soft palm presses to my cheek, and I lean into her when she lifts herself up a little so she can touch her cheek to mine.

When I open my eyes, she draws back with a whisper, "I'm here when you're ready to tell me what's wrong."

How does she always know how to strike into my heart?

With her kindness or her anger or even her fear.

She tugs at my soul so forcefully, it's as if she could draw deep light out of me, even though it's gone.

"How far away is this place?" Graviter asks.

"Far," I say. "We will need to head south toward the human city there."

"You mean Vadlig Odemark?" the dragon asks, his eyes widening. "The cursed wasteland."

Asha also appears surprised. "The city we escaped from?"

"Not into it," I clarify. "We need to keep west and head toward the peak of the mountains that sit on its western side."

The dragon makes a rumbling sound in his throat. "That is closer to Vadlig Odemark than is safe for dragons," he says, his brow drawn in a fierce furrow. "But if we fly west and then cut back to come at those mountains from behind, we can avoid detection from within the city."

"Fly?" Asha asks, warily eyeing Graviter's big face and then his scaled body.

He grins suddenly. "Yes, but not on me."

With that, he backs away and swivels toward the forest that rests before the clearing—the forest through which we traveled for five days.

"Torva Viridia!" he roars. "I know you're there." His fierce eyes glare across the trees. "Show yourself!"

I'm alarmed by the fact that whatever being Graviter is calling, I can't discern its presence.

All I see are trees and all I hear is the softest breeze.

Then the forest rustles violently, a storm of wind and sound, and another dragon, much smaller than Graviter Rex, shoots up from within the trees.

CHAPTER 48

The new dragon's scales are alternating green and blue, rippling between the colors of the forest until they settle on bright emerald.

Even across the distance, the dragon exudes a sense of intense peace. Of lush leaves, a breath of wind, and so much *life*.

My eyes widen because this dragon's presence feels like the undefined presence I sensed when we were traveling through the forest.

I'd detected another creature in the forest and a sort of *breathing*, not much more than a breeze around us that seemed to follow us along our path. Even with my wolf's eyesight, I didn't see this dragon. Not even an outline of it.

Its wings and body shiver as it hovers now above the forest, floating there, while its focus darts from Graviter Rex to Milena, where I laid her down on the warm stone, wrapped up in a fur.

"There you are, Torva Viridia," Graviter says with a huff.

"Graviter Rex," the new dragon calls in a distinctly

feminine voice. She sounds as angry as Graviter did when he first raged at us. "Do you mean to fight me?"

The air seems to rush out of Graviter's mouth, and his shoulders sink a little. His reply is quiet. "I do not."

"Yet you declared war on my rider and vowed to kill her."

Graviter bristles a little. "Milena Ironmeld has much to answer for."

"We all make mistakes," Torva snaps. "Especially when it comes to the ones we love. Betrayal from those closest to us cannot always be foreseen."

Graviter is quiet for a moment. "I concede that I did not foresee Thaden's duplicity, either."

Torva considers him for a moment, still hovering, her wings beating slowly, her focus flashing once more to Milena. "Then will you let me go to her?"

Graviter backs up a little, although there isn't really enough space for him to go anywhere. "You may."

Tucking her wings, Torva shoots toward Milena, landing beside her in a rush of wind that rustles the blue leaves on the tree Asha healed.

Her expression becomes increasingly downcast as she looks Milena over until tears form in her emerald eyes.

Finally Torva says, "Milena Ironmeld will not live another day." She takes a deep, shuddering breath. "There is nothing we can do but make her as comfortable as possible for her final hours."

"I'm sorry, Torva," Graviter says, his voice a sad growl.

Torva nods, her eyes glistening. "Thaden lured her here. It was the same night we heard that he had killed your son. She didn't think about her own safety or how it might appear if she went to him. She was heartbroken that he had chosen his father's path. She wanted only to bring him back to face justice. I flew her here, but he was ready to fight. I have never seen him so angry."

Her emerald scales pale as she looks at the tree and the monstrous creature that lies dead behind it. "He was always so peaceful. It was all a shock."

When we first arrived in this clearing, it was protected by both a monstrous bear with six powerful legs and a tree in which Milena was encased. The tree had transformed its trunk and branches into a spider-like creature, trying to trap Asha in its web.

The tree and the bear had both been implanted with a device like the one Malak used on me. If anything, those devices were even more elaborate and skillfully created than the one that changed me into a wolf.

Torva continues. "The moment we arrived, I was driven back by the dark magic in that tree and that monster. Each time I tried to approach, I nearly passed out. The dark magic... It was killing my light and destroying the peace in my soul."

She shakes her head. "Milena threw herself into the danger. She demanded to know why Thaden killed your son. They were shouting at each other and it was hard to hear them through the pall of darkness, but he spoke of you, Asha Silverspun."

Torva's focus swings to Asha, whose shoulders have tensed.

Asha has remained kneeling beside me but slowly draws away from me, as if she expects she will need to leap to her feet at any moment to face another threat. "Why?" she demands to know. "What did he know about me?"

"He knew everything that Milena knew," Torva replies. "Everything she also divulged to me. That you were imprisoned in the cursed city by a beast of Malak's making, and that your power of creation, should you be able to access it, would be limitless."

My breath stills. It feels like a lifetime ago that Asha and I stood together in her room in the tower, her cage in the sky, and I pressed my palm to her chest above her heart in the same way she'd pressed her hand to my heart when I wrapped her up in furs and kept her warm.

I told her that I saw her as two opposing natures constantly in conflict with each other. Fragile but strong. Fearful yet unafraid. Compliant but deeply defiant.

I told her there was only one respect in which she was constant.

She is limitless.

Now, Asha's jaw clenches and in her eyes, I see a flicker of the darkness that clouded her mind when she was exposed to Malak's dark metal.

For a moment, I can't stop my own tension from rising.

She's no longer in contact with the medallions or the hammer. They aren't influencing her any longer.

Yet there is the darkness.

"What did he say of me?" Asha demands to know.

"That he would find you and free you," Torva replies. "And that *you* would listen to him, even if nobody else would."

"'Free me'?" Asha's lips part and her forehead creases. "Listen to him... about what?"

Torva shakes her head. "He kept shouting that Lysander gave him no choice."

Nearby, Graviter has tensed. "My son gave him no choice?" he snarls. "What did Thaden mean by that?"

"Their speech was jumbled through the dark magic," Torva says quickly. "I heard only parts of it. Without context, I cannot give you clarity."

"Without clarity, misinterpretation is easy." I growl, fully aware that I have used partial truths and ambiguity many times to achieve a particular outcome.

I remember again the way that Thaden spoke to Asha when he was captive in my prison. He asked her why she was doing the bidding of a wolf when she could raze the entire city to the ground.

Torva continues. "But I heard one thing clearly: Thaden Kane demanded that Milena make you a hammer, Asha. He wanted to deliver it to you."

Asha's eyes widen, while mine narrow.

"Milena refused," Torva says, her voice wobbling. "And that's when she cut off her own hand so he could not force her to craft the hammer."

"*She* cut it off? Her own hand?" Asha's green eyes flash to me. "But she said…"

"She implied that her attacker cut off her hand," I say.

Asha's lips press into an unhappy line. "I don't like this. He wanted to free me? Speak with me? He thought I would believe him? Something isn't right here."

Once again, it feels like we're on the cusp of danger.

"Without clarity," I growl again.

Asha nods rapidly. "Misinterpretation could get us killed. It could get my family killed." She shakes her head, a near-wild movement. "He wouldn't have kept up his façade if he didn't want to keep my family alive to use them as leverage against me. But if he becomes volatile and thinks he has no other options, he may act without reason."

Across the way, Torva is downcast. "I'm sorry I can't provide the answers you need, Asha Silverspun. As soon as Milena cut off her own hand, Thaden raged at her. He entrapped her in the tree. He took her hammer and her three medallions. I couldn't stop him from leaving. He was already a skilled Blacksmith and his physical strength, now that he has merged with Lysander, is immense."

He's as strong as I am. When he first appeared and I had him imprisoned, he easily broke through his chains—although he pretended to be constrained at first. Bronze dragon scales extend across his right shoulder, up the side of his neck, and down his right arm. Also down his torso beneath his arm, extending to his waist.

Torva draws herself upright again as she focuses on me. "I heard what you said about a forge, Wolf. You cannot safely ride Graviter. His scales will rip up the skin on your legs. But my scales are soft. You and Asha can ride with me."

Graviter speaks up. "I can carry Milena in my talons."

Torva bristles. "You will break her back that way."

"I can hold on to her," I say quietly, glancing at Asha, knowing that she will no longer have the same physical strength she did when she had access to her power. "Between us, we can keep Milena safe on your back, Torva Viridia."

"Very well," Graviter says. "Gather your things and we will find this forge."

CHAPTER 49

The wind rushes past us as Torva Viridia sweeps her wings and carries us up into the air and across the cliff's edge.

My stomach plummets, but I focus on keeping myself on her back and holding on to Milena where she rests between Asha and me. We're both facing forward with Asha in front and me at the back.

Graviter hangs back behind us. According to him, if he takes off at the same time, the strength of his wing beats will knock Torva off course.

She doesn't disagree.

Before we took to the air, we retrieved our satchels from the edge of the forest, along with our fur coats, which we quickly pulled on.

Using a piece of broken tree bark, I scooped up the discarded black hammer and three medallions and dropped them into the toolbox Asha brought with her.

The device she pulled from my heart rests in there, along with her grandmother's silver medallion. That medallion was the last object that Asha's grandmother ever forged, and she poured all of the goodness of her heart into it. It helped Asha to overcome the darkness of Malak's medallion for a time.

Last of all, we gathered up the two onyx spears we brought with us. When Asha fought a monstrous wolf that rose up in the wasteland on her final day in the city—the day she saved me from death—she turned that creature to stone. It had tusks protruding from its face. Each tusk is long and thin and gently curved with a sharp tip at its pointed end.

She used the tusks as poles to fashion a sled on which she dragged me to safety, but they've been useful as spears since then.

The substance they're made of has proven to be unbreakable. Asha's magic can't shatter them.

Now, Graviter carries them in his talons as he finally rises into the air behind us—and that's the last I see of the snow-covered cliff and the tree Asha healed before I'm forced to face fully forward.

It's impossible to speak, as any sound I could try to make would be drowned in the rush of wind, but I described the location to Torva before we left so she can recognize it within the western mountains.

For the next hour, we travel farther west before turning to head southward. We're closer to the coastline than I've ever been, a salty tang filling the air.

Father once described the sea to me, the way the waves crash against the shore and the wind brings the taste of salt and brine to your tongue.

Soon enough, the salty taste gives way to the crispness of snow once more.

Torva angles a little west again, veering far wide of the cursed city that becomes visible in the distance, a mere blob that I could put my thumb over.

While the fae call the city *Vadlig Odemark*, meaning 'the

cursed wasteland', Thaden called it *Svikari Traidor*. The Home of Traitors.

Now I wonder if he came to the city thinking to free Asha from me, only to find her fighting for me. He would have come to see her as a traitor.

The sun is setting by the time Torva flies back toward the western peaks from the far side, her body casting a final shadow across the trees below us before the light fades altogether.

My heart squeezes hard within my chest as I glance down at the rooftop of my old home and the smaller buildings that rest alongside it.

Torva glides for a moment, circling the clearing before she picks a spot where she slips smoothly to the ground.

Snow has built up along the long side of the cabin, although not as much as I thought there would be. At its far end, I can make out the structures that appear to have remained intact—the smokehouse and forge.

As soon as Torva touches down, Asha adjusts her position and I can imagine her arms and legs are even more sore than mine. I have my wolfish strength to call on while she has had to rely on her now-human muscles to cling to the dragon's back.

Despite my physical discomfort, I have enough insight to know that my now-wooden movements are caused by more than the ride.

My father's statute has remained in the clearing.

His back is to me and I'm grateful for that, because I'm not ready to face him yet.

He's located closer to the cabin's entrance on the far side, giving Torva plenty of space to move around within the clearing at this end.

She folds her wings and crouches low, her question urgent. "Is Milena still alive?"

"She is," Asha calls, quickly checking Milena before dropping our satchels to the snow and turning carefully so we can coordinate our movements to slide off Torva's back with Milena secured between us.

Carefully, we lay her on the snow beside Torva, the fur still wrapped around the Blacksmith.

A moment later, Graviter's large shadow looms over us.

We hold on to each other while he glides to the snow in a rush of wind.

He nearly doesn't fit between the cabin and the trees, pulling up sharply at the last moment to drop to the ground and quickly fold away his wings.

He gives a *humph*, awkwardly squeezing himself closer to us.

All the while, my father's statue remains untouched.

Asha and I end up crouched beside Milena on the ground.

Asha's silver hair is messy around her face, from the flight and Graviter's landing, but she doesn't seem to care, her perceptive gaze racing across the clearing.

Within seconds, she seems to take in the cabin, the far buildings, the surrounding trees, the snow, and finally, my father's statue.

Her questioning eyes meet mine. Pale-green eyes like faded leaves. They're the only part of her that reminds me of her father, Kalith Silverspun.

Her voice is a whisper. "Erik, what is this place?"

The answer sticks on my tongue.

I was ready to tell her everything back on the snowy cliff. I want her to know what happened, how we first met. Not the price I paid for her life, but the reason why I believed, even then, that her life was worth risking everything for.

"Asha—"

Before I can continue, Milena gasps. Her dark-blue eyes fly open and she struggles within the fur. "Graviter is here! He's coming!"

Her mind must be stuck in the moment when Graviter first stormed toward us, before she was knocked out.

Asha's hand rests down on Milena's chest. "Be still. Graviter Rex has agreed to peace. He will not hurt us now."

It doesn't escape me how stern Asha's voice sounds. How harsh she has sounded each time she's addressed Milena.

When Asha was a child, Milena deliberately gave her the wrong hammer so it would appear that Asha was weak and powerless. For years, Asha was ridiculed and mistreated by her people because of it.

It was that ridicule that led to her being dragged out into the snow in a senseless act perpetrated by her peers.

Their actions led to the deaths of my family.

Milena's choice led to the deaths of my family.

"We will take you inside this place and make you warm," Asha says. "You will not die alone, Milena, but know this: We are not your allies. The harm you caused me and those I care about can never be forgiven."

Beside us, Torva Viridia has stiffened, her emerald eyes narrowing at Asha's harsh words. Then she softens, a slump to her shoulders, because there's no denying the pain in Asha's voice.

Milena's brow has smoothed out and now she's focused entirely on Asha. I expect the older woman's response to be jumbled and difficult to comprehend—just as her replies were muddled before Graviter arrived on the snowy cliff.

I'm surprised when she replies softly, but clearly. "It was my intention to keep you safe from my brother."

"You failed," Asha says. "And then you left." Her chest rises and falls rapidly. "You left me to the brutes and the beasts. You exposed me to my mother's switch and the back of my father's hand and my people's brutality. You left me unable to protect my siblings when they needed me the most. Unable to protect the humans. Unable to stand up when someone should have stood up—"

Her voice chokes. Tears glisten in her eyes, but the pure anger in her voice tells me they're tears of rage.

She takes a deep, shuddering breath, and the clearing around us is suddenly so quiet that the dragons may as well have stopped breathing. Both of them hang their heads low to the ground, as if Asha's words weigh them down.

"You had the power to stop all of that from happening, but you chose the easy path," Asha says. "You chose to protect yourself."

Milena is very still where she lies. And then, she whispers, "I did. I protected myself."

CHAPTER 50

Milena's admission causes Torva's head to lift, the dragon's eyes widening. It's clear it wasn't the response the emerald dragon expected from her rider.

Graviter has also raised his head, his eyes narrowed. When he first raged at us, he called Blacksmiths 'murderers'. He said that there was nothing but betrayal and darkness in their hearts.

Milena doesn't take her eyes off Asha. "From the moment I first saw you when you were a baby, I knew that the light magic within you was beyond any power any Blacksmith had ever wielded. Light magic!" she exclaims. "We are not creatures of the light and have never been. And I..." She swallows visibly. "I was afraid."

"Afraid of me?"

"Afraid of the justice you would bring. Even when you were a mere five years old, I saw it in your eyes. I saw the way you looked at us. At me."

"You feared me," Asha says. "You hated me."

"Yes!" Milena gasps. "Yes, I hated you. Because you could tear our world apart. Tear our power down."

"So you tore me apart first."

"I did." Her gaze wavers for the first time. "I convinced myself I did it to protect you from my brother. I told myself he was too cunning. He would find a way to exploit your power for his own purposes. And by then, I was writhing within his grip. Trapped. Unable to breathe because of his darkness, and when I saw a chance..."

Milena falters for the first time since she started speaking.

"And then..." Her forehead creases and her lips purse. "I had a reason to escape..." She struggles against the fur wrapped around her. "I had to go, but I don't remember..."

"Thaden Kane Ironmeld was born," Asha says.

Milena blinks up at her. The moment Asha speaks his name, Milena's face becomes completely blank and devoid of recognition.

My heart sinks to see it.

Every time we've asked her who attacked her, or any other question relating to Thaden Kane, she has been unable to answer.

Resignation is heavy in Asha's voice. "She can't tell us anything about him."

My jaw clenches. "We will find the answers ourselves."

At the sound of my voice, Milena's focus shifts to me. Then to the trees behind me, then to the buildings behind Torva.

The structures are partially blocked from Milena's view by Torva's body, but I'm startled when she fixates on the cabin's roof and the spot where a turret is hidden.

That was the turret from which Thoren shot the arrows that killed a Blacksmith.

"I know this place," Milena whispers, startling me.

Back on the snowy cliff, she called me by my birth name,

Erik, not *Vandawolf,* as every Blacksmith knew me then, and now it looks as if she recognizes my home.

She struggles within the fur again, wriggling her left hand free despite the pressure of Asha's hand and reaches for me, her eyes suddenly bright. "Is your father here?"

I can't stop myself from recoiling—away from her grasping hand and the unexpected hope in her eyes.

She falters a little at my reaction, her hand hovering in the air. "Is... Thoren here?"

I don't understand how she knows my birth name, let alone knows about my family. She was long gone from the city by the time Thoren and I were captured, and I can't see how she would have known about my father in such a way that she would ask about him.

My voice is a cold growl. "My family is dead."

Her choice to withhold a hammer from Asha led to their deaths, but it was *my* choices that killed them.

Her forehead creases. "But... I..."

She closes her eyes and tears trickle from them.

Torva takes glances between me and Graviter, who is an increasingly tense form nearby.

I'm not sure what the silent communication between them means, but Graviter seems to capitulate, sighing softly as his anger appears to dissolve.

"Milena," Torva says softly, nudging her side. "Please let us take you inside, where you can be warm."

"No!" Milena's protest is sharp.

Her eyes fly open and her hand darts out to wrap around my wrist.

I could easily shake her off, but she grits her teeth as she looks at me. "I'm dying. I know it. I can feel my life waning. I can feel the final rush of energy within me before death will claim me. There are things I need to say while I can."

Her strength wanes and her hand slips away from me. "You will allow me say them," she says. "And then you will let me die here in the snow."

CHAPTER 51

Milena's voice softens as she gazes up at me. "You look so much like your father."

"How did you know him?" I can't keep the growl from my voice. "How do you know my name?"

A tear trickles down her cheek. "I met your father in these mountains soon after he first arrived here. You see, this forest was my particular playground."

My brow furrows at the description she uses. "'Playground'?"

"Yes, Erik," she whispers, fully fixated on me in the same way she was fixated on Asha. "I was responsible for the monstrous leopards and the malformed butterflies and all the other vicious creatures that ran and crawled and flew in this forest. I did not have my brother's special power over living things, but I found other ways to manipulate life."

I narrow my eyes at her because if it's true that she knew about us, then I can't see how she wouldn't have told her brother. "But Malak didn't know we were here."

He was surprised on that day when he tracked us to our home, I'm sure of it.

"I didn't tell anyone." Milena sighs. "In my hunger for power and my determination to push the limits of what I could create, I had destroyed so much of this place. Your father, when I first came upon him, had just killed a leopard. He was kneeling to it, speaking words of respect for its strong spirit."

She closes her eyes and repeats the blessing that I, too, gave the beasts I killed. "'You have a strong spirit and you fought well'," she whispers. "'May you fill your belly in the Hall of Warriors and sleep by the warmth of the eternal light.'"

She opens her eyes. "That's what he said to that wretched creature. Then he rose up and turned to me, and I will never forget the fury in his eyes as he gripped his sword and asked me if he would soon need to speak a blessing over my dead body, too." The faintest smile crosses her lips. "It was clear he thought he could kill me."

Near to me, Asha has fallen silent. When I look at her, she's contemplating me with an expression I can't decipher. Her heartbeat is steady. Her hand has remained on Milena's chest. But there's a tension in her posture that wasn't there before.

No. Not tension.

Sadness.

I've told her very little about my family. She knows that I'm descended from the Einherjar and that, when my brother was born, our father left his people behind. She knows I didn't grow up in the city. And she knows that my father's creed was to protect the people he loved at all costs.

She knows that Blacksmiths killed my family.

"Nobody had ever challenged me like your father did," Milena says to me, her voice fainter now. "And then, there you were, you and Thoren, both little children, clearly unaware of the danger I posed to you. You were both so full of life and completely unafraid of me."

Her faint smile fades. "It was the first time in many years

that any child had looked at me without fear in their eyes. Even Blacksmith children were taught to stay away from me."

She takes a shallow breath and my heightened senses allow me to detect that the act of breathing is becoming more difficult for her now. "I told your father I would leave him be. I promised he would not be disturbed as long as he didn't come anywhere near the city."

Her focus slips away from me, lifting to the stars that are now appearing in the night sky. "This forest was mine. Nobody was allowed here except for me, and nobody would risk displeasing me. Not even my own brother."

She's silent for a long moment before she sighs.

With that exhalation, I hear the near-silence within her chest.

The slowing of her heart.

"My brother was broken," she whispers. "I couldn't allow another Ironmeld child to grow up unloved."

Tears drip down her cheeks as she stares upward, her focus glazed now, but her heart gives a final, strong *thud.*

With that heartbeat, it's as if a surge of energy must allow her to fight through the damage within her mind because she whispers, "I lied to Thaden. I told him that his father loved him, even though Malak never knew he had a son..."

Milena's whisper fades into silence.

A silence that stretches while night settles around us.

In the distance, the creatures of the forest begin scurrying, some more softly than others, while the wind picks up, blowing the snow off the leaves.

"She's gone," Torva says, lowering her head to Milena's chest.

Beside me, Asha is stiff.

"Milena's body is mine now," she says.

Her stern declaration makes me study Asha more closely, the tension around her eyes and lips, the set of her shoulders.

Torva raises her head, a puzzled crease between her eyes. "What did you say?"

Asha doesn't look away from the dragon, her voice harsh. "The Fae Queen sent me to hunt Milena. I had no issues with that. Milena deserved to pay for what she did. So I came to kill her. Thaden Kane merely got to her first."

Tension rises within me at the intense anger in Asha's voice and the fact that her description of her intentions isn't actually accurate.

It's true that she was hunting Milena at Queen Karasi's command. But it was part of a deal in which Asha had had no choice.

In exchange for my life, Asha promised to kill Milena Ironmeld and bring her dead body to Karasi as proof of her death. It was the only way Asha could keep me alive.

I move to speak, but Torva has already lurched forward, her talons closing around Milena's body. The peace she exuded just moments before has vanished.

In its place is a deep fury.

"You cannot have her body," the emerald dragon snarls. "The fae cannot have her!"

Asha leaps to her feet. "I am owed for the pain Milena Ironmeld caused me," she shouts, her voice sounding nothing like the compassionate person I know her to be. "I will take Milena's body to the fae and they will do whatever they wish with it. Hang it from the ramparts. Put her head on a spike. Burn her where all can see—"

"No!" Torva wrenches Milena's body upward before she leaps away from Asha and into the only remaining space near the trees.

Torva's wings shoot out, the force of their movement sending a violent whirlwind of air through the forest, making the trees bend and sway.

"No? Then you had better run, Torva," Asha snarls, stepping toward the dragon, as if she would come after Milena.

At that, Torva takes to the air, clutching Milena's body in her talons. The Blacksmith woman is still wrapped in a fur, but her dark hair flows behind her in the night.

Within seconds, they're a mere speck in the distance.

Asha stops still in the snow, standing beside the deep furrow that Torva's talons made when her powerful legs pushed her into the air.

Now, Asha doesn't shout or rage. She's startlingly quiet after her vicious outburst and, once again, her heartbeat is heavy.

I'm worried that Graviter will react to what she said and did, but when I glance back at him, he hasn't moved from his cramped spot, his head tilted and a sigh on his lips that rustles the trees.

I approach Asha cautiously. "Asha?"

Her shoulders slump. "I learned well from you, Erik."

As I draw level with her, she closes her eyes briefly.

"I learned well from the Vandawolf," she says.

Her use of my former name makes me even more wary.

"Asha?" My tension increases as I wait for her to explain.

She speaks slowly. "Torva's heart is so pure and good that she would have willingly caused herself pain if I asked her to. To help me, I'm certain she would have let me take Milena's body to the fae."

Asha meets my eyes. "Even though it would have meant that Torva, and any humans who love Milena, would have had to endure whatever cruelty Queen Karasi planned for Milena's body." Asha's voice hardens, a snarl once more, but now there are tears in her eyes. Angry tears. "The fae have no right to the body of a Blacksmith!"

"No, they don't," I murmur, casting my gaze up into the

night sky, where Torva flew. "So you gave Torva a reason to run."

Just as I gave Asha a reason to hate me enough to leave me to my fate.

Asha nods. "From you, I learned an important lesson: Sometimes, I must be a villain to achieve what's right."

CHAPTER 52

Many times I played the villain, making moves and countermoves to keep Asha safe, no matter how much she hated me.

But always I wondered if there was another way.

There should have been another way.

Graviter's voice breaks through the silence between Asha and me.

"That little forge will do," he says with a slight incline of his head at the structures behind him. "You should both seek shelter and warmth before the temperature plummets."

To Asha, he says, "If I am to help you make a hammer, there are things I must collect. I will leave now, but I will return by midnight."

Doubt floods Asha's expression. "But how?" she asks. "How will you help me make a hammer?"

He gives her a smile, all sharp teeth. Without explaining himself, he turns toward the cabin's entrance.

I'm alarmed when heat waves glimmer around his lips and he breathes out softly across the air. A wash of water runs to the side of the cabin, but it doesn't catch fire like I thought it might.

"There," Graviter Rex says. "I've removed the built-up snow from around this side of the entrance. You should be able to enter now."

Then he casts another smile at Asha. "By morning, you will have your hammer, Asha Silverspun. I'm certain of it."

Her brow is furrowed. So is mine. More so when his focus flicks briefly to me.

All the moves and countermoves I carried out while I ruled the human city—all the plans I set in motion—may as well be nothing now that I'm out here in the wilderness with dragons.

It feels as if I can only control my next breath.

Graviter eases to the side a little, away from the cabin, and I'm not certain how he's going to take flight from within the cramped space, but like Torva, he bunches his hind legs and uses them to leap higher than the cabin's rooftop.

His wings snap out and he deftly beats them twice to gain air before he's far above us.

Asha and I are alone outside my family's home.

She reaches for me, slipping her arms around my waist, dropping her head to my chest and murmuring, "Don't stay away from me, Erik."

I pull her close, feeling how cold her face is when she presses her forehead to my chin.

"We need to go inside," I say. "And hope it isn't built up with snow."

Yet I can't make myself move.

"Coming here was painful for you," she says. "We don't have to stay in this spot. We can trek through the forest and make camp a short distance away. We have enough furs to stay warm."

I close my eyes and drag in her scent.

"No," I whisper. "There's a hearth inside. Along with more furs. It will only get colder out here. To shun shelter would be reckless."

She gives me a small smile. "But would forcing your heart to do things you don't want to do be more so?"

I consider her question. A body may survive, but without a heart and mind, what is left of it?

As I contemplate her features, her pale eyes now more darkly blue in the dim light, her silver hair tangled around her face, I realize that to see her once again nestled in the snow... Even if she is wrapped in furs this time...

I tug her toward the cabin, scooping up our satchels along the way. The toolbox rests inside her bag and she picks up both onyx spears from the ground where Graviter left them.

My footsteps slow as we approach my father's statue, his sword's blade catching the light. I thought it might have rusted after all these years, but it shines a bright steel-blue.

I stand at his height now, although my shoulders are somehow even broader and my chest bulkier.

I force myself to stop beside him, contemplating his features, fighting the sadness that rises up within me.

Milena was right. I do look like him.

Asha reaches out to run her hand across his arm, and I don't try to stop her.

"A powerful warrior," she whispers.

"My father," I say.

She nods. She won't have missed the resemblance. "This was Malak's doing, wasn't it?"

"Yes."

"The same way I turned monsters to stone."

"Yes."

Her jaw clenches. "I did it with the same black medallion Malak wore."

She swings to me, her hand connecting with my chest. "I'm sorry you had to watch me do that. I can't begin to imagine the painful memories it would have brought back to watch me use the same dark power that took your father's life."

I catch her hand and press my palm over it, holding it to my heart. "But you did it to save *my* life."

Her expression softens, but she slowly shakes her head. "It couldn't have erased the past."

"You're right." My voice catches in my throat, a hard lump I can't get past and now all I feel is uncertain. "Will you...? Would you...?"

She tilts her head, quietly waiting.

Back on the snowy cliff, I started to tell her that the first time we met wasn't in the throne room, like she thought it was. That when we actually first met, I didn't know she was a Blacksmith.

We weren't enemies then.

She was just a girl in the snow, and I was a boy who fell in love with her in a heartbeat.

I count my breaths to steady the shakiness in my voice. "Will you come inside, help me make a fire, and allow me tell you everything?"

Her eyes are luminous in the dark, and it's hard for me to believe that she doesn't have access to her power anymore.

"Yes," she says.

"Even if some of it might hurt or surprise you?" I ask.

She doesn't falter. "I trust you, Erik. I want to hear everything you need to tell me."

I can only nod. We move away from my father's statue and head toward the cabin's entrance, finding the ground on this side of it slushy while the door is clear of snow.

I take a deep breath before I open it and step inside.

All of the scents from within the cabin rush at me, as if they were trapped all this time, bringing with them memories of fur and wolves and family.

The blood that was spilled here must have been long ago cleaned away by insects because there's no sign of it.

The weapons on the wall directly to the right have remained in place, including my father's broken war hammer.

The stairs at the far end of the space, and the loft around three sides, appear intact. Father built them to stand the test of time.

Asha heads straight for the hearth, busying herself around it, repositioning the remaining woody pieces within it before reaching for fresh logs from the small pile nearby.

I set about spreading out a fur next to the hearth before I reach for the tinder and light the fire with ease. Then I take the bucket that once contained clean water, step outside to gather snow, and bring it back to boil it.

We work in silence until the weight of the past lifts; these simple, familiar actions ease the hold I've kept on my memories.

I know Asha is listening, giving me the space and time to begin when I can.

I start where it's easy. "My wolf's name was Skirra."

CHAPTER 53

I tell her everything, speaking for a long time, stopping only to chew a small portion of our remaining food and gulp the cooled water.

I've learned to identify Asha's emotions. The small changes in her expression that match her sadness, anger, surprise, frustration, outrage, and far more rarely, happiness.

She asks quiet questions, especially about my deep light, and constrains her moments of shock, although her heartbeat gives her away, leaping and pounding when the things I say must be shifting her foundations or hurting her heart. I can see that the way I lost my family hurts her as if my family were her own.

I talk through it all, and by the time I reach our interaction in the throne room, my voice is hoarse.

"I convinced myself that the only way I could appease the humans who were screaming for your death was to deliver a punishing verdict on you. I would make you pay for the sins of your people by fighting the monsters in the wastelands. At the same time, there could be no hint that I favored you."

I clear my throat. "I needed to make you indispensable to

them, to convince them that you alone could fight those monsters. Then I put you as far away from the humans as I could get you. I chose that tower because of the way the sound carried from it to the one where I stayed. I could hear if anyone tried to attack you at night. And they did. They tried."

Her eyes have widened now, as if this final surprise is too much for her to restrain.

"They were the ones you killed, Asha," I say. "When I would come to your room at night and take you to the prison and ask you to interrogate and kill humans."

"I thought they were political assassinations," she whispers.

I shake my head. "I could tolerate dissent among my people. I didn't want to rule by fear. I knew they were conspiring to kill me from the beginning. But if they tried to hurt you—"

My jaw clenches with remembered anger—Skirra's rage—that would surface whenever Asha was threatened.

That anger clouded my reason until I wanted blood. "I wanted them to die by the hand they sought to cut off."

She's sitting opposite me on the fur now, her hands clasped in her lap. "When we met in the throne room, you looked at me as if you were trying to pull the thoughts from my head. When you took my hand, I thought you were testing me. I thought it was because you perceived my defects."

My jaw clenches. I hate that, even now, she describes her power that way.

"Were you wondering if I recognized you?"

I nod. "Even when I realized that you didn't, you were the only one who looked me in the eye. Before I was changed, there was no shortage of stares. After, you were the only one who saw *me*. Even as a beast, you saw me."

She takes a deep, shaky breath and then exhales it. "Back at the fae castle, you told me that this connection between us has only ever brought pain." She bites her lip, her eyes glistening with tears. "When you said that, I told you I wanted to go back, all the way back to the time before Malak changed you. I would ask you to run away with me. I would pull us all through the mud and slime, just as I pulled you through the wasteland when you were dying.

"I would carry Tamra and you would carry Gallium and your family would come with us too and we would never be lost." Her hand closes around my palm. "When I said that to you, you looked at me as if I'd broken your heart. I didn't understand why, but I do now."

Her voice lowers to a bare whisper. "We have both lost too much. But I won't lose any more. I won't lose my sister or my brother. And I won't lose you."

She slips forward onto my lap, her arms wrapping around me, her lips seeking mine.

Her kisses ease my frayed thoughts, calming the fears that, even now, push at me.

She traces a path to the base of my coat, tugging it apart, reaching for the bare skin beneath it. My stomach muscles tighten at her touch, my body responding to her nearness.

Her fingers are warm, her cheeks no longer pale, even though her eyes are still bright with tears.

Softly, she says, "We're alone until midnight."

I nod, not wanting to break this moment in which her touch is everything.

Her left hand rests against my side, her other hand reaching up to trace my jaw before she drops quiet kisses on my cheeks, my chin, and then back to my mouth.

"We're both free now," she says, searching my eyes. "I choose to be with you. As myself. For myself."

Neither one of us has power over the other any longer. I don't hold her captive. We aren't at the whim of the fae. She isn't fighting off the darkness in Malak's medallion.

I wrap my arms around her, my forehead pressing to hers as I inhale her scent, now tinged with a hint of wild snow.

"Erik? Will you fuck me?"

Fucking. It feels like entirely the wrong word for what we do. The way she shares her body with me is beyond the physical act, every kiss and every stroke carrying her thoughts and feelings and her trust in me to keep her heart safe.

With a groan, I answer her by capturing her lips, pulling her closer. My body hardens beneath her as she wraps her legs around my hips and pushes at my coat and tunic.

My clothing comes free, dropping to the floor beside us.

She reaches for her own upper garments, dispensing with them quickly before standing and removing her pants.

She's completely naked and seems fully at ease in front of me as she moves to drop back to the floor beside me.

Before she can descend, I rise to my feet, my arms slipping around her waist.

I capture her mouth with mine.

"Asha," I groan, sweeping her upward, guiding her legs around my hips as I drive us back toward the steps that lead up to the loft.

It's not so far away from the fire that we'll be cold and it will give me the access to her body that I crave.

I lower her down onto one of the steps, trailing kisses across her chest. I stop to kiss her breasts before I settle into a kneeling position at the base of the stairs.

She moans as my mouth closes over her breast, her hands tangling in my hair as I move lower, trailing kisses across her stomach. My lips brush across the top of one of her thighs and then the other while she closes her eyes and inches closer to the edge of the step.

When I lower my mouth to her center, she moans and pushes her pelvis toward me, her fingers tightening around my head.

I will never grow tired of how she tastes beneath my tongue —will never take for granted how close she invites me as she rocks against my mouth.

Her breathing grows rapid. I sense the tension growing in her stomach and the clench of her thighs, and everything in me wants to bring her to the crash like this, but she lurches forward, her hands landing on my chest and pushing me backward.

She can't hurt me, and I don't care about the hard floor beneath my back as she pulls at my pants. She removes them swiftly before she drops down again, straddling me.

I reach for her, gripping her hips as she takes hold of me and lowers herself onto me.

Damn. She takes my breath away.

My hands sweep upward, exploring her curves as she drives herself fully down and pleasure spikes through me.

She responds to my groan with a certainty that awes me, pulling my hand to her core, rocking against me, her moans full of need.

I give myself over to her wants, stroking her, holding myself back, maintaining my grip on my own pleasure until she drops her mouth to mine and whispers, "Let go."

I drive myself upward as she plunges down. Again and again, her wild breathing and her cries sending me into an upward spiral until she crashes hard against me.

She takes me with her into a crash that only makes me thirsty for more.

Her moans are still washing over me as I wrap my arms around her, my stomach muscles bunching as I sweep us upright, carry her around the stairs, and push her back against the nearest wall beside them.

I hesitate for the briefest moment, but she anticipates my question.

"Yes," she gasps as her back connects with the wooden

surface, her breathing erratic, her kisses demanding more as I drive into her again.

Her hands grip me hard, digging into my back, her legs hooked around my hips, her needy moans only increasing as I give in to the storm building between us.

Every thrust binds me to her. A connection between us that defies all the darkness we've escaped.

"Asha," I groan.

She captures my mouth, kissing me hungrily before she draws back, her eyes meeting mine, seeing me.

Always seeing me.

I move, harder and faster, until she arches into me with a scream on her lips, her fingers clawing into my back as her body thrashes against me, bringing on my own release.

My thoughts splinter, a breaking that feels endless.

I struggle to fill my chest, aware of the way she's also dragging at the air, her chest heaving.

"Erik," she whispers, her voice a bare rasp as she gasps for breath. "Don't..."

I wait for her to continue, my body shivering, my hands softening around her sides, supporting her.

"Don't betray me," she says.

My breath catches as I remember the question I would ask her every time I gave her Malak's tools and commanded her to kill another monster in the wasteland.

I would ask, *"Will you betray me?"*

And she would reply...

"Never," I whisper. I slip my arms behind her before I slide my body away from hers, not caring about the mess as I pull her close again.

As quickly as I can, I carry her to the fire, where we clean up with the cloths we find tucked inside the fur there. Then we settle beneath the warm pelts.

She lays her head onto my chest, nestling into my side and moments later, when I move to speak, I find her eyes closed.

I press a kiss to her forehead and let her sleep.

A soft howl makes me alert, my wolfish nature instantly responding to the call.

The fire is warm and so is the air around us. Midnight may be less than an hour away—the time when Graviter said he would return.

Asha is fast asleep, her breathing remaining even. She looks peaceful, even if seeing her here again takes me back years to fleeting moments in time when hope seemed possible.

Not wanting to wake her, I carefully extract myself from beneath the fur and quietly pull on my warm clothing.

Soft howls float through the air, calling me.

As quietly as I can, I exit the cabin into the cold and turn the corner into the clearing.

A white wolf sits at the edge of the trees.

My chest stills to see it.

I would know that white pelt anywhere.

I can hardly speak. "Kori?"

The wolf rises up onto its feet and that's when two more wolves step out of the shadows on either side of it.

One is a mere pup, darting forward and frolicking around the first wolf.

The third wolf moves more slowly and its coat is thinner and duller, slightly grayed.

But of course. It's been ten years.

The first wolf and the pup are too young to be Kori.

I take a knee and wait for the older wolf to reach me. "Kori."

He stops in front of me, but his head swings slowly from

side to side, looking past and around me, as if he's searching for something.

Someone.

I close my eyes and bow my head. "Thoren isn't here."

Kori gives a soft whine.

"I'm sorry," I whisper. "I couldn't keep him alive."

Tears drip down my cheeks and onto the snow, the first I've shed in this place.

Kori's body nudges up against mine and he rests his chin on my raised thigh, his faded eyes raised to me.

The way he looks at me, it's as if he already knew, because if Thoren were alive, he would never have abandoned Kori.

I stay like that for a long moment while the pup bounces forward, full of new life, scampering around me.

"You made a family for yourself," I say to Kori.

He gives a soft growl.

At which the spaces between the trees fill with wolves.

It's the largest pack I've ever seen. Most are white, their pelts clearly visible in the moonlight, although some are a pale gray.

They look strong and well-fed, which tells me there's enough food in this forest to sustain them. Which also tells me that the ecosystem must be repairing itself, for both predator and prey to flourish.

A resurgence of life to heal this forest.

A little more of my heart mends to see them and hear their chorus of soft growls and snarls, the yips of their pups, and the way they seem to defer to Kori.

He slips away from me, lifting his head, giving me a fierce growl, lips drawn back from teeth.

I answer it, giving him the respect he deserves, a deep snarl in the back of my throat.

At that, he turns and pads away, nudging the first pup toward its parent.

Within moments, the wolf pack has melted back into the trees.

But I'm not alone in this clearing for more than another few seconds.

An enormous shadow falls over me before Graviter Rex glides to the ground, making an impossibly quiet landing while his golden body catches the moonlight.

I wait for him to settle onto the ground, but I take a step back when I see a new presence floating next to him. It's a small whisp of light that dances across the air, leaving a glowing trail behind it. Ripples of light radiate from its center as it brightens and fades, gliding in the air beside Graviter.

The dragon inclines his head toward the dancing light. "Do not be alarmed, Wolf. This creature is a Celestial Star. She and her sisters live in the ether far above us. She has seen the births of gods and titans and now watches over the Valkyrie in the End Lands. I have invited her here to witness the making of Asha's hammer."

My heart leaps. The way the dragon speaks about the hammer indicates he thinks it really can be made.

I take a step toward the cabin, anticipation growing within me. "I'll wake Asha."

"Do not."

His soft reply startles me enough that I pause.

Graviter moves with stealth now, his focus swinging to the cabin as he speaks in a whisper, like a breeze through the air. "Asha must remain asleep."

I suppose he can hear her regular heartbeats as well as I can.

"Do not wake her," he says.

I'm on guard now. "Why not?"

He takes another step, and I realize that both of his front talons seem to be gripped around objects, but I can't see what they might be.

"I have seen her memories," Graviter says. "I have seen her risk her life and forsake her family to keep you alive because her connection with you is made of iron and her love for you is unbreakable." He lowers his head and now, his eyes glisten with tears. "She will not allow you to make this choice."

I search his eyes and the flicker of fire in them. "What choice?"

"The choice to give your life for hers."

CHAPTER 54

Graviter Rex makes no move toward me, but he turns one of his paws over and opens his talons.

A single lump of crimson coal rests between his sharp claws.

"Do you know what this is?" he asks.

"Crimson coal," I say.

His voice hardens. "But do you know what it really is?"

I consider him carefully, recalling the way Braddock once described the coal. "A human once told me that those rocks have a soul and that it is vengeful."

"As it should be." Graviter nods. "For these are the bones of dragons long buried, and they should never have been dug up without permission." He snorts, an angry sound. "The Blacksmiths of past generations understood and respected this, but Malak did not."

Well, that would explain its fire and volatility.

I ask carefully, "Why are you giving it to me now?"

"Because every part of Asha's hammer must be freely given. Nothing must be taken." His golden eyes are filled with sadness as he takes a step nearer to me. "You must hear everything I need to tell you and understand the consequences of your choice. I will not sway or coerce you. Your decision must be willingly and knowingly made."

"I'm listening."

He settles down onto the ground while the Celestial Star wafts through the air beside him, but his front paw remains tightly folded around whatever other object he's concealing there.

"I spent enough time with Milena Ironmeld to understand how a Blacksmith's power works," Graviter says. "They cannot access their power without the right metal acting as a conduit. Otherwise, their power is trapped in their bodies like water in a bottle."

"They need a hammer," I say, nodding. "With a hammer, they can make medallions that will answer their will with a single thought. And only with the hammer can they awaken those medallions. Otherwise, the medallions will fall dormant once separated from their body."

"Yes." Graviter lifts one of his talons. "But only with the right hammer. That is where the hammer-maker comes in. Milena once told me that a hammer-maker is a Blacksmith with the ability to discern not only the existence of another Blacksmith's power, but its true nature.

"By understanding that nature, she could choose the right primary metal and fold other metallic elements into it that would reflect and amplify a particular Blacksmith's power. That is how she could create the perfect conduit for them."

He exhales a heavy sigh. "I watched her make Thaden's hammer when he was five years old. She showed me the titanium she sourced—a metal particularly conducive to House Ironmeld's line, into which she folded a little mercury and a little copper, and then she beat the metal for hours, pouring her own magic into it. By the time she was done, the hammer she fashioned was receptive to Thaden's power."

"So she created it... as if it were one of her medallions?" My brow furrows. "I don't see how this helps Asha."

The golden dragon huffs softly at me. "Have you not heard me, Wolf? With the right metal and the *right* magic, a conduit can be created."

The furrow in my brow doesn't ease.

He doesn't rise or move toward me, but his voice lowers to a growl. "I ate the leaf that Asha created. I have seen her memories and all that will be. It is my belief that despite Milena's failings and her fears, she didn't make Asha a hammer because she *couldn't*."

My eyes widen at this theory.

"No hammer beaten with Milena's power would ever be a conduit to Asha's power," Graviter finishes.

I consider what he told me about how Milena made Thaden's hammer. How she beat it with her own power—a power that, by the time Asha turned five, would have been contaminated with darkness.

"Asha needs a hammer filled only with light," Graviter says. "Only the brightest, purest light will provide the conduit she needs to access her true power."

His eyes blaze at me. "She changed that tree *despite* Malak's darkness. The power she was able to access to do that was a mere trickle of what she's truly capable of." His gaze burns me. "With the right conduit."

I find myself, once again, studying his closed talons, where another object is concealed.

He said that to make Asha's hammer, she needs the right metal and the right magic.

"You have the right metal," I say, a sudden hope rising within me. "Don't you?"

Graviter slowly turns his paw over, opening his talons to reveal a large lump of gold. "This is dragon's gold. *My* dragon's gold, in fact. I have hoarded this lump of metal for centuries.

The hoarding process gives the gold living properties and makes it receptive to forming a bond. I had intended this gold for my son and so it contains all my love for my child." His voice cracks a little as he continues. "It is the right metal."

He extends his talons toward me and I take the lump of gold from him. It's heavy in my hands, but not so heavy that it can't be lifted.

"And the right magic?" I ask, recalling the way he told Asha and me that dragons are creatures of light, and he is one of the rare dragons who can share his light. "You mean your light, don't you?"

But my hope fades when he says, "No. I cannot forge this hammer. I hold too much anger for the death of my son. Using my light to assist Asha to rid herself of Malak's darkness was as far as my light could extend."

Now, he rises to his feet and edges toward me, his voice a low murmur. "Asha's hammer must be made by someone whose deep light loves her. Someone who is willing to give everything for her."

Someone whose deep light...

He can't mean mine. Mine is gone. And even if it weren't, I was never able to share it.

My shoulders slump as I consider the gold in my hands. "You said that a hammer must be made by someone who can pour their magic into it. My deep light can't be shared."

His eyes glisten with tears. "You forget, Wolf, I ate the leaf and saw it all."

Despite myself, I take a step away from him, wary of the pain in his eyes. "What are you talking about?"

"I saw what you did, Wolf," he says, now speaking in a low growl. "You drove one of those black spears down onto a mangled, silver medallion and woke the silver up. I saw the sapphire light that passed from your heart into that medallion. I saw the way the metal healed because of your light."

"No. It didn't *pass into* the metal." I shake my head. "Hitting it triggered it to resume its former shape. It was the impact, not my light." I continue backing away from him. "I can't share my light."

"You can."

My snarl is suddenly savage. "No, this is cruel. If I could share my light, I could have saved my father. I could have helped my brother. I was told—"

"One in every generation," Graviter snaps. "Just like dragons." He prowls closer as I fight the urge to rage at him.

My whisper is strangled. "No."

The dragon king leans forward, quiet flames licking around his mouth, hot enough to melt the snow on the nearby trees.

The liquid drips like tears onto the icy ground, a soft patter that curls around my anguish and tears everything away from me.

"I do not lie," he says.

My voice is empty. "Even if what you say is true, I have no light left."

Graviter gives me a sad smile. "But you do. I see it."

"How?" I ask disbelievingly.

His focus shifts to the cabin. "Asha," he says. "Every time you touched her. Every time you thought of her. Every time you lied and schemed to keep her alive. Every time you raged quietly against your fate and concealed your true intentions. Your deep light built again. Hidden from you beneath the weight of the darkness that rested within your heart."

"Malak's device," I murmur.

"Until she removed it," Graviter replies. "Look into your heart, Wolf. You will find what you thought you lost."

I close my eyes, seeking the light within my heart, taking myself back to the moment when I lifted the onyx pole above my head and struck it down onto her grandmother's mangled medallion.

"Remember who you are." That's what I said in that moment.

The bright, melodic *ting* rang in my ears, but all I thought about was that Asha needed the light in that medallion to help her fight the darkness of Malak's metal.

"Remember who you are."

My fingertips tingle and my chest hurts, as if there were a cage around my heart.

A cage behind which I've hidden myself for ten, long years.

I open my eyes to find that the flames dancing around Graviter's scaled face are now reflecting the faintest sapphire tinge.

My deep light. It's radiating out from me, pushing back at his power.

"Erik the Vandawolf." Graviter speaks gravely. "If you forge this hammer, you cannot hold back. You must give everything."

A new pain squeezes my chest. "I will need to burn out my light. Once and for all."

"You must," Graviter says. "It is the only way."

I take a deep breath, inhaling the crisp air and listening to the faraway howls of the wolf pack that survived despite the darkness around them.

Farther away is the city and the wasteland that surrounds it. Ashen ground that gives rise to monsters formed from the bones of dead creatures and the creation magic that seeps across the land.

A darkness that is growing and spreading.

Without a hammer, Asha can't heal any of it. And as for using my claws to fight Thaden and slice through his dragon scales, she can cut off my claws and use them herself.

She hasn't woken since Graviter returned. Her heartbeats from within the cabin tell me how deeply she remains asleep.

"She wouldn't let me do this," I say.

She told me she couldn't lose me. She would stop me. Fight me. Rage at me for even considering it.

"She will consider it a betrayal."

Did she sense what was going to happen? When she told me tonight not to betray her. And I told her that I never would.

"Destiny defies all," I whisper.

I look at my father's statue and remember his long-ago words.

"It's your destiny to keep this woman alive."

I raise my eyes to the dragon. "Tell me what to do."

CHAPTER 55

The honeyed scent of crimson coal wafts through the air.

Its glow extends across the waist-high anvil and the items resting on top of the metal surface: tongs, a regular hammer, a chisel, and the dragon's gold.

Before I step into the forge, Graviter casts his warm breath across it, clearing the snow and then drying the structure.

He rests down on the snowy ground directly opposite me while the Celestial Star continues to float at his side, the star's light somewhat subdued now as she waits for Graviter to perform the first task.

He holds one of the onyx spears within his grip.

I told him it was unbreakable, but he wasn't daunted.

"Do it," I say.

Graviter raises the onyx spear to his sharp teeth.

His fire flows from his mouth, its heat scorching, and with it comes his light magic, his own sapphire-blue energy combining with the flames.

He bites down on the spear, straining against its resilient

structure, which finally cracks and snaps in half. Now it's the perfect length for the handle of the hammer I will make Asha.

It will not be a small hammer or a delicate one.

It will be a war hammer to protect her through all the battles ahead of her.

Huffing, as if breaking the spear did indeed take more effort than he thought it would, Graviter hands me both halves.

I choose the half with the sharp end.

It will take the strongest power to shatter this handle, and I'm determined that by the time I'm done with it, it will be as strong a conduit to Asha's power as the dragon's gold.

"Asha will have a hammer like no other," I say.

The dragon king bows his head to me. "You have a strong spirit, Wolf, and you will fight well."

I incline my head at the warrior's blessing.

Then I reach for the light within my heart and let it loose.

It bursts around me, rushing through the air and pushing back at the flames that rise around the dragon's mouth.

Taking the tongs, I cast aside any remaining doubts and pick up the gold, thrusting it into the fire and submerging it within the flames.

I know that the moment I start beating the gold, the noise will wake Asha, but I won't stop, no matter what happens.

I count my heartbeats, just like I watched Asha do when she forged the weapons back in the city. Just as her mother did when her students forged their medallions.

One... Two... Three...

Within the fire, the gold now glows a perfect amber color.

I block out the knowledge that what comes next will create enough noise to draw Asha from her sleep.

Wrenching the gold from the flames, I don't hesitate, holding it tightly with the tongs while I grip the hammer, hit the metal, and send my light through it.

The forge fills with a new surge of sapphire light, and I'm

certain that it will be filling my eyes, just like it filled my father's, making them glow.

Energy strikes down my arm, through the hammer and into the gold.

The first *clang* echoes through the air like a clear bell.

I don't stop, hitting it again and again.

Across the way, the cabin's door flies open and Asha's figure appears in the doorway, her silhouette lit by the gentle fire within the building.

She's pulling on her boots and coat and trying to run to me at the same time, nearly tripping.

I told her how my father died.

I explained all about my deep light.

Her silver hair flies behind her as she runs directly toward me, her voice a frightened shout. "Erik! What are you doing?"

Graviter catches her before she can reach me. "No, Asha. Do not approach."

"Let me go!" She struggles against his hold, thumping violently at his paw, shoving at his talons, but her strength is human now and she won't have a chance of making him budge.

Her voice rises to a commanding shout, the kind that belongs to a warrior. "*You will let me go to him!*"

"I will not." Graviter growls.

She wrenches against his hold again, trying to kick herself free as her wild eyes seek mine. "Erik! What are you doing?"

I want to tell her not to be afraid, not to grieve for me, but the light thrumming through me has encased me now and speech is impossible.

I'm committed to my task, wholly and completely, and there's no going back.

When I don't respond, she screams at me. "Answer me!"

"He cannot," the dragon says. "His deep light is in control now."

Even though my focus is on the gold, on shaping its sides, I'm aware of Asha's struggle and the changes in her expression.

What breaks my heart is the hurt in her voice.

"Why would you do this?" she screams at me. "You know it will break me to lose you." Her voice rises to a roar. "*Why?*"

I want to tell her that I would do anything for her, and this is how I can mend the past and the future.

It isn't a betrayal. It's what I was always meant to do. From the moment I found her in the snow to the moment she gave me her heart.

But my arm is hammering and my light is blazing and all I can do is send all of my hope and love for her into the metal I'm forging.

Within my mind, I can hear Ayla Silverspun screaming at her students again.

"*You will forge until your hands bleed and your muscles break and still, you will keep on forging.*"

"I don't want a hammer this way!" Asha screams at me, her voice tearing at me. "I will hate you for this, Erik!"

Her fury is deafening.

"Stop!" she cries, suddenly breaking down, thrashing at Graviter's paw as she sobs. "Please, stop."

I don't. I can't.

For the next hour, I work until my arms ache, heating the gold and beating at it, and still I keep going, digging deep into the well of light within me.

Finally, the hammer's head takes shape, a double-sided block, evenly balanced, and I attach it firmly to the end of the spear.

I shape it for strength and resilience, speed and control. And when its shape is finished, I take the chisel and carve into it the same runes that were inked into my father's hands. Marks of bravery, loyalty, strength, perseverance, and finally, one he didn't wear: hope.

My hands are starting to shake and my light begins to fade by the time the final rune is finished.

Asha has slumped in Graviter's hold, but as my light sputters, her head rises again, dark tear tracks visible down her cheeks.

"Let me go, Graviter," she says, her voice hoarse from screaming.

"Not yet, Bright Heart," he says to her, lowering his head to hers while the Celestial Star drifts softly back and forth beside them both.

Asha has barely paid any attention to it and even now, her focus is entirely on me.

The chisel falls from my fingertips and my arms drop to my sides.

My light is nearly gone.

With a groan of exhaustion, I make myself pick up Asha's hammer, sliding it off the anvil. The weight is nearly too much for me to carry now that my muscles are giving way.

I count the heartbeats I have left. Maybe thirty at most.

As I stumble out from behind the forge, Graviter finally opens his paw.

Free of his hold, Asha launches herself across the space between us, throwing herself forward and sliding through the snow to catch me as I drop to my knees.

The hammer's head hits the ice beside me, but somehow, I manage to keep hold of the handle, trying to drag it closer to her side so that she will take it from me.

Her strong eyes are filled with pain as she cradles me. "Erik, what have you done?"

"Your hammer," I rasp, pulling it to her side, its head gouging a turret in the ice.

She doesn't take her eyes off me. Barely looks at it. "I don't want it," she says softly. "Don't you understand? I want *you*."

Twenty heartbeats left.

"Take it," I whisper, my eyes burning with tears I refuse to shed. "You have to take it."

She wraps her arms around me, her human strength straining under my weight as she pulls me to her chest. Her lips press to my forehead, and for a moment, I think she's going to shun the hammer altogether.

Then my hand brushes her arm and the hammer's handle makes contact with her skin.

That's all it takes for the clearing to burst into light. The brightest, most breathtaking glow as the conduit I created connects with her power.

Her eyes light up like gold in the sunlight and her hair glows as brightly as the moon.

Her power ripples out from her, banishing the darkness. Her light is so bright that Graviter Rex closes his eyes and the Celestial Star's form is no longer distinguishable from the air around it.

Asha gasps, her chest filling as she drags in air. Her head lifts, and with it, her arms, now filled with power, pull me close and envelop me, raising me up so that her cheek presses to mine.

"Erik," she breathes, her lips pressing to mine, her throat constricting.

"You're limitless," I whisper before the strength in my body gives way entirely and it's only because she's so strong now that I don't slip to the ground.

I did what I set out to do. I kept her alive and I gave her the power she never had before. But I need to tell her…

"I love you, Asha. I loved you from the moment I first saw you."

"*Don't*," she says, shaking her head, her salty tears on my lips. "Don't you dare."

Ten heartbeats.

Carefully, I extend my claws. "Cut them off. Make them into weapons."

"No." She wraps her arms more tightly around me, even though my claws could impale her, drawing me close as the weight of my death begins dragging me toward the snow.

"No, Erik. No!"

Her furious, limitless face blurs behind my fading vision.

"Vandawolf!" she screams, as if I've betrayed her.

It's your destiny to keep this woman alive.

Nothing in my father's words could have warned me that I would become a villain in her life over and over again.

Or that I would love her with my whole heart.

One heartbeat.

"Destiny," I whisper as the darkness finally claims me.

Find out how Asha and the Vandawolf's story ends in
A Soul Like Glass
the final book with no cliffhanger.

A SOUL LIKE GLASS
(KINGDOM OF BETRAYAL #4)

To save my family, I will become the betrayer...

Content information: A Soul Like Glass is fantasy romance, enemies to lovers, the fourth and final book in the Kingdom of Betrayal series.

Recommended reading age is 17+ for sex scenes, mature themes, violence, and language.

NO cliffhanger.

This series is part of The Ever Realms. A seven-series world by Everly Frost.

ALSO BY EVERLY FROST

KINGDOM OF BETRAYAL

(Fantasy Romance)

1. A Sky Like Blood

2. A Sin Like Fire

3. A Storm Like Iron

4. A Soul Like Glass

BRIGHT WICKED - COMPLETE

(Fantasy Romance)

1. Bright Wicked

2. Radiant Fierce

3. Infernal Dark

ASSASSIN'S MAGIC

(Dark Urban Fantasy Romance)

1. Assassin's Magic

2. Assassin's Mask

3. Assassin's Menace

4. Assassin's Maze

5. Rebels

6. Revenge

7. Rogue

8. Assassin's Match

SOUL BITTEN SHIFTER - COMPLETE

(Dark Urban Fantasy Romance)

1. This Dark Wolf

2. This Broken Wolf

3. This Caged Wolf

4. This Cruel Blood

DEMON PACK - COMPLETE

(Dark Paranormal Romance)

1. Demon Pack

2. Demon Pack: Elimination

3. Demon Pack: Eternal

SUPERNATURAL LEGACY - COMPLETE

(Angels and Dragon Shifters)

1. Hunt the Night

2. Chase the Shadows

3. Slay the Dawn

4. Claim the Light

DARK MAGIC SHIFTERS

(Dark Urban Fantasy Romance)

1. Wolf of Ashes

2. Bond of Flames

3. Crown of Fate

MORTALITY - COMPLETE

(Science-Fantasy Romance)

Mortality Complete Set: Books 1 to 4

1. Beyond the Ever Reach

2. Beneath the Guarding Stars

3. By the Icy Wild

4. Before the Raging Lion

STORM PRINCESS - COMPLETE

(Fantasy Romance)

1. Book 1

2. Book 2

3. Book 3

<u>Stand-alone fiction - dark romance</u>

Corrupt Me: Immortal Vices and Virtues

About the Author

Everly Frost is the USA Today Bestselling author of fantasy romance, urban fantasy and paranormal romance novels. She spent her childhood dreaming of other worlds and scribbling stories on the leftover blank pages at the back of school notebooks. She lives in Brisbane, Australia with her husband and two children.

amazon.com/author/everlyfrost

facebook.com/everlyfrost

instagram.com/everlyfrost

bookbub.com/authors/everly-frost

goodreads.com/everlyfrost

www.ingramcontent.com/pod-product-compliance
Lightning Source LLC
Chambersburg PA
CBHW030518120726
47904CB00005B/1523